Henry Handel Richardson was born in 1870 in Melbourne and was educated at the Presbyterian Ladies' College, the original of the 'superior' girls' school in her novel *The Getting of Wisdom*. She was the eldest daughter of Walter Lindsay Richardson, an indigent Irish doctor who had emigrated to Australia in the sixties 'in the hope of digging up a fortune', and who was, to some extent, the source of the tragic title figure of *The Fortunes of Richard Mahony*.

When Richardson was seventeen, she left Australia to become a student of the piano at the Conservatorium of Leipzig, where she spent more than three years. It became clear to her, however, that she had neither the ability nor the temperament to become a concert pianist, and she turned to writing instead. During this time she married J.G. Robertson, who later became Professor of German Literature and Language at the University of London.

Except for some travel on the Continent and a brief visit to Australia in 1912 to gather background material for *The Fortunes of Richard Mahony*, Richardson lived in England until her death in 1946. Despite the fact of her long residence outside Australia, most of her principal works with the exception of *Maurice Guest* and *The Young Cosima* have Australian backgrounds and characters.

In *The Adventures of Cuffy Mahony*, two stories of which are previously unpublished in book form, Richardson's mastery of the short story is made brilliantly apparent. The themes of separation, loss and acceptance through childhood, adolescence, marriage and ultimately death are superbly controlled and developed in this collection.

THE ADVENTURES OF
CUFFY MAHONY

By the same author

The Fortunes of Richard Mahony
The Getting of Wisdom
Maurice Guest
The Young Cosima*
(*published by Angus & Robertson)

THE ADVENTURES OF CUFFY MAHONY
and other stories

HENRY HANDEL RICHARDSON

SIRIUS QUALITY PAPERBACK EDITION
PUBLISHED BY ANGUS & ROBERTSON

For B.S.

Angus & Robertson Publishers
London • Sydney • Melbourne • Singapore • Manila

This book is copyright. Apart from any fair dealing for
the purposes of private study, research, criticism or
review, as permitted under the Copyright Act, no part
may be reproduced by any process without written
permission. Inquiries should be addressed to
the publishers.

First published by Angus & Robertson Publishers,
Australia, 1979
(This Sirius Quality Paperback edition incorporates
The End of a Childhood, first published by
William Heinemann, 1934, and two stories previously
unpublished in book form)

© Olga Roncoroni 1979

National Library of Australia card number and
ISBN 0 207 13511 8 (limp)
ISBN 0 207 13771 4 (cased)

Printed in Hong Kong

CONTENTS

PART ONE

THE ADVENTURES OF CUFFY MAHONY
  The End of a Childhood ... 1
GROWING PAINS Sketches of girlhood ... 39
  THE BATHE ... 41
  THREE IN A ROW ... 45
  PRELIMINARY CANTER ... 54
  CONVERSATION IN A PANTRY ... 60
  THE BATH ... 66
  THE WRONG TURNING ... 69
  "AND WOMEN MUST WEEP" ... 73
  TWO HANGED WOMEN ... 79
  SISTER ANN ... 84

PART TWO

TWO TALES OF OLD STRASBOURG ... 105
  LIFE AND DEATH OF PETERLE LUTHY ... 107
  THE PROFESSOR'S EXPERIMENT ... 127
THE COAT ... 161
SUCCEDANEUM ... 171
MARY CHRISTINA ... 189

PART ONE

THE ADVENTURES OF CUFFY MAHONY

The End of a Childhood

THE ADVENTURES OF CUFFY MAHONY

I

TWELVE months almost to a day after her husband's death, Mary Mahony received a letter that greatly perturbed her.

It was handed to her straight from the sorting-table. Recognising the writing, she put on her spectacles and unthinkingly slit it open. But she had not read far before her colour rose, and with a covert glance at her two subordinates — the telegraph-operator, who sat lazily picking his nose, had a sly and roving eye — she hastily refolded it and thrust it in her pocket.

There it remained; and all day long she was conscious of it, as of something hot or heavy. Not until evening, when the office was closed and the children lay asleep, did she draw it forth again. Then, alone in her little parlour, she pulled the kerosene-lamp to her and prepared to face the contents.

It was from her old friend Henry Ocock, and ran:

Wendouree House,
Ballarat.

My dear Mrs. Mahony,
My prolonged silence has not, I trust, led you to infer me grown in any way indifferent to your welfare. Far from it, you have, if I may say so, seldom been absent from my thoughts. But I have hesitated to intrude, without due cause, on a grief that I regarded as sacred. Now, however, when it may be assumed that Time, the great Healer, has assuaged the first bitterness of your irreparable loss, I venture to take up my pen on a subject of to me vital importance.

What I am going to say may, no doubt will surprise you. But the wish, the fond hope, I am about to express, is, believe me, no new one — I have cherished it longer than I should dare to tell you. Dear friend, I cannot but think you have always been aware how much I admired, how highly esteemed you — though doubtless still appraising you below your true worth. It would be impossible to minimise the heroism you have shown in battling with a concatenation of circumstances that would have crushed a lesser spirit. In my estimation, few women are worthy to be compared with you, and of this esteem and veneration I now offer you tangible proof, by asking you if you will do me the honour to become my wife.

I will not, in this connection — and I think you will understand me — make use of such terms as love and passion. We are neither of us in our first youth, and have each had our full share of Life's Trials. But my appreciation of your many excellent qualities of mind and heart have only increased with the years; and should you, dear friend, consider that these sentiments suffice, that you could, without trepidation, lay your fate in my hands, I assure you you should never have reason to regret it. — There are, besides, others than ourselves to think of. My children sadly need a mother's care, yours a father's guiding hand.

Let me entreat you not to reply too hastily. Take your own time — as long as you will — to consider my proposal.

Until then, believe me,
    Truly and devotedly yours,

                                Henry Ocock.

For a moment Mary continued to sit with this letter in her hand, staring a little stupidly over the top of it. Then she dropped it, even gave it a slight push away from her. In reading, she had grown more and more uncomfortable. Till she came to the bit about the children. At that, a kind of stiffening ran through her. What? *Her* children? — Richard's children? — to need the guidance of ... of Henry Ocock? "Well, upon my word!"

But, no, you couldn't ... she mustn't ... look at it that way.

Taking off her spectables — they were the cheap, ugly, steel-rimmed kind — she settled herself squarely in her seat, mouth and chin gripped fast in the hollow of one hand: an attitude she often fell into when unpleasant things had to be faced — bills for the mending of the children's boots, complaints from Head Office, the contrariness of columns of figures that would *not* tally.

Yes, unpleasant was the word: her first feeling was one of utter repugnance. The thought of marrying again had never occurred to her. She wasn't that sort. And now came Henry Ocock ... *Sir* Henry Ocock ... for the fraction of a second her mind lingered on the prefix. But in the next minute she heard Richard's voice saying: "Confound his impudence!" and with so much of the familiar Irish over-emphasis that she simply had to smile. Oh! she could just imagine how angry Richard would be. *His* wife ... Henry Ocock!

This violent personal antipathy she had never shared. She had even been given to standing up for Mr. Henry, preferring as she did to think that there was *some* good in everybody. And if Richard could now come back and see what a friend Ocock had proved, he'd have to admit she was right. Though of course if, all the time, Mr. Henry — Sir Henry — had had *this* up his sleeve .... But there! why go poking and prying into people's motives? (That was Richard again — not her.) Let her stick to facts. Where would she and the children be to-day, if Ocock had not come to their aid? Why, in the gutter ... or the Benevolent Asylum. Certainly not together; and that would have hit her harder than anything. Then again her transfer, six months ago, from that dreadful Gymgurra, to this more civilised place, with a forty-pound rise in salary, a decent *brick* house, and a large garden for the children to play in: all this she owed to Mr. Henry's influence. (Of course, that he had feelings just like anyone else, *she* had known since the day when she saw him ... made him ... cry.)

No, the truth had to be faced: Richard was gone, and she couldn't go on for ever letting herself be swayed and prejudiced by what he had thought, by his likes and dislikes. Times changed, and you changed with them. Looked at in this light, Ocock's letter was nobody's business but her own. For who else knew the circumstances that had led up to it? (Certainly not Richard.) And so, compressing her lips, she began by admitting — a little doggedly — that, in spite of its stiffness and pomposity, its "estimations" and "venerations" where he might have said "like" and "respect," ("concatenation" she'd never seen or heard of before) — in spite of everything, Ocock's letter was a generous one. Considering the — well, she wouldn't say "the snob he was" — but considering the enormous value he set on money and connexions and social prestige; remembering, too, the nobody he had been to start with, and the way he had climbed (and over *what* obstacles!) to the top of the tree; she thought it, now, more than generous of him, to put his pride in his pocket and stoop to a poor little up-country postmistress. (And not at all patronisingly: his wordiness, his difficulty in coming to the point, struck her as rather pathetic.) Yet to say "stoop" wasn't being quite honest either. For every one knew who *she* was ... or had been. Richard's name still counted for something. And if this affair had happened a few years earlier, she would have been the one to stoop, not he.

Even as it was, the favours wouldn't be all on Ocock's side. Nobody was more experienced than she in running a big establishment — the scale of living at "Ultima Thule" would have made Ocock himself open his eyes — how to keep it up to the nines, yet without undue extravagance. She would even undertake to manage him, too, if necessary; after Richard, no other man would prove difficult. And it would surely be worth a great deal to Mr. Henry, for once in his life to have some one to club with him and support him. His nearest relations — his damaging old father, his dissolute brothers, poor little Agnes with her fatal weakness — one and all, in their separate ways, had been weights to drag him down. With a different family at his back, he might have ended as Prime Minister. — She would even guarantee to get on with Agnes's children; though these were now in their teens, of an age bitterly to resent the coming of a stepmother.

Yes! had that been all. In any of these ways she could have made herself useful ... even indispensable. (Indeed, the idea of showing what she *could* do, in this line, made a kind of insidious appeal to her.) but it wasn't all; and it wasn't enough. He didn't want a housekeeper or a business companion; he wanted a wife. And it was here her courage failed her. She had been so essentially, so emphatically, a one-man woman; never had her inclination strayed; having Richard, she had everything she needed. Of course, he had caught her *very* young, very innocent. Perhaps, had she been just a little older, with more knowledge of life ... more *nous* ... for really, by nature ... yes ... well ... "Well, you know what I mean," said Mary to herself, a series of half-formed images, which she would have shrunk from completing, chasing one another across her mind. And at the thought of now having to begin all over again — at *her* age — with a stranger; at the thought of once more yielding her freedom, (which she had learned to value) of an invaded privacy, the intimacies of the bedroom — no! it was not to be contemplated, not for an instant; it simply could not be done.

And there was another thing. If she married, she might still have children — *his* children. And this was surely the crucial test. For the unloved man's embraces might be borne: they concerned yourself alone. But what must that mother feel, who had to see appearing in the children she loved — and that you could help caring for the little things you carried about with you for nine long months was unthinkable — ugliness of face and character belonging to the father? Eyes set too close together, or shifty eyes, or thin, cruel lips. Foxy ways . . . unscrupulousness — double dealing. She could imagine nothing, nothing more horrible.

But here she broke off, with an impatient click of the tongue. For this string of faults and blemishes, whose were they but Henry Ocock's as seen by Richard? Oh, it was hopeless, quite hopeless: Richard would have her under his thumb to the end; and even more than during his lifetime, when she could at least stand up to him and fight for her own opinions. Well, one thing she had to be thankful for: in *his* children there was nothing she need fear to see develop. No ugliness of face or disposition there! — And as she now sat and thought of them, and of what they meant to her, she saw that all this arguing and disputing, this palaver about what *she* could or could not put up with, was a mere foolish beating of the air. In matters that affected the children, she simply did not count. The sole query was, would they benefit? Did they stand to gain by her re-marrying?

She felt a sudden need of being near them, of having them before her eyes. Getting up she fetched a candlestick from the kitchen, lit the candle, and went into the bedroom. But, in passing the dressing-table, she caught a glimpse of her own shadowy figure; and yielding to an impulse she crossed to the glass, holding the light above her head.

There she stood and looked at herself: not as a mother, or a wage-earner, but a woman — and a woman somebody still thought worth marrying! On the wrong side of forty now, middle-aged, and for all the world to see — since she had never a moment left in which to care for her appearance. Her hair had worn best: it was still glossy and fairly thick, nor had the straight white centre parting spread. But it had gone very grey round the temples; and these, and her forehead, were furrowed with lines; while wrinkles fine as spiders' webs teased her lids, and ran out, fan-shaped, from the corners of her eyes. The sharp steel of the glasses, too, had cut a permanent red line on the bridge of her nose. The big dark eyes, which had once been her chief feature, might still, if freed from the disfiguring spectacles, have passed muster; but that was all. Of the lower part of the face the less said the better: the nose was pinched, the mouth thin-lipped and elderly; and all sorts of odd twists and creases were forming on her once smooth cheeks and chin.

And yet ... and yet ... such a store of energy still existed in her, that, give her but half a chance to recuperate, a spell, say, of nights unbroken by the rat-tat-tat of the night-mail, and the consequent shivering of her sleep to atoms: give her these, and she believed she would rise a different woman. Then, too, there would be no more knitting and screwing up of the brows, or biting of the lips, or straining of the eyes, over infinitesimal dots and dashes, or dizzy rows of figures. No more denying herself in order that the children should not go short; or pinching and scraping in order to make a pittance of a hundred-and-twenty a year stretch to twice its size. No more twelve-hour days on her feet — these hot, tired, throbbing feet — or hands rough and red with rough work. No more quailing before her subordinates — never, never again, anything to do with young men of their class! — a telegraphist who subtly, a postman who openly flouted her authority, both knowing their jobs much better than she knew hers. Oh! what it would mean to be rid of them, to retire into private life again, did not bear thinking about. Seized by a sudden fear, she turned from the glass.

In the dimity-hung double bed that stood against the wall, little Lucie, her bedfellow, slept the drunken sleep of childhood. Bending over her, she was lying face downwards, Mary turned her on one side, then passing a finger under the fair thick mass of curls, lifted them, for coolness' sake, and spread them out over the pillow. It was a very hot night; and on his little stretcher-bed in an adjoining cubby-hole, Cuffy lay drenched in perspiration. Here, his mother's first act was to take a clean little nightshirt from a drawer, sit him up, slip off the wet one and pop the dry over his head, he opening his eyes for a second, unseeingly, making a kind of growly noise in his throat, and dropping back fast asleep, before she had finished with the buttons. And, as she did this, other nights rose before her, scores of them, on which she, or Nannan — even Richard himself — had made the change. The habit dated from Cuffy's babyhood.

It was only a trifle, but it seemed to unlock the floodgates; and sitting down beside him, her elbows on her knees, her chin in her hands, remembering and remembering, she put the question that mothers have asked themselves since the world began: who would do these things for my children if I were not there? — But no, that sounded too like being dead. What she meant was, if I were prevented, belonged to some one else who had first claim on me, or the right to object. Some one, too, who, from what she knew of him, might easily turn jealous of her children and the love she bore them. Who might not even like them. And indeed, he and Richard having had such different natures, could she reasonably *expect* him to like Richard's children? The probability was, he wouldn't; and they would be pushed into the background, kept down: as mere stepchildren made to play second fiddle to his own.

But here, her mind taking a sudden leap, she came face to face with the bugbear that stalked her wakeful nights — the problem of Cuffy's education. For the present, he went every morning for a couple of hours' lessons to Mr. Burroughs, the clergyman; and it was enough: Richard had always been against forcing him. But after this? — say, a couple of years hence? Oh, when she thought of all the plans and ambitions they had nursed for their firstborn ... now blown to the four winds. Yet, even still, there was something in her, something obstinate, irrational, which refused to believe that Cuffy would be done out of public school and university. And now, as always when she reached this point, she declared to herself: "Well! ... if the worst comes to the worst!" — and with such emphasis that her lips moved to the unspoken words. What she meant was: though I have never for myself borrowed or owed a farthing, yet ... when it's a case of my children ... And then once more she went over in thought those it would be least galling to apply to for aid. Old Lady Devine, who was for ever making them presents; Tilly, childless now herself; and — yes, as long as he had been content to remain a friend, the list had also included Henry Ocock. Now, Ocock had put himself out of court. — But, even if she married him, could she expect him to share her ambitions and aspirations for a child that was not his own? Or even understand them? He was none too fond of untying his purse-strings. In all probability he would want to put Cuffy into business, or thrust him, half-grown, half-educated into a Bank.

And there were other things, too, that he might not, would not, understand.

The children had thriven in the past half-year; even Cuffy having at last begun to fill out and grow. This was partly due to them having a garden again to play in; they had always been used to gardens. But the chief reason, no good shirking it, was that an ugly shadow had been lifted from their lives. Children were not built to stand what hers had been through. And, her first grief over, she could not but feel glad for their sakes that Richard was gone. Whether she had really done right, in taking him away from the asylum, she sometimes wondered; when she saw how they had blossomed out since his death. And yet ... and yet ...

That they had not got off scot-free she realised — when it was too late. For it was all very well to plume herself on them being their father's children, in good looks and nice feelings. That wasn't the whole truth. They had inherited other, less desirable traits as well: Richard's ultra-sensitiveness, his finickiness (what they would and would not eat, what they chose or did not choose to wear) his Irish uppishness. In other words, they were both very highly strung; and, in consequence, the strain of his illness, and the unhappy years preceding it, had told on them more severely than if they had been ordinary children. Look at Lucie. In her seven short years Lucie had seen so many changes — the death of her little twin sister, the racketing from place to place, the collapse of one home after another, and, worse still the collapse of the father who should have been her mainstay — that she, too, had broken down, and was now little better than a bundle of nerves. Having lost so much, the child lived in a constant fear lest her last and dearest should also be snatched away. It was Mamma here, Mamma there; and on those rare evenings when she, Mary, stepped across the road for a chat with the Bank Manager's wife, she knew that on her return, no matter at what hour, she would find the child sitting bolt upright in bed, with frightened eyes and perspiring hands, convinced that Mamma had gone away, or was dead, and would never come back. Neither scoldings nor pettings took any effect.

Cuffy, always excitable, had shortly after his father's death developed a convulsive twitching and blinking of face and eyes that was distressing to see. The doctor said the habit was purely nervous, and would pass as he grew older. Meanwhile, there was nothing to be done; except sometimes hold up a glass to show him how ugly or how silly he looked. But did she think of him, of either of them, going among strangers thus handicapped, to be made fun of, or found fault with — perhaps even *punished* — for failings they had done nothing to deserve: at the mere thought of it, all her protective tenderness was up in arms. No; Richard's children they were, for good or for ill; and Richard's children they should remain.

No one but the father they were so like would be capable of understanding them.

And here, as if to brace her in her decision, words she had once heard, and which her memory had as it were stored up for use in this crisis, came floating into her mind. "Henry Ocock is harsh with children ... is harsh with children."

That did it: now she knew where she stood. Well, he shouldn't — she wouldn't give him the chance to be — with hers. On no one but herself should their lives and happiness depend.

Picking up the candle, she went back into the sitting-room where the letter lay, just as she had left it, open on the table. Without giving it a second glance, she took out pen and paper, and sat down to frame her reply.

Oh yes, she knew quite well what she was doing when she wrote: *Deeply as I appreciate your kindness, I cannot marry you.* Besides condemning herself to poverty, she was cutting herself adrift from the friend who had most power to make things easier for her. (Stung in his vanity, Ocock would hardly be big-minded enough to go on pulling strings on her behalf.) She was also, in a sense, taking leave of her womanhood. Many a year must elapse before either of the children could come to her aid. By then she would be old in earnest, and long past desiring. But she did not waver. Once more it had been brought home to her where her heart really lay.

And then, with the ink still wet on her name, she smiled to herself — a grim, amused little smile. In all this pro-ing and con-ing, this weighing of profit and loss, she had taken no count of the children's own inclinations: Richard's children, blessed (or cursed) with Richard's faculty for pronounced likes and dislikes, with his mercilessly critical eye. Now, it was with almost a feeling of compensation that she thought to herself: I wonder what *they* would have had to say of *him* ... as a father!

II

CUFFY would soon be nine now; and very proud he felt of it. Not quite so proud as if it was ten: ten was like a little platform, where you stood and looked at a row of steps going down to one (what were you before that?) and up to twenty. It was twenty he thought of when he said: "When I'm a man." Twenty was awfully old; any time after that you might die. Oh well, he knew people did go on being older — Mamma and Bowey both had grey hairs on their heads, and'd been alive so many years they didn't like to tell, but pretended they'd forgotten. But he didn't think he would. Specially not since he'd heard the text: who the God loves dies young. For if you loved God, as you *had* to, and God loved you back, then ...

Another proud thing was his satchel; that he carried his school-books in. This was a present from the same old Lady Devine who'd given them their piano, so that they could go on practising. Not *exactly* a present; she'd sent the money for it; and he'd been allowed to go by himself and buy it, at the shop down the town where they sold pens and paper. It was brown, and had two straps with buckles on them. He always let Luce fasten one, to make up for having to stop alone while he went to lessons. She came across the road with him, and stood and waved; and when he'd run along the rightaway and climbed the embankment to the top road, she was still there. And her pinny was always dirty, from falling down, and her socks hung over her shoes. Every time Mamma saw her she said: "For goodness' sake, child, pull up your socks!" (Yet wouldn't let her wear garters, because of spoiling the shape of her legs.) And when he came home at eleven she was dirtier still. He tore down the hill and she tore to meet him, and he kept her on the other side of him because of the dam, which Mamma was afraid she'd fall into and be drowned.

But he liked going to lessons; Mr. Burroughs was so nice. (The Reverend John Noel Burroughs his whole name was.) Mamma was in a dreadful hurry for him to get there punctually at nine; but once he was on the top road and she couldn't see him, he didn't run any more. For mostly Mr. Burroughs wasn't up yet; and he'd have time to spread out his books and maps and pencils on the table, and sometimes draw a whole ship, or a horse, before he came. And then he'd just have put on his overcoat on top of his pyjamas. And he'd laugh and say: "I *shall* have to pay another visit to the ant, shan't I?" (which meant he was a sluggard.) But he was *very* nice. He never made you feel you were only a little boy. He'd come and put his arm round you and say: "Now then, old chap, let's see what you've been up to!" — in your sums or parsing. And he didn't say: "That's wrong ... or three mistakes," but only, ever so polite: "*I* think it would look better this way, sonny!" — Really, sometimes in church on Sunday, when you saw him come up the aisle in his black gown with the white one over, and the blue silk thing hanging down his back, and his head bent and carrying his sermon, it made you feel quite shy, to think how *different* you knew him, sitting in his pyjamas with his arm round your neck.

Another nice thing about him was that he never laughed at you — no, not even when you "made your faces." Mostly, he'd pretend not to notice. But if they were very bad he'd say: "Let's take a breather, shall we?" — which was because the doctor had said you were to have lots and lots of play. And then they'd leave off doing lessons, and go out in the yard and play tipcat; or Mr. Burroughs would show him how to bowl. And when he got too hot he'd take off the overcoat and just be in his pyjamas.

Another time was when he'd asked that *silly* question about the book. Mr. Burroughs read books all through lessons, mostly with brown-paper covers on, to keep you from seeing what they were called; after one day he'd caught you trying to make the name out. Mamma said they were yellow-backs, and not proper books for little boys. But once there hadn't been a cover on, and it was such a funny name that he simply *had* to ask — Mr. Burroughs never minded you asking questions, he said they showed an intelligent mind. So *he* said: "But why is it spelt like that? In the Bible it's always 'goeth' when it says: 'He who goeth down to the sea to get on board a ship:' (which wasn't a text at all, he just made it up, because he liked ships so much, and now they lived so far away from the sea). And first Mr. Burroughs didn't know what he meant. But when he did, he didn't laugh, but just said, well, it hadn't got anything to do with "go," but was the name of a man — one of the wisest men that ever lived — and was called "Gertie." (But when he told them at home, feeling rather proud about it, *they* laughed like anything and wouldn't believe him; for Mamma said no man had ever been called "Gertie," that was a little girl's name. And only after he'd found out that it was a "foreigner name," then they had to. Privately, he thought it was too funny for words, and that he'd rather not be wise than have to have it for his.)

Then there was the time Mamma told on him; which he didn't think she ought to have done. He had to learn Latin now: Mr. Burroughs said you couldn't begin Latin too young. So he took *mensa*; and when Mr. Burroughs was surprised how quick he knew it, Mamma said it was because he'd made a tune to it, and sang it while he learned it. And Mr. Burroughs didn't even smile, but thought it was a "brilliant idea," and said they'd go on having it to music. So then he had to sing it when he said it, and Mr. Burroughs liked the tune so much that he went and fetched Miss Burroughs in —

he didn't have a wife, only a sister — to hear it, too. And she clapped her hands and said it was wonderful; and then they talked together, and he heard them say something about a "natural moddleation to a dommy-something" — but it couldn't have been *dominus*, for he had another tune for that: *dominus* sounded so *strict*. And Miss Burroughs said soon he'd have to learn the organ and play for them in church, and Mr. Burroughs said he'd have him in the choir, and then he'd teach him a plain song.

Miss Burroughs was a lovely lady. As tall as her brother, who was *very* high, with yellow hair, and the most beautiful teeth when she smiled, and a neck like a swan. Well, people called it that; but *he* thought a swan had a neck like a snake, and hers was thick and round. She was so kind, too. He never had to take any lunch with him; every morning she gave him a slice of bread and jelly to finish up with; and in all his life he thought he'd never eaten anything so delishous. — Mamma only made jam, not jelly.

Yes, going to lessons was most int'resting: there was always something new that you didn't know yet. How many masts a ship could have, f'r instance, and what ships were called because of them, and how they were rigged — Mr. Burroughs, he liked ships, too. And how to draw a circle so that it was eszackly round, with arms that went out from its middle, and what *they* were called. And all about the Greeks and Romans and what funny people they were. The Greeks wore short dresses and bare legs — like Luce — and the Romans rode on elephants when they went to war. Goodness! *that* must have been exciting. Nowadays, if you wanted to see an elephant at all, you had to go to the circus.

A funny thing happened about these Romans; he thought of it directly he began to learn them; and it had to do with their noses. And that was because every one in Yerambah said about Mr. Burroughs that he had a Roman nose. This was so awfully int'resting that it did something to him inside, and wouldn't give him any peace till he'd shown he knew (even though it sounded a little rude), and asked: "What does it mean when you say a 'Roman nose'? When the Romans are all dead and gone?"

This time Mr. Burroughs did laugh — not to offend you, though, he just sort of looked mischievous and half-shut one eye. "It refers to the shape, my boy! If you want to see a good Roman nose, look at mine. And then go home and look in the glass, and you'll see another!" Which made him turn all hot and funny-feeling; first to think *he* had one (when he was just beginning to learn about the Romans) and then because he'd got something the same as Mr. Burroughs, who everybody said was so handsome. — And home he went to the glass in Mamma's bedroom, and swung it low and examined himself. But his nose didn't show properly against his face, and he couldn't look sideways because Mamma hadn't got a hand-glass any more. And while he was there, she came into the room and found him and said: "What on *earth* are you doing, Cuffy? — staring at yourself like that! Looking to see how ugly you are?" — But he didn't tell her, for fear she'd tell again. He kept it as a secret with Mr. Burroughs.

He didn't tell Luce either; for hers was little and fat; and she mightn't have liked it — or like him having something Mr. Burroughs had, when she hadn't. She didn't enjoy him being away so long in the morning, and watched for him ever such a time, and was dreadfully glad to see him come back. But so was he. For though lessons were jolly, the rest of the day was jollier, when they had nothing to do but play. And play they did ... oh, how they played! Mostly just him and Luce. They knew some other children in Yerambah, and sometimes went to parties; but their best games were alone, by their two selves. Luce was quite happy as long as every now and then she could go and look at Mamma; and she always played what he liked: it was him who said what the game should be. Mamma thought they were "the queerest children," because they never wanted variety, but went on with one till they were finished with it. When it was cool it had been hopscotch, and they'd played till Luce's legs almost broke in two, and their boot-soles had hole in them. In hot weather it was "knuckle-bones," which they collected themselves, going down to the butcher to beg them. Then they sat all day long on the back verandah, at an old table Mamma made them out of a packing-case and some lids, and tossed the little bones up in the air, catching and scooping and driving them home, as pigs to market or horses to stall — till their own finger-bones were sore.

There was a swing in this garden; but it wasn't like the swings other children had, but was hung between two tall telegraph-posts, so that you could go ever so high. And the most lovely thing about it was that it was *dangerous;* for the seat was loose, not fastened on, but just with two notches in it to fit the rope. *He* wasn't a bit afraid of it coming off, and stood to swing, working himself up so far that he almost turned over, and Luce got frightened and fetched Mamma, and Mamma came and called out: "Stop it, Cuffy! Stop it at once!" Luce, she sat to swing, and felt seasick when she went the least little bit high. He'd never been seasick, not in his whole life, Mamma said so; but had always walked about a ship asking for his dinner.

Oh, yes, there were exciting things to do from the moment you waked, about six, and jumped out of the hot, crumply bed straight into the bath; which you could fill as full as you liked here, for there was plenty of water, even though it was red. And for breakfast, if you wanted to, you could take your bread and butter in your hand and eat it running round the garden, with peaches or figs or nectarines to it (when they were ripe); for there was lots and lots of fruit, and you were allowed it all — except almonds, which was because Mamma said Lallie had once died of eating them. There was a'normous long hose to water the garden with; and sometimes, when it was very hot, they would play it was a rainy day, and put on something very old, and umbrellas, and turn the hose over each other, to make them cool. Mamma didn't like this very much; she was afraid people would look through the fence and see you and call you "those queer children" again, and whatever were you doing? Besides, it made the verandah in such a mess.

But mostly Mamma was *very* nice now, and never cross — or hardly ever: only if the Inspector was coming; or when she was bothered about her "statement"; or if you broke a plate; or climbed up on the roof and walked about on it, making a noise on the iron like thunder. Then she thought you might fall off and kill yourself.

And in the evening, when it was dark ... well, then he had a sort of secret with Mamma; one even Luce didn't know (like his nose with Mr. Burroughs). It was when Bowey was giving Luce her bath to go to bed. After the office was shut and the sun had gone down, Mamma used to bring the rocking-chair out on the front verandah, where she never went and they weren't allowed to go in the daytime, because the office-window, where you asked for letters and stamps, opened off it. But at night it was quite private. And then, though he never, never did when it was light, he was much too big — well, then somehow, when nobody was looking, he'd find himself sitting on Mamma's knee; even though his legs were so long now that they hung over it right down to the ground.

And there they'd sit, just Mamma and him, nobody else knowing about it; and it was most awfully comfortable, when you were tired, quite the most comfy place, with a kind of shelf for your head, and Mamma's arms keeping you from falling off, and her chin against your hair. You just sat there and didn't talk, not at all ... you wouldn't have liked to; it was too close for talking. Besides, there was nothing to say.

Really what you did was just to lie and stare at things. Sometimes the moon was up and sometimes it wasn't. But you could always see the dam and the top road and the hill. This was the hill the sun went down behind every night; and when there were thunder-storms they came up behind it. Then, half the sky would still be all blue — or starry — and half one 'normous black cloud that rushed along as if it had wings, and made Luce very afraid. Once, one of the little houses on top of the hill had been struck by lightning, and the firebell had rung after everybody had gone to bed, making such a terrific noise that everybody got up again; and the house had first been nothing but flames that stretched miles up into the sky, and then was burnt down. They went to see it next morning and it was just a black smoky mass, with nothing left: Mamma said that was the worst of wooden houses, they burnt like matchboxes. But *she* believed the people in it had set fire to it themselves, to get money.

The time the comet came, too, it was over this hill. They were allowed to get up to see it. Bowey wakened them when it was ready, and put their ulsters on and brought them out; and they sat on the edge of the verandah and looked ... so long that Luce nearly went to sleep again. But he didn't; he stared and stared at it — tail and all — to make sure he'd never forget. But he wouldn't forget the rest of the stars either; the whole sky was chock-full of them. That was because there was no moon, and because it was right in the middle of the night. (When the moon was round and big, like a bladder hanging up at the butcher's, you couldn't see the stars, it put them out.)

Sure as sure, though, just as he was lying thinking all this, thinking, too, what they'd play at to-morrow, and what he'd ask Mr. Burroughs at lessons, and how pretty Miss Burroughs was; then, Bowey would call out from the back verandah, where the bathroom was: "Your bath's ready, Cuffy!"

But he didn't move; and Mamma, she mostly made a kind of sigh and said: "Oh, dear! there she goes again. I really must call her over the coals."

And he, just to stay sitting; "But why *should* she say 'Master Cuffy' ... if she doesn't want to? Other children's servants don't."

But Mamma knew why he did it, and only said: "Don't ask silly questions. Off you go now! Or the water will be cold." And she tipped down her lap till he had to stand on his feet.

But still he hung back. "Why does Bowey always have to give me my bath? Why can't I do it myself? ... why can't I?

I'm nearly nine now, and I learn Latin, and ... and you could look at my ears after!"

Mamma laughed. "There would be a great deal more of you than your ears I'd have to look at. But you know quite well Bowey wouldn't like it. She's bath'd you both ever since she came. And it wouldn't do to offend her."

"Why not? We pay her money."

"There are some things all the money in the world wouldn't buy. And what Bowey did for me was one of them."

Cuffy knew quite well what Mamma meant. But not for anything would he have shown it. Papa and his illness were fast getting to seem like a dream, a nasty dream — being chased by a black horse, or trying to run with your legs in water — that you put far away from you, and did your best never, never to remember.

Back he whisked to his original theme.

"Well, can I when I'm *truly* nine? Mamma! Say yes!" — and he pumped her arm up and down.

"Oh well, perhaps. We'll see — now, *do* you want Bowey to have to come and fetch you?"

Grudgingly Cuffy dragged his feet to the door. There, however, he stood to finger and break a morsel from the edge of a damaged brick; went back to the verandah's edge to flip it into the roadway; then took aim with an imaginary ball down the length of the verandah (oh, *why* did children, no matter how tired, so hate to go to bed?) and only at a second, impatient shout from the bathroom disappeared into the house.

He left his mother deep in thought. What he said was true: very soon he would be a big boy, "little Cuffy" no more: the day of long legs and lankiness was at hand.

And together with an inevitable regret, at seeing the child she had fondled change and pass, came the baffling problem of his future. What should she do? How give him the education to which, as Richard's son, he had a right? Opposed, too, no doubt, by relatives and friends, who would think her ambitions for him exaggerated, absurd, and only likely to unfit him for his after life. Yes, she would have to fight for him. — And as she sat there, looking out into the shadowy silence of the bush street, where a line of tall gum-trees stood, but never a street-lamp, and where no vehicle moved after dark, Mary's face wore the dogged look with which she fronted and overcame obstacles; tempered by a touch of the selfless ecstasy which her children — or the thought of her children — alone had power to wake in her, who stood with her feet so firmly planted on this earth.

III

SHE decided to make the journey to Melbourne. In this, she was encouraged by Mr. Burroughs, whom she went to church one Sunday specially to consult. — As a rule nowadays she was no churchgoer. Her Sundays were spend in making up arrears of office-work, in overhauling the children's clothing, in cooking and baking for the week to come. ("If God bothers his head about me at all, He'll understand.") — And after service Mr. Burroughs, still in cassock and surplice, his stole — he had taken it off while coming down the aisle — dangling from one hand, stood in the porch and chatted to her, nodding and smiling at his departing congreations, or taking aim with a stone at some inquisitive dog. (Really, delightful man though he was, he had very little dignity as a clergyman.)

He entirely agreed with her that the time was coming for Cuffy to leave home.

"The boy has ability — learns quickly, remembers well. What he needs, to make a man of him, is to be among boys of his own age." And in relating the incident to his sister, he added: "Otherwise, he'll turn into a regular oddity. He has all the makings of one in him. Mammy-fed — that's what he is. Nothing but women round him, and only a girl to play with."

So, at midwinter, Mary applied for and was granted "leave of absence;" and wrote announcing her arrival to some of her old friends. Just as she expected, she had heard no more of Henry Ocock, Sir Jake was the most influential person she knew. Through him she would obtain particulars of the Melbourne Grammar School, the terms, and rules of entry; and find out how the land lay with regard to a possible scholarship.

It was to Sir Jake, too, she supposed, that the hated appeal for a loan would eventually have to be made.

Next, she fell to furbishing up her clothes, turning, sponging, pressing; inking the seams of black gloves; persuading old bonnet-plumes back into curl with the aid of a silver fruit-knife; cutting out and stitching a couple of new frocks for Lucie. The child went with her, of course; there was never any question of leaving Lucie behind.

Cuffy would stop at home with Bowey and the Relieving Officer, the latter by special request a woman, whom Bowey could put up and do for. Hence, another of Mary's jobs before she set out was thoroughly to clean the house. for the older she grew, and the poorer, the more fanatically she clung to a spotless nicety — it was all that was left her — and no stranger on entering should ever be able to point to an "Irish curtain," or a dusty corner; her carpets were hooked down, not nailed, and the beds could every one be washed under. And having dragged the dining-room furniture out into the middle of the floor, she was horrified at the state of the walls: bare, they showed brown and fly-stained, and bore numberless traces of greasy little fingers. She might just as well, while she was about it, give walls and ceiling a fresh coat of whitewash.

There was nothing unusual in this; she had always to be her own handyman nowadays; taking sewing-machine and clocks to pieces, cleansing the parts and fiddling with them, till she got them fixed and going again. (And oddly enough, thus late in the day, she had discovered in herself an unsuspected interest in machines: they seemed to her to have more meaning in them, more *sense*, less room for vagaries, than most other things in life.) Once, to retrieve a dead mouse, she had been obliged to take the action of the piano apart. Whitewashing four walls and a ceiling was child's play in comparison. So, tying up her head in a handkerchief, and binding an apron round her waist, she climbed with her bucket to the top of the tall wooden step-ladder. And soon the great flat brush was sucking and splashing, the thick, milky drops were flying.

At times like these the children were bidden to keep out of the way. Thus they were in the garden when the accident happened.

What caused it, she never knew. Perhaps, in trying to drive her brush into an awkward corner of the ceiling, she had leaned too far to one side; or the bucket, perched on top of the steps, might have threatened to tip over, and she have made too hasty a grab at it. However it was, she lost her balance, struggled desperately to regain it — the bare walls offered no hold — and came down with a crash, bucket and steps on top of her. The noise, and the scream that escaped her in spite of herself, reached Bowey, who was scrubbing the kitchen; and in the old woman came running, drying her hands on her apron, loud-voiced with alarm.

"Mrs. Mahony, Mrs. Mahony! Now what *have* you done? Whatever have you done now!"

"*Hush*, Bowey! — you'll frighten the children. It's all right, I'm not dead. Quick, help me up before they come. It's my leg I think — oh! my leg." And while Bowey pulled away steps and bucket, and lugged and tugged at her, Mary bit her lips, white with pain.

"Fetch me a drink of water, and then I'll try — no, stop, I *can* straighten it, it's not broken — thank God for that! Oh, Bowey, don't be so silly." For, in her relief, Bowey had flung her apron over her head and sat down to cry. "Help me to the bed. I'll rest for a bit."

There she remained, sick and giddy, the injured leg bound round with cold-water bandages. The children came running in, full of interest and excitement. *They* knew, from bitter experience, what it meant to hurt your legs, graze your knees bloody, and have to sit still with cloths tied round them. Now Mamma had done it; and it was rather fun to perch on the edge of the bed and talk to her while she drank her tea. Other days she never had time to talk.

Next morning, though she ached from top to toe, Mary managed to drag herself into the office, where she sat to work, her leg — by now it was discoloured, and acutely painful to the touch — stretched out before her on a stool. But in spite of all her care it grew worse instead of better; and by the end of the third day, being still unable to stand, she gave the journey to Melbourne up as lost. Here she would need to stay.

Having handed over charge to her deputy, who had now to lodge at the primitive hotel, she strove to resign herself to an inactivity that was new to her. Not that she was idle: she mended, darned, knitted, without stopping. Yet soon it began to seem to her, who had so seldom been off her feet, that all she really did was to lie there, hour after hour, day after day, listening to time tick past, waiting for an improvement that *would not* come.

Every remedy she had ever heard of for the relief of a bruised bone, she tried: bathing, poulticing, fomenting: everything, except sending for the local doctor. She knew no good of him; and, anyhow, her belief in doctors was small; she having always been behind the scenes as it were in medicine. Or perhaps her long dependence on Richard, and Richard's skill, had shaken her faith in anyone else. And when at length she yielded to Bowey's entreaties and sent for Dr. Forrest, it was just as she expected. The most ordinary little up-country practitioner, he had nothing fresh to suggest; her merely confirmed her in her treatment, and bade her to go on with it. Time alone, said he, was needed for complete recovery.

While he was there, a strange thing happened. From so

much thinking and worrying, her brain had grown very woolly: and, as she lay listening to him stumbling over his words, watching his fumbly hands, she had a kind of lapse of memory, in which he got all mixed up in her mind with some one else, a doctor just like him, who had sat beside her and asked her questions — oh, years and years ago, on Ballarat, when her first baby was born, and Richard had been too nervous to attend her himself. And this confusion spread and grew till the past seemed much more real than the present, and she was once again the frightened girl-wife, lying on her first sick bed. — Even after he had gone, she could not shake herself wholly free.

The children and their chatter roused her, and Bowey carrying in a tray. But at night there was nobody to call her back, and she would drift, and drift, till she was very far away. Otherwise, she had nothing to do but lie and count the throbs (in the darkness they thudded like little hammers), struggling to make herself believe they were getting easier; when all the time (and she knew it) they were growing steadily worse. Then, her courage failed her; and she, who had never been given to brooding, finding it simpler just to shoulder her burdens and plod on — she, too, now fell to questioning Providence, trying to dig out a meaning in, a reason for what had happened. "It all seems so *stupid*. What's the use of it? What good can it do anyone?" But more often she reproached herself: "Oh, *why* couldn't I have left those walls alone! *So* dirty they were not." And to these words, oddly enough, there would come an answer. Somebody or something, that was like, and yet not like herself; something that stood aloof, looking coldly on, would say: *"You* could never have done that. It isn't in you." To which she, her real self, gave back hotly: "I can't bear *dirt* ... if that's what you mean!" But as to this, the thing that was her, yet not her, refused to be drawn. The sole response, given in an icy tone, was: "No use talking now. It's too late. As one's made, one's made" — which sounded like a knell. And *was* the finish; for to: "Oh, I know that, I know! But *why* was I made like it? Who's responsible?" never a word came in reply.

Night after night she went through the same performance, to which the unbearable thought was added: "Oh, *what* would become of *them*, if ... if ... " or "Shouldn't I after all have thought twice, before ... " Until one night she became conscious that she was talking aloud, getting audible answers. Then, panic seized her, lest she should be going out of her mind; and, having faced this new horror till day broke, she took a sudden decision, and sent a cry for help to the friend who had never yet failed her; whose great good sense would know what it was best to do.

And as fast as train and coach would carry her, Tilly came: a Tilly greatly altered since the death of her child; in many ways but a shadow of her former self; gaunt-looking and lean, where she had once been round and comfortable. But at sight of Mary's predicament all her old energy revived. In two twos she had grasped and taken command of the situation.

More horrified than she dared to show by the appearance of the wound, which by now was dark, and very puffy, she would hear of nothing less than Melbourne, and a Melbourne doctor.

"What? Leave you here and let that ignorant brute lose your leg for you? Not me!"

Mary's faint objections of the expense, of a "leave" that was all but up, passed unheeded. The wires were set in motion, the authorities informed, those good friends, the Devines, called on to do their share. After which, Tilly spent half one night at the sewing-machine, manufacturing a loose dark garment, without fastenings, that could be slipped on over the patient's head. Then, since a journey in a crowded coach was out of the question, she took a door off its hinges, placed a mattress on it, saw Mary laid on this improvised stretcher, and carried out to a cart with its flap down, for the long bush-drive to the nearest railway-station.

A further protest of: "Oh, but I *couldn't* leave Lucie behind, Tilly — it's quite impossible. The child has never been parted from me. She'd fret herself sick," again received scant quarter.

"Then all I say is *let* her! Is *this* a time, I'd like to know, to pander to a spoilt child's whims!"

And it was of no use trying to explain. All the explanations in the world would not have made Tilly understand.

Lying in the cart, Mary raised herself on her elbow for a last look at her two: they stood hand-in-hand, the long-legged, the small and fat, among the little crowd that had gathered to watch her departure. Excitement had for the moment even dried Lucie's tears. It was not for her to set them re-flowing. So all she said, and in a matter-of-fact tone, was: "Now *do* be good, chicks, and not give Bowey any trouble; she'll have her hands full. And I shall soon be back. Till then, mind you look after Lucie, Cuffy — whatever you do, take care of her."

Cuffy he just nodded. He thought she *needn't* have said that about being good, in front of everybody. Or about Luce either. For he always did — besides, she'd said it ever so often before. So he only nodded, and looked at the horse and the man who was driving it, instead of her. Anyhow, he didn't care much to look at Mamma these days: her face was so red and hot-looking, not a bit like it ought to be. He didn't like to see her dressed so funny either, lying out there in a cart for all these people to stare at. He wished she'd hurry up and go. — And soon she did; for Aunt Tilly was dreadfully afraid they'd miss the train — though what she said to the man was: "Now if you let your horse break into a trot I'll brain you!" Then she climbed up and sat beside Mamma, with a bottle and a parasol; and the horse walked away with them through the township.

But all the same it was a *very* exciting going-away. And it was *his* door Mamma was lying on; because it was the smallest. Now, there was only a hole where the door had been. You could look through it at night to where Luce slept with Bowey. Mamma had said it was a good job he had holidays, because of Luce. But it didn't really matter, for Luce never wanted to play now, only to stop with Bowey. As long as she could do that, she left off crying.

So he played alone. Just at first Mamma's going left a sort of hole in him (like the door.) But after that he thought he was really rather glad. For when she wasn't there he didn't need to think so much about her. She wasn't *nice* to think of, since she fell off the steps — not able to walk properly, and her face so red and swollen. He wanted her to look like she always had.

But even though he could manage to forget her face, he wasn't really happy. Because of a secret he knew — one he never told anybody, not even Luce. As long as he was out in the garden it didn't bother him much. But when he went to bed, before he was sleepy, then it was just like a lump in his chest. It was something he'd heard Aunt Tilly say to Bowey, when she didn't know he was listening. How, if Mamma's leg didn't get better, she might have to have a wooden one. And that was *simply dreadful.* He'd once seen an old man with a wooden leg, strapped on where his own leg stopped — just a long thin stick, with a lump at his knee — and at the thought of Mamma having to go about as hideous as that, he could have cried. Of course, ladies had dresses which covered it up; but you couldn't stop the noise it made on the floor, going clump, clump, clump; or the way the old man had to roll about when he walked — oh, no, no! he couldn't *bear* to think of Mamma like that, truly he couldn't. Why, the larrikins would shout after her in the road. And when he went to school (and she'd promised him faithfully he should) she might come and see him, and then the other boys would laugh and make fun of her behind her back, and he'd feel so ashamed he believed he'd die. Only to think about it made his sheet get twisted like a rope, and the blanket fall down to the floor. And Bowey heard him and came in and picked it up, and scolded him for not being asleep. (As if you could *make* yourself go to sleep, if your eyes didn't want to!)

In the daytime he played his hardest. But heaps of days went by, a whole week of them, and it began to be dreadfully dull, always playing alone. Bowey wouldn't let him ask other children in: "I don't know if your Ma would like it." In despair he took to doing things he *knew* Mamma didn't like: hanging over the garden-gate to see if somebody mightn't go past; or swinging on it . . . till the cross-bar broke, and he had an awful time fixing it up so that Bowey shouldn't know. After that he did another thing he wasn't allowed to: opened the gate, and went into the street and swung on the chains that were put on posts along the footpath, to keep you from falling into the gutters (which were ever so deep) when it was dark or you were tipsy. But while he was there, some rude children came from the state-school and asked if his mother knew he was out. And he felt himself go so red that he didn't remember the proper answer, which was, yes, she'd given you sixpence to buy a monkey and were *you* for sale. Instead, he jumped up and ran back into the garden.

But then one day he had an idea — a perfectly scrumptious one, and Luce liked it, too. They'd make a flag for when Mamma came home — people always had flags when anything specially nice happened. Bowey had given them their threepences for the week, Mamma'd told her to. He'd spent his; for always, as soon as he got it, he tore up to the little lolly-shop by the Chinese Camp, where you got a simply enormous lot of chocolate-pipes for threepence (because they were gone whitey); but Luce still had hers, and thought it was a *lovely* idea, and would give it. (Instead of putting it in her money-box.) So on Monday, when Bowey was busy washing and hadn't time to see them, they ran down the street to the township, and bought a beautiful piece of turkey-stuff, bright red, and ever so large; and he cut a stick for it, and they made holes in it and tied on, so that it was a flag. Only it looked very bare, flags mostly had something painted on them; so they decided they'd *write* something on theirs; and went indoors and picked some beads off one of Mamma's cushions, and got a needle and cotton from Bowey's workbox, and began to stitch "Mamma" in white beads on the red stuff. It was *awfully* difficult; Luce was a perfect donkey, and couldn't do anything, and his hands weren't much good either. Most of the beads broke, when you tried to poke the needle through them; and when he went to fetch some more, all the others on the cushion began to run away and he couldn't stop them. (He had to turn it with its face to the wall.)

It made him perspire all over to sew, it was such hard work. And the letters *wouldn't* go straight. It took ages; and he'd only just go MAM done when suddenly there was a telegram from Aunt Tilly saying they were coming back — the very next day! Then, he was far too excited to sew any more. He and Luce rushed about the garden shouting; and he made a song that went: Hurray, hurray, hurray, Mamma will be home to-day! (Which was *nearly* true.) But in the night he didn't believe he hardly slept at all, because of that about the wooden leg, which wouldn't go out of his head.

They started to watch for the coach long before it was time. They played at hearing it, and ran races down to the corner of the road to see. Bowey didn't tell them they weren't to, to-day.

And at last they *did* truly hear it — the horses' feet and the wheels rumbling — and he tore in and got the flag (they'd hidden it in the summer-house, so that Bowey shouldn't know), and then they both stood and held it, as high as ever they could. (Only there was no wind to make it fly.)

And first they saw the red through the trees, and then the whole coach. And no wonder it was so long coming, the horses were only just *lolloping* along; because it wasn't the coach that carried the mails. And it came to where they were, and pulled up, and the driver twisted his reins round the brake, and climbed down and opened the door. And after he had fetched a carpet-bag, Aunt Tilly got out . . . backwards, her behind first. (By now his heart was thumping so loud he thought people would hear it, because in a minute now he'd know about the leg.) But then . . . why, what was this? Instead of Mamma getting out next, the coachman shut the door, and got back on his box, and untwisted the reins and shook them at the horses. Hi! What was he doing? Why was he taking Mamma away again? Cuffy's eyes felt as if they were popping out of his head, and his mouth got so dry it stuck together. He just managed to make it say: "But where's Mamma? Hasn't she come?" — And all of a sudden, as he said this, his heart started to knock his chest so hard that what it had done before hadn't been knocking at all.

And now Aunt Tilly turned round and was coming to them; and to Bowey, too; and first she looked most dreadfully, *dreadfully* angry, and then her face sort of shrivelled up, till she hadn't any eyes left, and her mouth sort of went right inside her cheeks. And then she began to cry . . . cry like anything . . . and took out her handkerchief and tried to stop, and couldn't, and was angrier still, and said, ever so fiercely: "No, she hasn't. She couldn't. Your Mamma will never come again. She's dead."

IV

IN after years, Tilly would volunteer in self-defence: "Upon my soul, I never *meant* to blurt it out like that. I was going to prepare 'em . . . break it gently, and so on. But when I saw those two chits standing there clutching that bit of rag — well, I don't know, but if you ask me, I think it was this what got me. Anyhow, there it was: I started to cry, and it just jumped out. But I've often thought since, it was probably best so after all. They had to know. And the sooner the better. Besides, it's not my way to go beating about the bush. — Never shall I forget though, how that child *blushed*!"

For, as the hard, cruel words came flying at him, like so many stones, all the blood in his body seemed to rush to Cuffy's face and stop there, scorching and burning. He forgot everything else — Luce, the flag, Mamma not coming — he'd only one thought: to get away from Aunt Tilly, somewhere where she . . . where nobody could look at him any more. And so he turned and ran, ran for his life, to the top of the garden, in behind the big cactuses, holding his fingers to his ears so that he shouldn't hear if she went on talking, or if they shouted for him to come back. And sat there, his ears stopped up, his eyes shut, his face like as if somebody had smacked it hard all over.

Later on, when time brought wisdom, he saw that what had driven the blood to his head, his heels to flight, was shame: the shame that was always to overcome him in face of another's shamelessness. But as a small boy, he just went on sitting there, conscious of nothing but his hot and angry cheeks. Nor, till he made sure nobody was being sent to fetch him, did his fingers relax their hold.

Nobody came: and gradually his face cooled off, his heart stopped thumping. Then he was able to think; and his thinking was: it can't, it *can't* be true! . . . somebody must be telling it wrong, or not know properly. Mamma would *never* go away and die, and leave them like this. That was something that simply couldn't happen. — And with the feeling that to hear more about it might somehow make things different, he got up and went down the path to the house.

This was quiet as quiet, not a sound anywhere: and for a second the wild hope raced through him that the coach had come back, while his ears were stopped, and taken Aunt Tilly away again. (Oh, if only . . . if *only!*) First the drawing-room . . . nobody there. In the dining-room there couldn't be anybody either, it was so still: but he just went round the door to see — and oh, goodness gracious! behind it, on the sofa, sitting close together, were Aunt Tilly and Bowey: and what they looked like, he would never, never forget. They weren't making not the very littlest sound, which was why he hadn't known: they were too *deep* in crying for that, their faces all wrinkles, their eyes shut and gone in, their mouths stretched right across their cheeks, their heads nodding and nodding like china mandarins. — Once more he turned and fled.

Back in the garden he stood about, not knowing what to do or where to go; and, in standing, picked the little new leaves and buds off the Japanese honeysuckle. Everything looked just like it always did, and yet was somehow quite different. He felt as if he'd never really seen things before: the summer-house, the gum-trees, the swing, the wood-stack, Bowey's empty kerosene-tins. They all looked like strangers, the garden, too — oh, but what was he doing? The tree he was pulling the leaves off now was not the honeysuckle at all, but the elderberry, which he simply *loathed*, and never touched if he could help it, it had such a horrid smell. — This garden they were so fond of, where he and Luce had played and played.

Luce! Where was she? What had become of her? Rushing indoors again he looked everywhere, going into every room (only not the dining-room). And at last, from a teeny-weeny noise, he found her: squeezed as far as she could go, right up by the wall, under Mamma's bed. Alone, forgotten, she had crawled in there and hidden herself, safe from every one but Mamma. She wasn't crying any more, but her face was fat with it, and she wouldn't come out, he couldn't make her. So he went in beside her, and said: "It's all right, Luce, it's all right, I'm here, I'll take care of you." And they just went on lying there together. Till all of a sudden, feeling how hard the bare boards were (which was all Mamma would ever allow under a bed) he remembered how he'd dreaded the thumping noise a wooden leg would make on the floors. And that was too much for him. Turning his head away, and hiding his face in his sleeve, he began to sob and cry, like a small little child. And went on for what seemed like hours, till he couldn't cry any longer.

Blowing her nose — so loud that anybody out in the street could hear it — Aunt Tilly sent Bowey to find them and bring them to be told "all about it". (The whites of her eyes were red and blotchy, her face shone like an onion.)

"Well now, you poor children, I suppose you'll be wanting to know just what happened. Well, my dears, it was exactly as I said all along. This darned fool of a doctor here never found out the real trouble, which was a piece chipped off the bone, which caused all the mischief. And when we got to Melbourne it was too late, the doctors couldn't save the leg; and when they went to cut it off, your poor Ma was too far gone to stand it, and just pegged out. After she went away from here she was light-headed most of the time, and didn't know what she was talking about; but *I* knew how she worried about what was to become of you two if she had to go; and I gave her my solemn promise I'd look after you. And so I will . . . for her sake. For she was the best friend I ever 'ave had, and the oldest, too. We'd known each other since she wasn't much bigger than you — long before she ever met your Pa, that was. She used to live with me and my poor sister — Polly we called 'er then; little nimble busy Polly."

Hastily Cuffy averted his eyes; for, the way her face began to twitch, he thought she was going to cry again. (Besides, they knew all about when Mamma was Polly. She'd told it them heaps of times.)

However, Aunt Tilly just sniffed hard up her nose, and swallowed in her throat, and dabbed her eyes with a handkerchief, and went on: "Well, you're not really big enough yet to understand all what that means; but anyhow, my dears, I saw to it that she got a nice grave — one out in the main avenue, easy to get at, not tucked away in a corner. And it'll have a stone on it, too, with her name and age and a text, all proper and right, as soon as the earth sinks. And if you're good and do as you're bid, you shall go to Melbourne one day and see it, too. — But now I must get started to work. There's so much to think about and see to that I don't feel I know whether I'm standing on my head or my heels."

Hand-in-hand Cuffy and Lucie went back to the garden, and sat down on the wood of the woodstack. There they stayed: they didn't know what to do with themselves, and the day seemed to have lasted years already. Very soon the rattle of the sewing-machine came out to them; and this went on and on; for the first thing Aunt Tilly did was to sew mourning for them, out of some old black dresses of Mamma's (the kind of stuff you didn't ever make *boys'* clothes of!). But *she* didn't know that, or how to sew them, and the things she made were simply awful: Mamma would *never* have let them go out such sights. Luce's dress pinched her under the arms, and one leg of his knickerbockers hung down longer than the other. But when he showed her it, she didn't take any notice, and said a little thing like that didn't matter. (*Never* would he be able to go to school in them!)

But it hurt even worse to see her opening Mamma's cupboard and fetching out Mamma's clothes and turning them over and cutting them up, just as if they belonged to her. In vain he protested: "When Papa died we only had bands on our sleeves. Mamma wouldn't let us wear black."

At these words, and at the tone they were said in, Aunt Tilly gave him a very queer look, and left off sewing Luce a petticoat.

"Now look here, my boy, just you listen to me. I'm not going to stand any nonsense. You're older now by a year than you were when your poor Pa died, and I'll see to it that you do what's right by your Ma. She was the best woman that ever walked this earth, or ever will; she hadn't her like — as you children'll know some day to your cost. And when you do, you'd be scandalised to think you hadn't paid proper respect to her memory. So now not another word! Black you'll have, and black you'll wear!"

The stuff scratched like ants walking over you. At night, when Aunt Tilly was asleep, Bowey sewed tape round inside the necks to keep it off you. (Bowey knew what funny skins you had.)

Next, Aunt Tilly went all through the house with her spectacles on, and a pencil and paper, examining the furniture.

"What's she doing that for?"

"You'd better ask her yourself, my poor lamb," said Bowey; and how she said it showed *she* didn't like Aunt Tilly much either. — They were always "poor lambs" to Bowey now; she never scolded, and cried so that he didn't often go near her, for fear he'd have to cry again, too. (Aunt Tilly didn't know he ever had. And shouldn't.)

Once more he plucked up his courage. "Why are you doing that?" — Even to his own ears his voice didn't sound very *polite*.

"Why do you suppose?" said Aunt Tilly crossly; she was getting up all red and hot from looking under the sofa at its legs. "For my own amusement?"

"I don't know," said Cuffy simply and truthfully.

At this she whisked off her spectacles and made a face as if she was going to bite him. But then changed her mind, and said, just irritated-like: "Sakes alive, Cuffy! you're not a baby any more, to be asking such silly questions. Why, you'll soon be man; and have got to learn and behave like one. Now just listen to me. It's not a bit of good you carrying on. Your poor Ma's gone; and all the weeping and wailing in the world won't being 'er back. It's the end of 'er. But there's you two children left to be seen after and provided for *some'ow*, and money's what's needed to do it with. The things 'ave got to be sold, my dear — and for what they'll bring. Your Ma doesn't need them any more. She won't miss them — where she's gone."

"But we can't live without furniture!" Never had Tilly seen such wide, astonished eyes. — Oh, was there ever such a stupid child! You could wear your tongue out, explaining.

"Or do you mean we're not going to live here any more?"

"Why, *of course* not, you silly! How could you? Why, the new P.M.'ll be in before we can say Jack Robinson, and'll need the place for his own furniture."

"Where are we going?" — Cuffy's mouth felt so dry it would hardly speak.

"Well, that's just what's not fixed yet. I'm waiting for your Uncle Jerry, to talk things over."

But Uncle Jerry lived ever such a long way off; and it was two whole days before he got there. Awful days, that seemed as if they'd never end. He just *mooned* about, kicking things with his feet, and feeling more mis'rable than he'd believed he ever could any more (after Mamma dying). But he didn't say a word to Luce: he was afraid of making her cry again. As it was, Aunt Tilly *despised* Luce, thought she was an awful baby, always liking to be *with* somebody and never alone — she even tried to make her not sleep in Bowey's bed. And when every night she found her in it just the same, she said she was a very naughty girl.

Then it was Cuffy's turn to try and explain. Which was hard, because he didn't have the right words. "It's not *really* naughty, Aunt Tilly. Luce's always been like that. She can't help it."

"Can't help it? Never did I hear such nonsense! A great girl of eight! — Well, I know this, my boy, there's precious little of your poor Ma in either of you. It's your Pa you take after, both of you, more's the pity. He was just such another. What *she* had to put up with, her life long, simply doesn't bear telling."

In these wretched days, funny things went on in his, Cuffy's, mind. For one, he'd never known how much he'd hoped and *believed* everything could stay like it was, and they just go on living with Bowey and the furniture. He hadn't *wanted* to know different, that was it: he'd just been a stupid boy. He hadn't known either till now how fond he was of the "things". Even still he couldn't imagine life without them. They'd always been there, and everywhere Mamma and they went, they'd gone too: the big green leather armchair, the leather sofa, Papa's bookcase with the books in it, Mamma's bed, and her brushes with the ivory backs that had turned all yellow. Oh, he simply couldn't bear to think of anybody else using them, or sitting in them, or sleeping in them. Mightn't Uncle Jerry, when he saw how much you liked them . . . and how *mis'rable* it made you . . . mightn't he perhaps say you might keep them, he'd let you?

But this fond hope was quickly routed. To begin with, Uncle Jerry was in a dreadful hurry. Aunt Fanny was ill, which was why he hadn't gone to Melbourne to Mamma's funeral; and now he'd only got a very few days' leave, which mostly went in travelling. He told this directly he got there; so you couldn't expect him to sit down and listen to *you*. After he'd kissed Luce and him, and said how most awfully sorry he was about Mamma, who'd always been his favourite sister, and who he'd never forget, he went into the dining-room with Aunt Tilly and shut the door, to talk business.

But no sooner they'd started to talk than they began to quarrel. Well, not exactly quarrel; but to talk *very* loud, and with a tremendous lot of arguing. He could hear them from the garden, going on and on, till at last he couldn't stand it any longer, and went close up by the window (where the elderberry tree grew) to try and hear. And it was Mamma they were talking about, all Mamma's business; and without ever asking him or Luce a thing. (Oh, *why* did he have to be so young? Why wasn't he allowed to talk, too?)

Making himself small, he crushed up under the window-sill; and then he could hear every word. Aunt Tilly was only a poor woman (why, he'd thought she was *ever* so rich!) and had a husband on her hands who'd never be good for anything again; but she was quite ready to do her share — though *some* might think she'd done it already, what with the illness, and the doctors' fees, and the funeral, and paying for a first-class grave. Still; as she said. But fair was fair and right was right, and after all, in *her* case, there wasn't any blood-tie, nor any real claim on her: what she'd done she'd done solely out of friendship. — But Uncle Jerry, he was poor, too; he'd only got his salary from the Bank to live on, and that was no prince's, but a damnably tight fit, with a wife to keep, and three children to educate; and though he wouldn't go so far as to call Fanny extravagant, yet they needed every penny he had to get along; and if he now took on two fresh burdens, why, it simply couldn't be done. Besides, there was Fanny to be considered, and it would come damnably hard on Fanny; for it would mean she had to deny herself every luxury — all those little comforts he was just beginning to be able to allow her.

But here the eavesdropper's courage, smitten to the core, failed him altogether. And not caring whether they heard him or not, how loudly his boots scratched the flagstones, he scrambled to his feet and ran away. Behind the cactuses, which was the most secret place he knew, he flung himself face downwards on the ground. His heart was full to bursting. Nobody . . . *nobody* wanted them, him or Luce, any more.

Thus it happened that, when the thunderbolt fell, he was as unprepared for it as Luce herself.

("I leave it to you, Jerry, to tell 'em what we've fixed. I've had my fill of it. It's been nothing but trying to din into them what's *got* to be, ever since I'm here.")

Uncle Jerry came out into the garden and called him, and talked a lot to him. Again about how sorry he was about Mamma, and how he'd never stop missing her, even though he hadn't seen much of her lately, through living so far away. But a sister was a sister. And then, how she hadn't left any money behind to keep them, and what a lot of this was going to cost, and how times were so hard and money so scarce that he'd barely got enough to pay for Aunt Fanny and his own children. The extra expense would be a sad drain — though of course he'd do it, for Mamma's sake. And ever so much more which wasn't easy to understand.

Not till Uncle Jerry'd been talking for a long time did it get plain what he really meant. Which was that he and Luce were not to stay together *any* more. One of them was going to live with Aunt Tilly, and one with Aunt Fanny.

The blow was so unexpected, so crushing, that, even if he'd been able to *think* of anything to say, he couldn't have said it. His throat sort of shut up. He just stood and stared at Uncle Jerry without really seeing him.

But the next minute things began buzzing round in his head like angry bees. Here were two more he'd never thought of. One was that, even though they weren't able to stop with Bowey, they would not both be going to live with Aunt Tilly. Or not allowed to be together. (And of all the dreadful things that had happened, this last was the worst.) Hurriedly he tried to think some thoughts about Aunt Fanny. But he couldn't . . . because he didn't know her; he'd never even seen her! He only knew Mamma didn't like her *very* much; Mamma always said Aunt Fanny was jealous of her, for being Uncle Jerry's favourite sister. And how she'd always been so expensive and extravagant, wanting the best of everything for herself and the children, and poor Uncle Jerry having to slave and slave, and never able to put by anything for a rainy day. But that was all, and he didn't like it; and he simply couldn't imagine . . . And suddenly, compared with this stranger, Aunt Tilly, in spite of her rude, rough way of talking, became something to hold on to, cling fast to — a very anchor of refuge — because she'd known Mamma so well, and all about Papa.

None the less, he just couldn't bring it over his lips to beg: "Have us both, oh, have us both!" For Aunt Tilly didn't want both of them; and it was such a new and dreadful feeling not to be wanted.

Instead, as the next best thing, he managed to say: "Oh, Aunt Tilly, please, *please*, let Luce stop with you! I'll go to Aunt Fanny." — His voice amazed him by coming out quite low and bass, as he said it.

And Aunt Tilly wasn't at all unkind. She looked at him a minute, and then said: "Now, Cuffy, now, my dear, you *must* be reas'nble. You're not old enough yet to understand, even if I told you all about it. But your uncle and me have gone into the whole thing and talked it out, and this is the only way to fix it."

"But why?" (Some day he would have a real bass voice altogether.)

"Well, for one thing, because your Aunt Fanny's only got little *girls*, and won't be bothered looking after a boy."

"But why not? I'm . . . I'm all *right*," he gave back desperately. "I wouldn't be a scrap of trouble — *I* can wash and dress myself, and Luce can't . . . not always. And I don't mind playing with little girls — truly I don't; I've always played with Luce." And as Aunt Tilly still only went on shaking her head, he cast about, once more, for words to describe Luce's funninesses. "You see, she doesn't *know* Aunt Fanny and these children. And she's so dreadfully shy, and when she is, she gets so silly and frightened. — And . . . and then . . . I said I'd look after her."

"Yes, I know you did. But in this world, my boy, it's not always possible to stick to one's promises. You'll find that out as you go on. Things happen of 'emselves and put a stopper on it. — Anyhow, there it is. Your Aunt Fanny's mind's made up, and nothing *I* can say will change it."

And as Cuffy still stood fixing her, she added: "It's no good looking at me like that. I've done all *I* can — with money so tight, and your Uncle a dead weight on my hands."

"*What* uncle?" (This was as rude as rude; for he knew quite well who she meant.)

"Why, your Uncle Purdy, of course. Lies there like a log, and'll never do a stroke of work again."

"He's not my uncle!" But, in saying it, his voice broke, and that was the end of it.

Luce, oh, Luce! . . . his poor fat little cry-baby sister, who'd never once been away from Mamma (or him; or Bowey). The agony of imagining what might happen to her was too much for him: he had to go and do hard, *cruel* things (to a bird, to the piano). Never, never, he knew it now, had he been so fond of anybody as Luce. Even Mamma being dead didn't seem to matter so much.

Uncle Jerry was starting home next morning; there was only to-day left to tell Luce and get her ready. — But when they did, it was the funniest thing: she didn't cry at all, no, not one single drop. She just stood and gaped at them, with her mouth half open, looking more of a silly than ever. And she stopped like this — all day. Bowey said the shock had been too much for her, and she didn't properly understand what was going on. And kept saying: "Cry, my poor lamb, cry, it'll do you good." Herself she cried like anything, while she was packing Luce's things in one of Papa's little old leather portmanteaux. But Luce didn't seem to mind, and stood staring at her clothes as if she didn't recognise them; till he couldn't help it either, and went and hid, and howled and howled. But not even when he took her to the summer-house and said: "Never mind, Luce, just you wait. As soon as ever I've saved up enough money I'll come and fetch you, and we'll run away — somewhere where they'll never find us again." Even then she only said: "Will you, Cuffy?" — just as if she didn't really care, and though he swore it on his "finger wet".

Uncle Jerry had hired a buggy to drive over from the railway in, because the coach was so slow; and now he had to drive it back. Early next morning he went and fetched it; and Luce's box, with a rope round it, because the lock wouldn't hold, was tied on behind. Luce was just the same as yesterday, and let Bowey dress her without a word — Bowey said it was like dressing a doll, for she didn't do a thing for herself, and held out her fingers to have her gloves put on as if she was a little baby. Then they kissed her good-bye and she was lifted up and put in. But Uncle Jerry remembered something he'd forgotten and got out again; and Luce sat up there by herself in the buggy, with a face like underdone pastry, all alone with the horse. She was most *dreadfully* afraid of horses; and it gave him a pain right through him only to look at her and think how afraid she was. Still, he went on doing it; but she never once looked at him, or turned her head, or called out good-bye . . . or anything. She just drove away.

Then his own turn came.

It was eleven o'clock — the time he used to get home from lessons. And Luce would be standing at the gate watching for him, in her dirty pinny; and Bowey'd scold because he dropped his satchel down anywhere; and Mamma be sitting in the office, wanting to hear how he'd "done". Now, everybody was gone (Bowey, too) except him. And the rooms were quite empty: after the auction men had brought carts and taken away all the furniture. The house was the only thing left. — And suddenly it came over him with a rush that he simply couldn't leave it like this. And though Aunt Tilly and the luggage was standing in the road, afraid of missing the coach (though it had been *told* to fetch them!) he tore back up the garden and hurriedly felt through his pockets. What was the dearest thing he had? Why, his knife, of course; the new one with three blades Mamma had given him last birthday, which he'd been so proud of. Just for a second, it was so precious, he wavered; then, making a hole, he put it in, pressed it down as far as he could, and filled in the earth again . . . like a grave. It wouldn't grow into anything; but it would always be there, something to remember — something to remember them by.

The coach! And Aunt Tilly shouting like mad where was he. Cleaning his hands on his seat, back he flew. — And now there was a most awful fuss till the bags and boxes were arranged, and counted, and they could climb in themselves. (Aunt Tilly was the dreadfullest old fidget he'd ever known, and kept on asking the driver if he was quite sure they'd catch the train, till he was ashamed of her.)

They were the only passengers; and as soon as they'd got through the township, she untied her bonnet-strings and put her feet up on the cushions and went to sleep. Though she groaned each time the coach gave a lurch or a bump. (In her sleep.) Very gingerly Cuffy opened the window, which she'd shut because of the dust, and stood at it, with his back to her, pretending to look out. He didn't want her to see his face. For all of a sudden, as the last familiar landmarks went by, something funny happened to him. The dreadful, hot, *angry* feeling he'd had in his inside ever since he'd heard Mamma was dead, and would never come back (it'd made him angry with everybody and everything, Mamma, too): well, now, suddenly he didn't seem to feel angry any more; and, as he realised it, the tears began to race down his cheeks, like mad, and without him being able to do a thing to stop them. And they went on running; and were so blazing hot that they burnt. He didn't make the least little sound though. He'd rather have died than let Aunt Tilly know.

But after a time, as tears will, they ran dry; and then, very gradually, other and pleasanter thoughts insinuated themselves. The coach. He always had liked travelling in a coach — specially if there was heaps of room. And after the coach would come the train (a train-journey nobody could help enjoying!) and then another coach; it'd be far the longest journey he'd ever gone! And that wasn't all. Aunt Tilly (oh gommy! she did look a sight when she went to sleep) had once said something about a pony . . . for him to ride to school on. Oh, perhaps, perhaps . . . even though he *couldn't* like her, he thought she was a silly, common old woman . . . oh, please,

please, dear God, let there be a pony! And let me soon see Luce again, let her come and live with Aunt Tilly, too, and stop there, so as I can teach her how to ride. (As he prayed, he saw himself leading a pretty brown horse, with Luce sitting on it, and him telling her everything what she had to do. And she wasn't a bit scared of it any more; because *he* was there, and she knew he —— Ho! but that was wattles: yes, there they came, a whole crowd of them, in full flower . . . he'd smelt them before he saw them! And shutting his eyes, the better to drink in the adored scent, he sniffed and sniffed, till the dust all but choked him, and his head went giddy.

And, from now on, his spirits continued steadily to rise, hope adding itself to hope, in fairy fashion. Just as mile after mile combined to stretch the gulf, that would henceforth yawn, between what he had been, and what he was to be.

GROWING PAINS

Sketches of Girlhood

THE BATHE

STRIPPED of her clothing, the child showed the lovely shape of a six-year-old. Just past the dimpled roundnesses of babyhood, the little body stood slim and straight, legs and knees closely met, the skin white as the sand into which the small feet dug, pink toe faultlessly matched to toe.

She was going to bathe.

The tide was out. The alarming, ferocious surf, which at flood came hurtling over the reef, swallowing up the beach, had withdrawn, baring the flat brown coral rocks: far off against their steep brown edges it sucked and gurgled lazily. In retreating, it had left many lovely pools in the reef, all clear as glass, some deep as rooms, grown round their sides with weeds that swam like drowned hair, and hid strange sea-things.

Not to these pools might the child go; nor did she need to prick her soles on the coral. Her bathing place was a great sandy-bottomed pool that ran out from the beach, and at its deepest came no higher than her chin.

Naked to sun and air, she skipped and frolicked with the delight of the very young, to whom clothes are still an encumbrance. And one of her runs led her headlong into the sea. No toe-dipping tests were necessary here; this water met the skin like a veil of warm silk. In it she splashed and ducked and floated; her hair, which had been screwed into a tight little knob, loosening and floating with her like a nimbus. Tired of play, she came out, trickling and glistening, and lay down in the sand, which was hot to the touch, first on her stomach, then on her back, till she was coated with sand like a fish breadcrumbed for frying. This, for the sheer pleasure of plunging anew, and letting the silken water wash her clean.

At the sight, the two middle-aged women who sat looking

on grew restless. And, the prank being repeated, the sand-caked little body vanishing in the limpid water to bob up shining like ivory, the tips of their tongues shot out and surreptitiously moistened their lips. These were dry, their throats were dry, their skins itched; their seats burned from pressing the hot sand.

And suddenly eyes met and brows were lifted in a silent question. Shall we? Dare we risk it?

"Let's!"

For no living thing but themselves moved on the miles of desolate beach; not a neighbour was within cooee; their own shack lay hid behind a hill.

Straightway they fell to rolling up their work and stabbing it with their needles.

Then they, too, undressed.

Tight, high bodices of countless buttons went first, baring the massy arms and fat-creased necks of a plump maturity. Thereafter bunchy skirts were slid over hips and stepped out of. Several petticoats followed, the undermost of red flannel, with scalloped edges. Tight stiff corsets were next squeezed from their moorings and cast aside: the linen beneath lay hot and damply crushed. Long white drawers unbound and, leg by leg, disengaged, voluminous calico chemises appeared, draped in which the pair sat down to take off their boots — buttoned boots — and stockings, their feet emerging red and tired-looking, the toes misshapen, and horney with callosities. Erect again, they yet coyly hesitated before the casting of the last veil, once more sweeping the distance for a possible spy. Nothing stirring, however, up went their arms, dragging the balloon-like garments with them; and, inch by inch, calves, thighs, trunks and breasts were bared to view.

At the prospect of getting water playmates, the child had clapped her hands, hopping up and down where she stood. But this was the first time she had watched a real grown-up undress; she was always in bed and asleep when they did it. Now, in broad daylight, she looked on unrebuked, wildly curious; and surprise soon damped her joy. So this was what was underneath! Skirts and petticoats down, she saw that laps were really legs; while the soft and cosy place you put your head on, when you were tired . . .

And suddenly she turned tail and ran back to the pool. She didn't want to see.

But your face was the one bit of you you wouldn't put

under water. So she had to.

Two fat, stark-naked figures were coming down the beach.

They had joined hands, as if to sustain each other in their nudity ... or as if, in shedding their clothes, they had also shed a portion of their years. Gingerly, yet in haste to reach cover, they applied their soles to the tickly sand: a haste that caused unwieldy breasts to bob and swing, bellies and buttocks to wobble. Splay-legged they were, from the weight of these protuberances. Above their knees, garters had cut fierce red lines in the skin; their bodies were criss-crossed with red furrows, from the variety of strings and bones that had lashed them in. The calves of one showed purple-knotted with veins; across the other's abdomen ran a deep, longitudinal scar. One was patched with red hair, one with black.

In a kind of horrid fascination the child stood and stared ... as at two wild outlandish beasts. But before they reached her she again turned, and, heedless of the prickles, ran seawards, out on the reef.

This was forbidden. There were shrill cries of: "Naughty girl! Come back!"

Draggingly the child obeyed.

They were waiting for her, and, blind to her hurt, took her between them and waded into the water. When this was up to their knees, they stooped to damp napes and crowns, and sluice their arms. Then they played. They splashed water at each other's great backsides; they lay down and, propped on their elbows, let their legs float; or, forming a ring, moved heavily round to the tune of: *Ring-a-ring-a-rosy, pop down a posy!* And down the child went, till she all but sat on the sand. Not so they. Even with the support of the water they could bend but a few inches; and wider than ever did their legs splay, to permit of their corpulences being lowered.

But the sun was nearing meridian in a cloudless sky. Its rays burnt and stung. The child was sent running up the beach to the clothes-heaps, and returned, not unlike a depressed Amor, bearing in each hand a wide, flower-trimmed, dolly-varden hat, the ribbons of which trailed the sand.

These they perched on their heads, binding the ribbons under their chins; and thus attired waded out to the deep end of the pool. Here, where the water came a few inches above their waists, they stood to cool off, their breasts seeming to float on the surface like half-inflated toy balloons. And when the sand stirred up by their feet had subsided, their legs could be seen through the translucent water oddly foreshortened, with edges that frayed at each ripple.

But a line of foam had shown its teeth at the edge of the reef. The tide was on the turn; it was time to go.

Waddling up the beach they spread their petticoats, and on these stretched themselves out to dry. And as they lay there on their sides, with the supreme mass of hip and buttock arching in the air, their contours were those of seals — great mother-seals come lolloping out of the water to lie about on the sand.

The child had found a piece of dry cuttlefish, and sat pretending to play with it. But she wasn't really. Something had happened which made her not like any more to play. Something ugly. Oh, never . . . never . . . no, not ever now did she want to grow up. *She* would always stop a little girl.

THREE IN A ROW

MISS ETHEL marched ahead carrying the candle, and so cupping it with her hand that the light fell full on her round, horn-rimmed spectacles, making these look like gigantic eyes.

"I'm sorry, girls," said she, throwing open a door, "this is the best I can do for you — every other room's full. But I know you won't mind turning in together. May's such a shrimp that you can put her between you and never know she's there."

Dutifully the three who followed at her heels chorused: "Oh, not at all," "We shall manage," "Very good of you to have us, Miss Ethel," as instructed by their respective Mammas.

But once the door had shut on their hostess they gathered round the bed — a narrow half-tester — in which they were expected to lie three in a row, and let their real feelings out.

"The old toad! Playing us such a scurvy trick!"

"On such a night, too!"

"And when she wrote she'd have heaps of room!"

"It's those Waugh girls from Bendigo that've done it. *Their* father's a judge! But anything's good enough for us."

"I wish I hadn't come," piped Patty, the youngest, a short, fat girl of eleven.

"Oh, you! — with your bulk you're safe for the lion's share. But what did the old hag mean by her cheek about me?" snapped May, who had come to the age of desiring roundnesses. "A shrimp, indeed!"

"Don't know I'm sure," said thirteen-year-old Tetta, not quite truthfully. (May's was just a case of the "girls from Bendigo" over again.) Tetta was getting rid of her clothes at top speed, peeling off her stockings, leaving one here, one there, her combinations on the floor where they fell. Then, holding her nightdress like a sail above her, she shot her arms into the sleeves, and was ready for bed while Patty was still conscientiously twisting a toothbrush round her gums, and May had got no further than loosening the buttons of her frock.

"Tetta! — you haven't done your teeth . . . or anything."

"Don't want to. And I'm giving my teeth a rest. A dentist told some one I know it wore teeth out if you were always brushing them," gave back Tetta easily.

The "Lazy Liar!" this evoked was cut through by her shrill: "Oh Lord, girls, *feathers*!" as she stooped to examine the build of the bed. This was that the bed had a distinct slope, out from the centre and down at the sides — she tried each in turn. And having let a few seconds elapse, for fear the others had noticed her wrigglings, she said mildly: "Look here, Mabs, if you like I'll take the middle. I don't mind being a bit crushed."

"Oh, no, you don't!" retorted May suspiciously, suspending her hair-brush. "I know what it means, my dear . . . when you're so willing to oblige." May was ratty with herself for being behindhand — even that stupid Pat had raced her. But to go to bed *properly* meant almost as much work as getting up in the morning.

"Well, for goodness' sake, put some biff into it. The mean bit of candle she's given us won't last for ever."

"No, I promised my mother to brush my hair twenty times every night and morning, and I'm not going to break my word for anyone," said May dourly; and pounded away with upraised arm. At which young Patty, who in her efforts to come in second had rather scamped the prescribed "folding" of her clothes, suffered a pang of conscience, and turned back to refold them. But Tetta thought: though she brushed it a hundred times it would never be anything but bristly. Yes, that was just what it was like — the bristles in a brush.

Now she and Pat lay stretched out, a sheet drawn over them, a hump of feathers between. Oh, it was a shabby pretence at a "double" — why, there was really hardly room for two. And when at last May came to join them — she had gargled her throat and cleaned her nails (just as if she was going to a party) — the rumpus began.

For Tetta said: "Blow out the candle first." This stood on the dressing-table, and it would have fallen to her, who lay on that side, to rise and extinguish it. May, the goose, doing as she was told, had then to climb over and in between them in the dark. There was a moment of wild confusion: dozens of legs, a whole army of them, seemed to be trampling and kicking in an attempt to sort themselves out. Tetta had taken a grip of the head-curtain, and so kept her balance, but Patty, unprepared, found nothing to hold to on the bare side of the bed, and, as May finally and determinedly squeezed herself in, slid to the floor with a cry and a thump.

"You pig!" from Tetta. "You did that on purpose."

"Well, what next I wonder! . . . after you two had taken all the room. Anyhow, now you'll just *have* to get up and make a light again."

Grumblingly Tetta swung out her feet and groped her unknown way. "Now where has that table gone to? Oh, *damn!*" For, coming suddenly and unexpectedly upon it, her elbow caught the candlestick and sent this flying. There was a crash; and the candle could be heard rolling over the bare boards.

"Now you've done it, you clumsy ass! Ten to one old Ethel'll come pouncing in on us."

"If I get a bit of china in my foot it'll be me who pounces." Tetta was on her knees, cautiously fumbling for the matches. These found and one struck, the candle was recovered; but the candlestick lay in fragments.

"Spill some grease on the floor and stick the candle to it," suggested May.

With some difficulty Tetta contrived this hold, clutching her nightgown to her out of reach of the flame. Then she crossed to the other side of the bed to see to Patty, who still lay where she had fallen, snivelling over a bruised arm and a hefty bump on the forehead.

As there was no butter handy, Tetta poured water into the basin, soaked a sponge and held it to the wounded place, to keep it from swelling — and over this the floor got rather wet and messy, for the half-burnt, guttering candle, some three inches high, shed its meagre circlet of light only on the opposite side of the room — then prodded the bruised arm to try for a broken bone. Patty was *quite* sure she had.

"Nonsense, Pat, it's only been your funny-bone," and Tetta rose to her feet.

But the sight of May sprawling meanwhile at her ease in the centre of the bed was too much for her. "It's all your greedy fault, pushing and shoving like that so that *you* can lie on your back. Well, you can't! There's only one way to lie and that's spoons — on our same sides. Now then, Pat!"

But Pat whimpered, if she had to sleep on the outside she'd never sleep at all, she'd always be expecting the whole night to fall out again. She'd rather lie on the floor.

"Well, why not? That's quite a good idea," struck in May brightly. "Then we should all have room."

"I wouldn't, Pat," said Tetta emphatically, with another glance at May's luxurious recumbency. "At least not if you don't want tarantulas crawling over you in the night . . . and perhaps centipedes, too. There's sure to be squads about this dirty old house."

Before she finished speaking, Patty had leapt on to the bed, her bare feet drawn up out of danger's way.

"Now then, Mabs milady, shunt! You've just *got* to let her in the middle. Are you ready?" — and with the same breath Tetta puffed out the candle and sprang to secure what little space was left.

With due care they arranged themselves, back fitted to front; and for a few seconds, tightly wedged though they were, it seemed as if there might be peace.

Then May said: "My mother always says it's dangerous to go to sleep on your left-hand side. It makes your heart swell up. And you could die in the night."

There was a faint squeal from Patty. "Here, let me . . . I'm not going to" — and the bed rocked under her determined efforts to turn to her right.

"Well, if she does, we've all got to. *Are* you ready?" sighed Tetta once more.

Gingerly and in unison they heaved.

But: "Tetta, you've taken every bit of sheet!" from May.

"I haven't!"

"You have!" And the sheet, reduced to a rope, was tugged violently to and fro. "If you think I'm going to lie with my back all bare . . . It's bad enough to have it hanging out over the edge."

"The answer to that is, you shouldn't have such a big behind."

"It's not! I haven't!" cried May, justly indignant. "It's not a scrap bigger than your own. Now if you had Pat's running into you, you *might* talk! Hers is simply enormous; it reaches down to my legs."

"Oh, it *doesn't*!" wailed Patty, on the verge of tears again.

"It's *not* true — it's *not* enormous."

"Oh, shut up, you blubberer! What's the matter if it is?" snapped Tetta, losing patience. "And anyhow the Turks admire them." But the Turks were heathens, and Patty was not consoled. She lay chewing over her injuries, to which another was now added: "It's no good . . . I simply can't . . . I'm suffocating," she said in a weak voice. "My head's right down in the crack between the pillows. I haven't *any* of my own."

"Here, take half mine," said Tetta, and shoved it towards her. May, who liked a pillow to herself, gave hers a hasty pull, which over-shot the mark. Down and out it slid, she, attempting a rescue, after it. "Ooh! I'm standing in water. The whole floor's swimming"

Said Tetta when order was once more restored: "The only thing to do'll be to hold on. Here, Pat, you put your arm over me and round my stomach, and May hers round you. That's it."

In her case it answered. But May, seeking an extra firm grip, was unlucky enough to let her fingers stray on Patty's front, and this was too much for the fat girl, who was ticklish. She began to squirm, and the more May tried to hold her fast the more she wriggled, screwing herself up, defending her middle with arms and elbows, fighting with her knees, all to the accompaniment of a shrill and unconquerable giggle.

The result was that May and Tetta found themselves standing one on each side of the bed.

"You'll have to take the fool round her bally neck."

"Well, then I shall probably strangle her in her sleep," said May darkly as she climbed in again.

They linked themselves anew, and once more there was a brief spell of drowsy silence.

But it was, oh, such a hot night, and before long, out of the heat and the darkness, May's voice was heard in a distracted: "But Pat! . . . you're all wet."

"I'm not, oh, I'm *not!*" tragically protested the one thus accused. Called abruptly back from a half-slumber, her mind in its confusion had jumped to the day of infant peccadilloes.

"Idiot! I didn't mean that. But we're simply sticking together like melting jellies."

"And oh, I do want a drink so dreadfully badly! I think I'll die soon if I don't have one," moaned Patty.

"That comes of being so fat. — Fetch her one, Mabs,"

ordered Tetta, stifling the girlish equivalent of an oath, as she applied yet another match to the stub of candle.

But May tilted the jug in vain. "I believe . . . yes, you *have*! . . . you've used up every drop. Well, Tetta Riley, if you don't deserve to come to want some day!"

"There couldn't have been more than a cupful to start with. I suppose the tank's going dry. Besides, who cleaned their teeth I'd like to know? — Well, Pat, there's nothing else for it, you'll have to suck the sponge."

And this Patty did, to the encouraging remark from Tetta that it was only her own dirt she was eating.

But the problem of sleep had become a very real one. And the night seemed to grow hotter with every minute that passed.

Here Tetta had a new idea: they should try one of them lying crossways at the foot. Yes . . . that was all very well . . . but which? And over this there ensued a wordy dispute. Patty was too fat; she'd stick out too much . . . besides being so hot to put your feet against. Tetta, on the other hand, or so she argued, was too tall: "My head'd hang over one side, my legs the other." No, it must be May or no one, and sourly and unwillingly the victim dragged herself to the bottom of the bed and lay athwart it. But she couldn't possibly sleep without a pillow . . . what was she to do for a pillow?

"Why, make a bundle of your clothes and ram them under your head."

"My clothes? That I've got to wear to-morrow? All crumpled and creased? Think I see myself!"

"Oh very well then, take mine! Thank the Lord I'm not such a darned old fad as you." And by the last flicker of the dying candle, Tetta darted round the room, redeeming her scattered undergarments, her skirt, her petticoat . . . and not omitting her prickly suspenders.

"There. Now turn over so that you face the foot."

"No, I mustn't do that. It'd mean lying on my left side."

"What tommyrot! Not if you put your blinking head the other way round!" cried Tetta in exasperation.

But this May could not be got to see; or else she would not see it; and, by now both dog-tired and half-silly for want of sleep, they barked and bit their way through what gradually deteriorated into a kind of geometrical wrangle, and ended by Tetta snarling: "It's easy to see *you've* never done any Euclid!"

This was a spiteful thrust; for May had failed at close of

term to get her remove, and so to reach a class in which she, too, would have been held capable of writing *Quod erat demonstrandum*. And ordinarily, for decency's sake, you did not allude to her misfortune. But to-night bonds were loosed.

After this a silence fell . . . but not the silence of peace. May, galled to the quick, lay revolving a means of revenge.

Presently to ejaculate: "Oh, Tetta . . . oh, your feet! . . . take them away . . . oh, *puh*!"

"What the . . . what in the name of Christmas do you mean by that? When I have had two baths today!"

"Then all I can say is, your *shoes* must be high!"

In answer to this, involuntarily, but very fiercely, the libelled foot shot out in a straight kick. It landed on May's nose — the soft and gristly part that is so tender. With a scream May sat up and clapped her hands to it, and now, thoroughly hurt and unnerved, fell to sobbing: "Oh, my nose, my nose! You've broken it, you beast — you dirty beast! It's bleeding . . . I can feel the blood dripping from it."

Yet another of the precious matches went in verifying this. True enough a few drops of blood *were* oozing, and the upper lip had had a nasty jab against the top teeth. Once more the sponge was requisitioned, and its last remaining moisture squeezed from it.

In compensation for her injuries May now demanded to be allowed to occupy Tetta's place at the head of the bed.

"Wait. First I'm going to find out what the time is. We seem to have been here for years. It must surely be nearly morning now;" and with this, Tetta opened the door and crept on tiptoe into the passage, where a clock hung.

Returning, she said hoarsely and dramatically: "Look here, you two, it's not even half-past twelve yet! There's still six blooming hours before we can get up . . . can possibly get up. And the candle's done, and there's no more water, and only two matches left. I'm fed up to the neck . . . I can't stick it a minute longer. I'm going out."

"Going out? What do you mean?"

"Where to? What for?"

"What do you think? On the verandah, of course. To get cool. This room's as hot as . . . yes, as hot as *hell* . . . when you come back into it."

"Tetta Riley! . . . your language! If only my mother could hear you!"

"Oh, bing, bang and bung your mother! I'm sick of the very sound of her."

"I'll tell her every word you've said."

"Oh, go to — to Sunday School!"

"I do. And I will. And I'll tell them, too. And you can just *get* out on your old verandah, and stop there. It'll be jolly good riddance to bad rubbish."

"I'm going. But you're coming, too. Think I mean to leave you two snoring here while I kick my heels outside? Oh, no, my dears, not me! Up you get — and double-quick! Both of you."

And meekly, without a further word, the two so commanded obeyed. For when Tetta, the easy-going, spoke like this — in what was known as her "strong-minded" voice — they were her humblest servants. Nor did they resent her mastery. Patty the sheep invariably trotted tail-down after her elders; but May, for all her spirit, was at heart Tetta's devoted crony; and as a rule each made a friendly allowance for the other's failings; a slommicky laziness on the one hand, an ultra-prim exactitude on the other.

Now, at Tetta's direction, skirts were slipped over nightdresses, jackets buttoned on top. And turning their backs on the hideously crumpled battlefield of the bed, they spread a blanket on the verandah's edge, laid pillows and bolster on this, and stretched themselves out, three in a row, with a sheet atop of them.

Oh! the relief was, to escape from those fondly clinging feathers, those steep, sloping sides. Hard the boards might be, as hard as your own bones, but they were at least dead level. Besides that, you were free from the heat of your neighbour's body, and could toss and turn as you chose.

The sweetness, too, of the summer-night air, after the shut-upness of the stuffy room. Pat, who had staggered tipsily in her companions' wake, drew but a couple of full breaths and was fast asleep. May, correctly arranged on her right side, took longer: privately, she thought what they were doing not quite *nice*, and wondered what her mother would say when told of it.

But Tetta lay wakeful. For one thing, it was so light. Not from the moon, for there wasn't any; it was the stars that did it. The sky was as thick with stars as . . . well, she who lived on the sea-board had never seen anything like this bush sky: it was just as if some one had taken diamonds by the handful, no, the bucketful, and flung them out without caring — hundreds and thousands of diamonds, all sharp and white and glittering, with hardly an inch of space between, and what there was, gone a pale dove-grey.

"Oh, gosh, what tons! I never knew there *were* so many stars, did you?"

But there was no reply. So she just lay there, with her hands clasped under her neck, and stared up at the sky till her eyes smarted. And then something else came into her head — a familiar thought, and one she often amused herself with. It had to do with her own identity. Did there, she was given to wondering, somewhere or anywhere on earth exist a replica of herself? Was there, hidden away in some corner of the globe, another girl called Tetta Riley, thirteen years old, with a stub nose with freckles on it, and all her other little funniosities, who had grown up as she grew up, and who felt and thought like her? Herself, finding it hard to believe in her own uniqueness, she was inclined to think there might, there must be; and when, as now, she had nothing better to do, she would send her mind round the world in a fanciful search after her second self. To-night, in face of this starry splendour, she let it stray to what she believed to be "other worlds", as well, chasing her thought among the stars and planets and the Milky Way, leaping from star to star . . . over gaps of palest grey . . . till her head spun, her eyes dazzled; and sleep, descending, gathered her too into the fold.

PRELIMINARY CANTER

PEGGY's hair was so thick that she had to wear it in two plaits instead of one; so long that when she sat down and let these fall over her shoulders, their ends curled up in her lap. Nell, whose own hair hung lank and short about her neck, was never tired of playing with them, pushing a finger in and out between twists so sleek and smooth that they felt like a rope come alive.

The two girls were in their favourite place, the hayloft. For here, if you pulled the ladder up after you, nobody could follow you; though *you* could see what was going on in the yard below: the men with the horses and carts, or customers taking a short cut to the shop. But you were quite safe from the other girls; and that was what she and Peg wanted — to be alone together. The others teased so that it made you simply furious. F'r instance, once when Peggy said she'd ever so much rather have had fair hair than dark, and she, Nell, cried out at her, the other girls pulled faces, and winked, and turned their eyes up to heaven till you could have killed them.

Here, she and Peg sat with their behinds burrowed into the hay, most comfortable, and all alone.

To-day was rather a special day; for Nell had something in her blazer-pocket so secret and important that it almost burned her through the stuff. This was a present for Peggy, and . . . well, now the moment to give it had come, she was feeling just a teeny bit uneasy. How dreadful if Peg didn't like it — after all the trouble she had had to buy it. Her pocket-money — she got threepence a week, got it honestly, not like one girl they knew, who sometimes sneaked a threepenny-bit from her father's till, under the old bookkeeper's nose. Well, for three whole weeks now, she, Nell, hadn't spent a penny of *her* threepence (instead of at once blueing it on chocs; she'd almost forgotten what they tasted like) and with her savings she'd bought Peggy . . . a hair-slide. Ninepence-halfpenny the exact price was, and she'd been fairly stuck how to raise the extra halfpenny without waiting another week. In the end, there had been nothing for it but to pinch a stamp from her father's desk, and sell it.

This slide was now in her pocket, neatly wrapped in fine tissue paper. But the longer it stayed there the more unsure she grew. The point was, it was intended for a place on Peggy's head . . . well, for the one piece of her that wasn't *quite* as pretty as the rest. This was at the back of her neck where the plaits went off, each on its own side. They seemed to leave such a big gap of white skin showing . . . perhaps because they were so dark themselves. Peggy of course didn't know this — you couldn't see yourself behind — but she, Nell, did; and every time the patch caught her eye, it gave her a slight stab that there should be *anything* about Peg that wasn't quite perfect. Once, too, she'd heard Madge Brennan make a simply horrid remark about people who went bald very young. Peggy didn't understand; but *she* did, and bled for her. It was then she'd made up her mind to get the slide.

Another worrying thing was that she'd been lured away from the plain, useful one she had gone into the shop meaning to buy, and had taken one set with . . . diamonds. Not *real* diamonds, of course; but they looked just like it. And now she was afraid Peggy might think it too showy for everyday. And not know how to explain it either to her dreadfully big family of brothers and sisters, most of them older than her. They said such rude things sometimes. And her mother, too. One evening when she, Nell, had been waiting in the rightaway, hoping yes, truly, only *hoping* Peggy would be allowed out again after tea, the mother, a great big fat woman with an apron over her stomach, had opened the window and called out: "Now then, Nellie Mackensen, just you be off! I won't have you always hanging about here at meal-times." As if she wanted their old tea! Her own mother said Peggy's mother was cross because there were so many of them and she'd so much to do. But it did make you rather wonder what she'd say to the diamonds. (Perhaps she'd throw them out of the window.) Oh dear, things were most frightfully complicated. It would have been much better, she saw it now, if she'd bought, say, a nice little diary-book, that Peggy could have carried in her pocket.

But she hadn't. And the slide was there. Faintheartedly she

drew it forth.

Peggy, who had been talking all the time — Peg's pretty mouth was always either talking or laughing — spotted the little parcel at once and said: "Hullo, what's that, — For me? A present for me? Truly? Let's see! Oh, Nell, you dear! . . . a brooch . . . just exactly what I've wanted."

Nell felt herself go red as a beetroot. "Well, no, not a *brooch*, Peg," she said in a small voice. "It's a . . . it's for your hair . . . behind . . . a hair-slide."

Peggy's enthusiasm fizzled out. "A slide?" she echoed disappointedly. "But — what for? Wherever could I wear a slide?"

The fatal moment had come. Nell swallowed hard. "Why, I thought . . . you see, I thought it would look most awfully nice, Peg, if you . . . put it on at the back . . . I mean on your neck . . . where the hair leaves off."

But all Peggy said, and as disbelievingly as before, was: "On my *neck?* Gracious! I should never be able to make it stick. Besides, every time I move my head it'ud run into me."

"Then you don't like it?"

"Oh, yes, it's all right. But whatever made you think of a slide, Nell?" pressed Peggy, and reflected peevishly: just fancy going and buying a thing like that, when there are such squads of things I really do want.

Nell's voice was abject with apology as she replied: "Well, you know, Peg darling, I've always meant to give you something — something private . . . for yourself . . . from me. And — But oh, you don't like it, I can see you don't," and her lips began to tremble.

"Of course I do, silly! But what I'm asking you is, *why* a hair-slide?" persisted Peggy, with a doggedness of which only she was capable.

There was nothing for it: the truth had to come out. "Well . . . I don't think you know, Peg, but — well, just at the back of you . . . where there isn't any more hair — just there, it sometimes looks so bare."

Now it was Peggy's turn to crimson. Very angrily. "*What?* So that's it, is it? I suppose what you mean to say is I'm going bald?"

"Oh no, no, indeed I don't . . . I *don't* . . . mean *any*thing like that."

"Well, I don't believe you. And I think you're simply horrid."

"I *don't*! It wasn't me at all. It was Madge Brennan — I heard her . . . say something. And I thought . . . oh, I thought . . ." But here Nell fairly broke down and put her knuckles to her eyes.

"*Who?* Madge Brennan? That pig-eyed sausage? Said that about me? That I was getting bald? Well, of all the *filthy* cheek!" And, everything else forgotten over the personal injury, Peggy went off into one of her hard white rages, when you might as well have tried to melt a stone. "Oh, I'll pay her out for it, I'll pay her out!"

Nell's cheeks were beginning to get a gloss on them with tears. "Oh, now . . . you're so mad . . . you can only think about her. And when I haven't spent a penny — I mean I haven't tasted a choc — not for donkey's years. I've done nothing but save and save. But you don't care . . . you don't care a bit."

But Peggy had been too badly stung to resist stinging in her turn. "Well, if you must know, I think it was perfectly ridiklous doing all that, just to buy something so — so *rude*. Why not find out first what I really wanted? — instead of listening to Madge Brennan. That's not how to give a present . . . to somebody you make out to be fond of. Oh, I say, hang it, don't bellow like that!" For Nell had flung herself face-downwards in the hay, and was sobbing convulsively. All her money gone; and Peggy offended . . . and furious. She hadn't meant to say one word about the baldness: it had just been dragged out of her. "And now you'll never, never forgive me!"

"Rot. Though I don't know if I'll ever be able to like you *quite* so much again. As for this, of course I'll keep it; but it'll have to stay in a drawer. I'd sooner be hung than wear it, as long as *that* putty-faced Jane's about!" said Peggy, and gave the slide such a vicious jerk that it fell to the floor. But even as she spoke she was wondering if, since she had prepared the way for its disappearance, she couldn't exchange it on the sly for something else. What about a nice silk handkerchief, with a coloured border, to be worn in the breast-pocket of her blazer?

"But not altogether, Peg? — you won't leave off caring altogether?" wept the giftgiver, callous now to any but the deeper issue. "For oh, I do love you so."

"No, of course, not altogether." But Peggy wasn't really thinking what she said; for she didn't stop to swallow before she added, in a kind of stiff, iron voice: "I shall make my mother buy me a hair-restorer right away."

(Oh, why hadn't *she* thought of this?) "But you don't need it, truly you don't, Peg, it's as thick as thick . . . all over," moaned Nell, now only too eager to perjure herself. "It's just the loveliest hair that ever was."

"Oh, get out! You only *say* that: you don't mean it."

"Honest Injun I do! And I wouldn't tell you a lie. For I love you better than anybody in the world."

"More than your mother? Or father?

"Much more. And there isn't anything I wouldn't do for you, word of honour there isn't!"

"Well, then, I tell you what. You take this thing back where you got it, and make them give you something else instead."

At the cruel suggestion Nell's heart dropped to her boots. "Oh, Peg!" she wailed, feebly, imploringly.

"There you are! Didn't I say it was all words?"

"No, it isn't . . . I . . . I *will* do it!" (Though her little-girl courage shrivelled to the size of a pea, at the thought of facing Mr. Massey the draper over his counter: he had a long angry kind of black beard, and great round spectacles, that gave him enormous fish eyes.) "But then . . . oh, Peg, then you will like me again, won't you? — as much as before. And like to come up here. You do, don't you? You'd rather be here than *any*where else?"

"Well, do it first, and then I'll say. But listen! That's somebody calling. Oh, Nell, it's Rex — the new man. Come on, let's go. He jumps us."

A bass voice shouted: "Now then, you two, what are you up to up there? Oblige me by letting that ladder down at once!"

They hastened to obey, lowering the ladder by its ropes. Then themselves crawled through the trap-door and climbed down backwards, Peggy leading, fastidiously mindful of her skirts. But when they reached the last rung, some way short of the ground, they faced about to meet two long arms, two big hairy hands, which, gripping each twelve-year-old securely round the middle, swung her high before setting her on her feet. Carelessly now the short skirts fluttered and ballooned.

"Oh, Rex, one more — *just* one!" coaxed Peggy. And up again she flew.

But at the sight of Nell's swollen eyes and blistery-looking cheeks, the man rubbed the tip of his nose with a finger.

"Hullo! what have you been doing to her? Quarrelling, eh?"

Peggy made her sauciest face, wrinkling her nose, sticking out her chin, showing the tip of her little pink tongue. "Who asks no questions gets told no lies!"

"Eh? What? What's that?" and with a laugh Rex dived to catch her. She skipped from his reach, there was a chase, a scuffle, and then for the third time up she went. "There! — that's for you, you little flirt, you!"

Deftly twisting the curls that served her in place of hair-ribbons, Peggy turned, once she and Nell were out of earshot, and said, in her most innocent tones: "I can't think *why* he called me a flirt, can you?"

Now the correct answer, the wished-for and expected answer was: because you are one. But, though Nell knew this quite well, and at any other time would have given it, partly to please Peg, partly because it made her happy to see Peg happy, to-day she was too numb to care. So her only reply was a flat and toneless: "No."

Deeply aggrieved, Peggy threw her a slide-glance which stood for: oh, very well, my lady! and at once ran on, glibly and enthusiastically: "I *do* like Rex, don't you? — better than any of the other men. He's got such positively gorgeous eyes — they look as if they could never stop laughing. He's so strong, too; just like a lion — I believe he could fight lions with his hands. (I say, *did* you see the hairs on them?) And when he jumps you, it makes you feel as if you're never going to come down again — and don't want to.— Well, I must hop it, or I'll be late for tea. Now, don't *forget* — what you promised. 'Bye."

"'Bye," said Nell limply, and went on walking by herself, heavy of heart and leg. Oh yes, she liked Rex, too, he was so kind and jolly you couldn't help it; even though she didn't show off before him, or put on airs so's to make him notice her. But Peggy — well, there were times . . . and this was one of them . . . when she felt that she didn't love Peg a bit — no, not the least little tiny bit. Love her? She *simply hated* her.

CONVERSATION IN A PANTRY

IT WAS no use, she simply could not sleep. She had tried lying all sorts of ways: with the blanket pulled over her or the blanket off; with her knees doubled up to her chin or stretched so straight that her feet nearly touched the bottom of the bed; on her back with her hands under her neck, or with her face burrowed in the pillow. Nothing helped. Going on in her she could still feel the bumps and lurches of the coach in which she had ridden most of that day. Then the log that had been smouldering in the brick fireplace burnt away in the middle, and collapsed with a crash; and the two ends, rolling together, broke into flames again. These threw shadows which ran about the ceiling, and up and down the white walls, like strange animals.

She was spending the night with Alice, and they had had a fire "just for luxury", and had sat by it for nearly an hour before going to bed. It would be her last chance of anything like that, Alice said: in schools, you never had fires, and all lights went out to the minute. And their talk had been fearfully interesting. For Alice was in love — she was over seventeen — and had told her about it just as if she was grown up, too; looking into the fire with ever such a funny little smile, and her blue eyes quite small behind her thick, curly lashes.

"Oh, don't you wish we could see into the future, Trix? And what it's going to bring us?"

But though she said yes, she wasn't sure if she did, really; she liked surprises better. Besides, all the last part of the time Alice talked, she had been screwing up her courage to put a question. But she hadn't managed to get it out. And that was one reason why now she couldn't sleep.

With a fresh toss, she sighed gustily. And, where her tumblings and fidgetings had failed, this sound called her companion back from the downy meadows.

"What's the matter, child? Aren't you asleep yet?"

"No, I simply can't."

Alice sat up in bed, and shook her hair back from her face. "You're over-excited. Try a drink of water."

"I have. I've drunk it all up."

"Then you must be hungry."

"Well, yes, I am perhaps . . . a little."

"Come on then, let's forage." And throwing back the sheet, the elder girl slid her feet to the floor.

One tall white figure, one short, they opened the door and stepped out on the verandah.

Here it was almost as bright as day; for the moon hung like a round cheese in the sky, and drenched everything with its light. Barefoot they pattered, the joins in the verandah floor-boards, which had risen, cutting into their soles. Had they to pass open windows, dark holes in which people lay sleeping, Alice laid a finger on her lips. From one of these came the sound of snores — harsh snores of the chromatic kind, which went up the scale and down, over and over again, without a pause.

Turning a corner, they stepped off the verandah and took a few steps on hard pebbly ground. Inside the pantry, which was a large outhouse, there were sharp contrasts of bluish-white moonlight and black shadows.

Swiftly Alice skimmed the familiar shelves. "Here's lemon-cheesecakes . . . and jam tarts . . . and gingersnaps . . . and pound cake. But I can't start you on these, or you'd be sick." And cutting a round off a home-made loaf, she spread it thickly with dairy butter, topped by a layer of quince jelly. "There, that's more wholesome."

Oh, had anything ever tasted so delicious? . . . as this slice eaten at dead of night. Perched on an empty, upturned kerosene-tin, the young girl munched and munched, holding her empty hand outspread below, lest the quivering jelly glide over the crust's edge.

Alice took a cheese-cake and sat down on a lidded basket. "I say, *did* you hear Father? Oh, Trix, wouldn't it be positively too awful if one discovered *afterwards*, one had married a man who snored?"

The muncher made no answer: the indelicacy of the question stunned her: all in the dark as she was, she felt her face flame. And yet . . . was this not perhaps the very chance she had been waiting for? If Alice could say such a thing, out loud, without embarrassment . . . Hastily squeezing down her last titbit — she felt it travel, overlarge, the full length of her gullet — she licked her jellied fingers clean and took the plunge.

"Dallie, there's something I . . . I want to ask you something . . . something I want to know."

"Fire away!" said Alice, and went on nibbling at the pastry-edging that trimmed her tartlet.

"Yes. But . . . well, I don't quite . . . I mean I . . ."

"Like that, is it? Wait a tick," and rather more rapidly than she had intended, Alice bolted her luscious circle of lemon-cheese, picked up her basket and planted it beside the tin. "Now then."

Shut away in this outhouse, the young girl might have cried her words aloud. But leaning over till she found the shell of her friend's ear, she deposited them safely inside. Alice, who was ticklish, gave an involuntary shudder. But as the sense of the question dawned on her, she sat up very stiff and straight, and echoed perturbed: "*How*? Oh, but Kid, I'm not sure — not at all sure — whether you ought to know. At your age!" said seventeen to thirteen.

"But I must, Dallie."

"But why, my dear?"

"Because of something Ruth said."

"Oh, Ruth!" said Alice scornfully. "Trust Ruth for saying the wrong thing. What was it?"

"Why, that . . . now I was growing up . . . was as good as grown up . . . I must take care, for . . . for fear . . . But, Dallie, how can I? . . . if I don't know?" This last question came out with a rush, and with a kind of click in the throat.

"Well, well! I always have felt sorry for you children, with no mother but only Ruth to bring you up — and she for ever prinking before her glass. But you know you'll be perfectly safe at school, Trix. They'll look after you, never fear!"

But there was more to come.

It was Ella, it seemed, Ella Morrison, who was two years older than her, who'd begun it. She'd said her mother said now she mustn't let the boys kiss her any more.

"And you have, eh?"

Trixie's nod was so small that it had to be guessed at. Haltingly, word by word, the story came out. It had been at Christmas, at a big party, and they were playing games. And she and some others, all boys, had gone off to hide from the rest, and they'd climbed into the hayloft, Harry MacGillivray among them; and she rather liked Harry, and he liked her, and the other boys knew it and had teased them. And then they said he wasn't game to kiss her and dared him to. And she didn't want him to, not a bit . . . or only a teeny weeny bit . . . and anyhow she wasn't going to let him, there before them all. But the other boys grabbed her, and one held her arms and another her legs and another her neck, so that he could. And he did — three times — hard. She'd been as angry as anything; she'd hit them all round. But only angry. Afterwards, though . . . when Ellie told her what her mother had said . . . and now Ruth . . .

But she got no further; for Alice had thrown back her head and was shaking with ill-repressed laughter. "Oh, you babe . . . you blessed infant, you! Why, child, there was no more harm in that than . . . well, than in this!" And pulling the girl to her she kissed her soundly, some half-dozen times, with scant pause between. An embarrassing embrace, from which Trixie made uneasy haste to free herself; for Alice was plump, and her nightgown thin.

"No, you can make your little mind easy," continued the elder girl on recovering her breath. "Larking's all that was and couldn't hurt a fly. *It's what larking leads to*," said Alice, and her voice sank, till it was hollow with mystery.

"What does it?"

"Ah!" said Alice in the same sepulchral tone. "You asked me just now how babies came. Well, *that's how*, my dear."

"Yes, but . . ."

"Come, you've read your Bible, haven't you? The Garden of Eden, and so on? And male and female created He them?"

"But . . ."

"Well, Trix, in *my* opinion, you ought to be content with that . . . in the meanwhile. Time enough for more when . . . well, when you're married, my dear." Not for the world would Alice have admitted her own lack of preciser knowledge, or have uncovered to the day her private imaginings of the great unknown.

"But suppose I . . . Not *every* lady gets married, Dallie! And then I'd never know."

"And wouldn't need to. But I don't think there's much fear of that, Trix! You're not the stuff old maids are made of," said Alice sturdily, welcoming the side issue.

Affectionately Trixie snuggled up to her friend. This tribute was most consoling. (How awful should nobody want you, you remain unchosen!) All the same she did not yield; a real worm for knowledge gnawed in her. "Still, I don't quite see ... truly I don't, Dallie ... how you *can* 'take care', if you don't know how."

At this outlandish persistence Alice drew a heavy sigh. "But child, there's surely something in you ... at least if there isn't there ought to be ... that tells you what's skylarking and what isn't? Just you think of undressing. Suppose you began to take your clothes off in front of somebody, somebody who was a stranger to you, wouldn't something in you stop you by saying: it isn't done, it's not *nice* ?"

"Gracious, yes!" cried Trixie hotly. "I should think so indeed!" (Though she could not imagine herself *beginning*.) But here, for some reason, what Alice had said about a husband who snored came back to her, and got tangled up with the later question. "But, Dallie, you have to ... do that, take your clothes off ... haven't you? ... if you ... sleep in the same bed with somebody," was what she wanted to say, but the words simply would not come out.

Alice understood. "But *only* if you're married, Trixie! And then, it's different. Then everything's allowed, my dear. If once you're married, it doesn't matter what you do."

"Oh, doesn't it?" echoed Trixie feebly, and her cheeks turned so hot that they scorched. For at Alice's words horrid things, things she was ashamed even to think, came rushing into her mind, upsetting everything she had been taught or told since she was a little child. But *she* wouldn't be like that, no, never, no matter how much she was married; there would always be something in *her* that would say "don't, it's not nice".

A silence followed, in which she could hear her own heart beating. Then, out of a kind of despair, she asked: "Oh, *why* are men and women, Dallie? Why have they got to be?"

"Well now, really!" said Alice, startled and sincerely shocked. "I hope to goodness you're not going to turn irreligious, and begin criticising what God has done and how He's made us?"

"Of course not! I know everything He does is right," vowed Trixie, the more hotly because she couldn't down the naughty thought: if He's got all that power, then I don't see why He couldn't have arranged things differently, let them happen without ... well, without all this bother ... and so many things you weren't supposed to know ... and what you were allowed to, so ... so unpleasant. Yes, it *was* unpleasant, when you thought of undressing ... and the snores ... and

— and everything.

And then quite suddenly and disconcertingly came a memory of Alice sitting looking into the fire, telling about her sweetheart. She had never known before that Alice was so pretty, with dimples round her mouth, and her eyes all shady. Oh, could it mean that . . . yes, it must: Alice simply didn't *mind*.

Almost as if this thought had passed to her, Alice said: "Just you wait till you fall in love, Trix, and then it'll be different — as different as chalk and cheese. Then you'll be only too glad, my dear, that we're not all the same — all men or all women. Love's something that goes right through you, child, I couldn't even begin to describe it — and you wouldn't understand it if I did — but once you're in love, you can't think of anything else, and it gives you such a strange feeling here that it almost chokes you!" — and laying one hand over the other on the place where she believed her heart to be, Alice pressed hard. "Why, only to be in the same room with him makes you happy, and if you know he's feeling the same, and that he likes to look at you and to hold your hand — oh, Trix, it's just Heaven!"

I do believe she'd even like him snoring, thought Trixie in dismay. (But perhaps it was only *old* men who snored.) Confused and depressed, she could not think of anything to reply. Alice did not speak again either, and there was a long silence, in which, though it was too dark to see her, Trixie guessed she would have the same funny little smile round her mouth and the same funny half-shut eyes, from thinking about George. Oh dear! what a muddle everything was.

"But come!" cried Alice, starting up from her dreams. "To bed and to sleep with you, young woman, or we shall never get you up in time for the morning coach. Help yourself to a couple of cheese-cakes . . . we can eat them as we go."

Tartlets in hand, back they stole among the moon-blanched verandah; back past the row of dark windows, past the chromatic snores — to Trixie's ears these had now a strange and sinister significance — guided by a moon which, riding at the top of the sky, had shrunk to the size of a pippin.

THE BATH

IT WAS December and a scorching afternoon: a north wind blew; and the pale wind-streaked sky, the little verandahed houses, the glaring roads, the very air itself, all were white with heat and dust. In comparison the bathroom struck cool, being windowless, and lit only by a raised skylight. A good-sized room, it was really made for bathing in, was made to get wet, a concrete floor sloping towards a drain in one corner. Except for a large hanging mirror and a wooden table, it held nothing but a huge old zinc bath, the sides of which were streaked rust-brown from the tidemarks of the many waters that had filled it. Over the broad end hung a shower-ring. This dripped without ceasing, drops forming continuously on its under-surface, gathering volume, depending perilously, then falling on the zinc with a toneless thud. The water that oozed out when the large old-fashioned cock opened was not unlike muddied milk, and for the most part lukewarm. But it gushed freely, making up by abundance for its tepidness and want of clarity.

To-day it ran very red, for a storm overnight had churned up the mud bottom of the reservoir.

Four half-grown girls had come dancing into the room, and eight hands were busy; for all four had cried as one: "A bath! Let us have a bath!"

And while the water raced and sang, shoes were kicked off and clothes fell, a bit here, an oddment there, in their owners' haste to be rid of encumbrances.

First ready was a fattish little blonde; though, as the eldest of the party, she had set to work more sedately than the rest. But, in her hurry to reach the water, one of the four had pulled a knot, and a brown and a red head were bent over it.

Meanwhile, Blonde sat on the side of the bath, swinging one leg. Her skin was of a delicate transparency, through which veins showed blue as forget-me-nots. A wonderful prong, running down the chest, forked and lost itself in the whiteness of the barely-hinted breasts. Round her throat were two lines that might have been scored by a thumb-nail in wet clay; and below the ribs were two more — the lines of sitting beauty — deeply indented and wavy, like the lines carved by ripples on the sea-shore.

The knot unravelled, Red Head was out of her clothes in a twinkling, and now advanced, shoulders hunched, arms crossed and hugging their uppers. While she stood waiting for the tide to rise, rubbing the sole of one foot up and down the other leg, she made her brown-haired little companion, the youngest of the four, and still skinny and straight as a boy, look very dark; for, in Red Hair, the promise of a pale face powdered with freckles was fulfilled: her skin was white as milk from top to toe, and velvety as rose-petals to the touch.

Last came the knot-puller — a tall, slim, brown-eyed creature with a sallow face, flushed pink at the moment from heat and hurry, and a head of short golden curls. Against the others she stood out for the richness of her colouring; her skin was the shade of old, old ivory, tinting to amber, to a dusky gold, in all crevices: where the curls met her neck, and in the hollows of her armpits. Her young breasts — at this moment laid flat, for she was stretching with the abandon of a cat, both hands clasped tight behind her neck — ended in rings the colour of blue grapes dashed with sepia.

By now the bath was full to the brim. And while the four still lingered, chattering, twittering, exulting in their freedom, there was the sound of a heavy foot in the passage outside. And the room had three doors, none of which locked. Whrr! Like a herd of startled wild things, all made for the water at once, a phalanx of cream, white, and dusky legs whisking over the side with incredible rapidity. Amber came off worst: she was too tall; crouching did not help her. So she lay at full length, the others half-leaning, half-sitting on her, to keep her down. But the threatened intrusion passed; and with a fresh run of giggles and trills the bathers rose to their feet. — The water that trickled down their skins left visible traces, like tears on a grimy face.

Then the shower was pulled. Amber and Brownie stood under it, holding their heads to the gush and hiss, Amber raising an arm to screen her eyes, the little one pressing her face against her companion's ribs. And, bristling and stinging, the shower flew off at right-angles, squirting madly out into the room. Blonde and Red Head dodged and scuttled. Then it was their turn. Blonde would not wet her hair; she leant her head and shoulders far back, stretching her lined throat, meeting the brunt of the water on her chest; or, stooping forward, let it hammer down the ridgeway of her spine.

Next, all tried to get under water at the same time. The result was wildest confusion; for the one below kicked, and splashed, and rolled over three slippery bodies, in her efforts to come to the surface. — Taking Blonde by the toes, the others floated her up and down.

An elderly woman looked in: the bathers gathered water in their joined palms and pelted her, in a perpendicular shower. Then they played at leaping. The game was: to go to the end of the room and take a running jump over the side, to see who could splash highest. Red Head was awkward, slipped and fell face downwards, to be half-drowned by the one who came after. This led to a free fight. The weapons were a big and little sponge: inflated to their fullest, they were hurled against any portion of a body that offered; and tireless hands, which scooped and flung, tweaked and slapped. The walls ran water, the concrete floor was a-swim with it.

In the midst of these gambols, a clock struck five. Like ghosts surprised by the dawn, the four were out of the bath in a trice and a-scramble for the towels that hung behind a door. There was a hasty rubbing down of sides and fronts; towels seesawed over backs, knees bent, curly toes wriggled dry. Grasped in two hands garments were poised for a moment high in air, then dropped into place, blotting out faces in the transit. And soon, of all that had lain bare, no more was visible than four damp-ringed, motley-coloured heads. — Though the long glass had given back in full the madcap riot of the bath, none had troubled to cast so much as a look at her naked self. Clothed, it was otherwise: here a sodden mass of curls was twitched and fingered, there the sit of a frock stroked into place.

Now a voice was heard calling — an urgent voice, that brooked no delay. Without a further backward glance each in turn followed the summons, vanishing swiftly. Four times the door opened and shut; till the room was empty. The splashed walls and swimming floor drained dry; the bath-water gurgled off; and the mirror's surface lay blank, no conjurer being at hand to call to life the lovely shapes that slumbered in its depth.

THE WRONG TURNING

THE way he helped her into the boat was delicious, simply delicious: it made her feel like a grown-up lady to be taken so much care of — usually, people didn't mind how you got in and out of things, as you were only thirteen. And before he let her step off the landing he took her strap of books from her — those wretched schoolbooks, which stamped her, but which she hadn't known how to get rid of: her one chance of going for a row was secretly, on her way home from school. But he seemed to understand, without being told, how she despised them, and he put them somewhere in the boat where they wouldn't get wet, and yet she didn't need to see them. (She wondered what he had done with his own.)

He was so *nice;* everything about him was nice: his velvety brown eyes and white teeth; his pink cheeks and fair hair. And when he took his coat off and sat down, and rolled up his sleeves and spanned his wrists on the oars, she liked him better still: he looked so strong . . . almost as if he could have picked the boat up and carried it. He wasn't at all forward either (she hated cheeky boys): when he had to touch her hand he went brick red, and jumped his own hand away as quick as he could.

With one stroke they were off and gliding downstream . . . oh, so smoothly! It made her think of floating in milk . . . though the water was *really* brown and muddy-looking. Soon they would be quite away from the houses and the little back-gardens and allotments that ran down to the water, and out among the woods, where the river twisted like a snake, and the trees hung over the edge and dipped their branches in . . . most romantically. Then perhaps he would say something. He hadn't spoken yet; he was too busy rowing, making great sweeps with the oars, and not looking at her . . . or only taking a peep now and then, to see if she saw. Which she did, and her heart thumped with pleasure. Perhaps, as he was so clever at it, he'd be a sailor when he was a man and go to sea. But that would mean him travelling far away, and she might never see him again. And though she'd only known him for a fortnight, and at first he hadn't liked to speak, but had just stood and made eyes at her when they met going home from school, she felt she simply couldn't bear it if he did.

To hide her feelings, she hung one hand over the side of the boat and let it trail through the water — keeping it there long after it was stone cold, in the hope that he would notice it and say something. But he didn't.

The Boy was thinking: I wonder if I dare tell her not to . . . her little hand . . . all wet like that, and cold. I should like to take it in both mine, and rub it dry, and warm it. *How* pretty she is, with all that fuzzy-wuzzy hair, and the little curls on her forehead. And how long her eyelashes are when she looks down. I wish I could make her look up . . . look at me. But how? Why, say something, of course. But what? Oh, if *only* I could think of something! What does one? What would Jim say, if he wanted to make his girl look at him?

But nothing came.

Here, however, the hand was jerked from the water to kill a gnat that had settled on the other.

This was his cue. He parted hastily with his saliva.

"I say! Did it sting?"

She suppressed the no that was on her lips. "Well . . . yes . . . I think it did, rather." And doubling her bony little schoolgirl fingers into her palm, she held out the back of the hand for his inspection.

Steadying the oars, the Boy leant forward to look, leant so far that, for a wild moment, she believed he was going to kiss the place, and half instinctively, half from an equally strong impulse to "play him", drew it away. But he did not follow it up: at the thought of a kiss, which *had* occurred to him, shyness lamed him anew. So nothing came of this either.

And we've only half an hour, thought the Girl distractedly. If he doesn't say something . . . soon . . . there won't be any time left. And then it will all have been for nothing.

She, too, beat her brains. "The trees . . . aren't they pretty? — the way they hang right down in the water." (Other couples stopped under these trees, she'd seen them, and lay there in their boats; or even went right in behind the weeping willows.)

But his sole response was: "Good enough." And another

block followed.

Oh, he saw quite well what she was aiming at: she wanted him to pull in to the bank and ship his oars, so that they could do a bit of spooning, she lying lazy in the stern. But at the picture a mild panic seized him. For, if he couldn't find anything to say even when he was rowing, it would be ten times harder when he sat with his hands before him and nothing to do. His tongue would stick to the roof of his mouth, dry as a bone, and then she'd see for sure how dull he was. And never want to go out with him again. No, thank you, not for him!

But talk wasn't everything — by gum, it wasn't! He might be a rotten hand at speechifying, but what he could *do*, that he'd jolly well show her! And under this urge to display his strength, his skill, he now fell to work in earnest. Forward swung the oars, cleanly carving the water, or lightly feathering the surface; on flew the boat, he driving to and fro with his jaws grimly set and a heightened colour, the muscles standing out like pencils on his arms. Oh, it was a fine thing to be able to row so well, and have a girl, *the* girl, sitting watching you. For now her eyes hung on him, mutely adoring, spurring him on to ever bolder strokes.

And then a sheerly dreadful thing happened. So lost was he in showing his mastery, in feeding on her looks, that he failed to keep his wits about him. And, coming to a place where the river forked, he took the wrong turning, and before he knew it they were in a part where you were not supposed to go — a bathing-place for men, much frequented by soldiers.

A squeal from the Girl roused him; but then it was too late: they had shot in among a score of bathers, whose heads bobbed about on the surface like so many floating footballs. And instantly her shrill cry was taken up and echoed and re-echoed by shouts, and laughter, and rude hullos, as the swimmers scattered before the oars. Coarse jokes were bandied, too, at the unwarranted intrusion. Hi! wasn't there nowhere else he could take his girl? Or was she coming in, too? Off with her togs then!

Crimson with mortification at his blunder, at the fool he had made of himself (before her), the Boy savagely strove to turn the boat and escape. But the heads — there seemed to be hundreds of them — deliberately blocked his way. And while he manoeuvred, the sweat trickling down his forehead, a pair of arms and shoulders reared themselves from the water, and two hands grasped the side of the boat. It rocked; and the Girl squealed anew, shrinking sideways from the nearness of the dripping, sunburnt flesh.

"Come on, missie, pay toll!"

The Boy swore aloud.

But even worse was to come. On one bank, a square of wooden palisades had been built out round a stretch of water and a wooden bath-house, where there were cabins for the men to strip in, platforms to jump from, ropes strung for those who could not swim. But in this fence was a great gap, where some of the palings had fallen down. And in his rage and confusion the Boy had the misfortune to bring the boat right alongside it; and then . . . then . . . Inside the enclosure, out of the cabins, down the steps, men were running, jumping, chasing, leap-frogging . . . every one of them as naked as on the day he was born.

For one instant the Girl raised her eyes — one only . . . but it was enough. She saw. And he saw that she saw.

And now, to these two young creatures, it seemed as if the whole visible world — themselves, boat, river, trees and sky — caught fire, and blazed up in one gigantic blush. Nothing existed for them any more but this burning redness. Nor could they escape; there they had to sit, knee to knee, face to face, and scorch, and suffocate; the blood filling their eyes till they could scarcely see, mounting to their hair-roots, making even their finger-tips throb and tingle.

Gritting his teeth, the Boy rowed like a machine that had been wound up and was not to be stopped. The Girl sat with drooped head — it seemed to have grown strangely heavy — and but a single wish: to get out and away . . . where he could not see her. For all was over between them — both felt that. Something catastrophic had happened, rudely shattering their frail young dreams; breaking down his boyish privacy, pitching her headlong into a reality for which she was in no wise prepared.

If it had been hard beforehand to find things to say, it was now impossible. And on the way home no sound was to be heard but the dip of the oars, the water's cluck and gurgle round the boat. At the landing-place, she got out by herself, took from him, without looking up, her strap of books, and said a brief good-bye; keeping to a walking pace till she had turned the corner, then breaking into a run, and running for dear life . . . as if chased by some grotesue nightmare-shape which she must leave far, far behind her . . . even in thought.

"AND WOMEN MUST WEEP"

SHE was ready at last, the last bow tied, the last strengthening pin in place, and they said to her — Auntie Cha and Miss Biddons — to sit down and rest while Auntie Cha "climbed into her own togs": "Or you'll be tired before the evening begins." But she could not bring herself to sit, for fear of crushing her dress — it was so light, so airy. How glad she felt now that she had chosen muslin, and not silk as Auntie Cha had tried to persuade her. The gossamer-like stuff seemed to float around her as she moved, and the cut of the dress made her look so tall and so different from everyday that she hardly recognised herself in the glass; the girl reflected there — in palest blue, with a wreath of cornflowers in her hair — might have been a stranger. Never had she thought she was so pretty . . . nor had Auntie and Miss Biddons either; though all they said was: "Well, Dolly, you'll *do*," and: "Yes, I think she will be a credit to you." Something hot and stinging came up her throat at this: a kind of gratitude for her pinky-white skin, her big blue eyes and fair curly hair, and pity for those girls who hadn't got them. Or an Auntie Cha either, to dress them and see that everything was "just so".

Instead of sitting, she stood very stiff and straight at the window, pretending to watch for the cab, her long white gloves hanging loose over one arm so as not to soil them. But her heart was beating pit-a-pat. For this was her first real grown-up ball. It was to be held in a public hall, and Auntie Cha, where she was staying, had bought tickets and was taking her.

True, Miss Biddons rather spoilt things at the end by saying: "Now mind you don't forget your steps in the waltz. One, two, together; four, five, six." And in the wagonette, with her dress filling one seat, Auntie Cha's the other, Auntie said: "Now, Dolly, remember not to look too *serious*. Or you'll frighten the gentlemen off."

But she was only doing it now because of her dress: cabs were so cramped, the seats so narrow.

Alas! in getting out a little accident happened. She caught the bottom of one of her flounces — the skirt was made of nothing else — on the iron step, and ripped off the selvedge. Auntie Cha said: "My *dear*, how clumsy!" She could have cried with vexation.

The woman who took their cloaks hunted everywhere, but could only find black cotton; so the torn selvedge — there was nearly half a yard of it — had just to be cut off. This left a raw edge, and when they went into the hall and walked across the enormous floor, with people sitting all round, staring, it seemed to Dolly as if every one had their eyes fixed on it. Auntie Cha sat down in the front row of chairs beside a lady-friend; but she slid into a chair behind.

The first dance was already over, and they were hardly seated before partners began to be taken for the second. Shyly she mustered the assembly. In the cloakroom, she had expected the woman to exclaim: "What a sweet pretty frock!" when she handled it. (When all she did say was: "This sort of stuff's bound to fray.") And now Dolly saw that the hall was fully of *lovely* dresses, some much, much prettier than hers, which suddenly began to seem rather too plain, even a little dowdy; perhaps after all it would have been better to have chosen silk.

She wondered if Auntie Cha thought so, too. For Auntie suddenly turned and looked at her, quite hard, and then said snappily: "Come, come, child, you mustn't tuck yourself away like that, or the gentlemen will think you don't want to dance." So she had to come out and sit in the front; and show that she had a programme, by holding it open on her lap.

When other ladies were being requested for the third time, and still nobody had asked to be introduced, Auntie began making signs and beckoning with her head to the Master of Ceremonies — a funny little fat man with a bright red beard. He waddled across the floor, and Auntie whispered to him . . . behind her fan. (But she heard. And heard him answer: "Wants a partner? Why, certainly.") And then he went away and they could see him offering her to several gentlemen. Some pointed to the ladies they were sitting with or standing in front of; some showed their programmes that these were full. One or two turned their heads and looked at her. But it was no good. So he came back and said: "Will the little lady do *me* the favour?" and she had to look glad and say: "With pleasure," and get up and dance with him. Perhaps she was a little slow about it . . . at any rate Auntie Cha made great round eyes at her. But she felt sure every one would know why he was asking her. It was the lancers, too, and he swung her off her feet at the corners, and was comic when he set to partners — putting one hand on his hip and the other over his head, as if he were dancing the hornpipe — and the rest of the set laughed. She was glad when it was over and she could go back to her place.

Auntie Cha's lady-friend had a son, and he was beckoned to next and there was more whispering. But he was engaged to be married, and of course preferred to dance with his fiancee. When he came and bowed — to oblige his mother — he looked quite grumpy, and didn't trouble to say all of "May I have the pleasure?" but just "The pleasure?" While she had to say "Certainly," and pretend to be very pleased, though she didn't feel it, and really didn't want much to dance with him, knowing he didn't, and that it was only out of charity. Besides, all the time they went round he was explaining things to the other girl with his eyes . . . making faces over her head. She saw him, quite plainly.

After he had brought her back — and Auntie had talked to him again — he went to a gentleman who hadn't danced at all yet, but just stood looking on. And this one needed a lot of persuasion. He was ugly, and lanky, and as soon as they stood up, said quite rudely: "I'm no earthly good at this kind of thing, you know." And he wasn't. He trod on her foot and put her out of step, and they got into the most dreadful muddle, right out in the middle of the floor. It was a waltz, and remembering what Miss Biddons had said, she got more and more nervous, and then went wrong herself and had to say: "I beg your pardon," to which he said: "Granted." She saw them in a mirror as they passed, and her face was red as red.

It didn't get cool again either, for she had to go on sitting out, and she felt sure he was spreading it that *she* couldn't dance. She didn't know whether Auntie Cha had seen her mistakes, but now Auntie sort of went for her. "It's no use, Dolly, if you don't do *your* share. For goodness sake, try and look more agreeable!"

So after this, in the intervals between the dances, she sat with a stiff little smile gummed to her lips. And, did any likely-looking partner approach the corner where they were, this widened till she felt what it was really saying was: "here I am! Oh, *please*, take *me!*"

She had several false hopes. Men, looking so splendid in their white shirt fronts, would walk across the floor and *seem* to be coming . . . and then it was always not her. Their eyes wouldn't stay on her. There she sat, with her false little smile, and *her* eyes fixed on them; but theirs always got away . . . flitted past . . . moved on. Once she felt quite sure. Ever such a handsome young man looked as if he were making straight for her. She stretched her lips, showing all her teeth (they were very good) and for an instant his eyes seemed to linger . . . really to take her in, in her pretty blue dress and the cornflowers. And then at the last minute they ran away — and it wasn't her at all, but a girl sitting three seats further on; one who wasn't even pretty, or her dress either. — But her own dress was beginning to get quite tashy, from the way she squeezed her hot hands down in her lap.

Quite the worst part of all was having to go on sitting in the front row, pretending you were enjoying yourself. It was so hard to know what to do with your eyes. There was nothing but the floor for them to look at — if you watched the other couples dancing they would think you were envying them. At first she made a show of studying her programme; but you couldn't go on staring at a programme for ever; and presently her shame at its emptiness grew till she could bear it no longer, and, seizing a moment when people were dancing, she slipped it down the front of her dress. Now she could say she'd lost it, if anyone asked to see it. But they didn't; they went on dancing with other girls. Oh, these men, who walked round and chose just who they fancied and left who they didn't . . . how she hated them! It wasn't fair . . . it wasn't fair. And when there was a "leap-year dance" where the ladies invited the gentlemen, and Auntie Cha tried to push her up and make her go and said: "Now then, Dolly, here's your chance!" she shook her head hard and dug herself deeper into her seat. She wasn't going to ask them when they never asked her. So she said her head ached and she'd rather not. And to this she clung, sitting the while wishing with her whole heart that her dress was black and her hair grey, like Auntie Cha's. Nobody expected Auntie to dance, or thought it shameful if she didn't: she could do and be just as she liked. Yes, to-night she wished she was old . . . an old, old woman. Or that she was safe at home in bed . . . this dreadful evening, to which she had once counted the days, behind her. Even, as the night wore on, that she was dead.

At supper she sat with Auntie and the other lady, and the son and the girl came, too. There were lovely cakes and things, but she could not eat them. Her throat was so dry that a sandwich stuck in it and nearly choked her. Perhaps the son felt a little sorry for her (or else his mother had whispered again), for afterwards he said something to the girl, and then asked *her* to dance. They stood up together; but it wasn't a success. Her legs seemed to have forgotten how to jump, heavy as lead they were . . . as heavy as she felt inside . . . and she couldn't think of a thing to say. So now he would put her down as stupid, as well.

Her only other partner was a boy younger than she was — almost a schoolboy — who she heard them say was "making a positive nuisance of himself". This was to a *very* pretty girl called the "belle of the ball". And he didn't seem to mind how badly he danced (with her), for he couldn't take his eyes off this other girl; but went on staring at her all the time, and very fiercely, because she was talking and laughing with somebody else. Besides, he hopped like a grasshopper, and didn't wear gloves, and his hands were hot and sticky. She hadn't come there to dance with little boys.

They left before anybody else; there was nothing to stay for. And the drive home in the wagonette, which had to be fetched, they were so early, was dreadful: Auntie Cha just sat and pressed her lips and didn't say a word. She herself kept her face turned the other way, because her mouth was jumping in and out as if it might have to cry.

At the sound of wheels Miss Biddons came running to the front door with questions and exclamations, dreadfully curious to know why they were back so soon. Dolly fled to her own little room and turned the key in the lock. She wanted only to be alone, quite alone, where nobody could see her . . . where nobody would ever see her again. But the walls were thin, and as she tore off the wreath and ripped open her dress, now crushed to nothing from so much sitting, and threw them from her anywhere, anyhow, she could hear the two voices going on, Auntie Cha's telling and telling, and winding up at last, quite out loud, with: "Well, I don't know what it was, but the plain truth is, she didn't *take!*"

Oh, the shame of it! . . . the sting and the shame. Her first ball, and not to have "taken", to have failed to "attract the gentlemen" — this was a slur that would rest on her all her life. And yet . . . and yet . . . in spite of everything, a small voice that wouldn't be silenced kept on saying: "It wasn't my fault . . . it wasn't my *fault!*" (Or at least not except for the one silly mistake in the steps of the waltz.) She had tried her hardest, done everything she was told to: had dressed up to please and look pretty, sat in the front row offering her programme, smiled when she didn't feel a bit like smiling . . . and almost more than anything she thought she hated the memory of that smile (it was like trying to make people buy something they didn't think worth while). For really, truly, right deep down in her, she hadn't wanted "the gentlemen" any more than they'd wanted her: she had only had to pretend to. And they showed only too plainly they didn't, by choosing other girls, who were not even pretty, and dancing with them, and laughing and talking and enjoying them. — And now, the many slights and humiliations of the evening crowding upon her, the long repressed tears broke through; and with the blanket pulled up over her head, her face driven deep into the pillow, she cried till she could cry no more.

TWO HANGED WOMEN

HAND in hand the youthful lovers sauntered along the esplanade. It was a night in midsummer; a wispy moon had set, and the stars glittered. The dark mass of the sea, at flood, lay tranquil, slothfully lapping the shingle.

"Come on, let's make for the usual," said the boy.

But on nearing their favourite seat they found it occupied. In the velvety shade of the overhanging sea-wall, the outlines of two figures were visible.

"Oh, blast!" said the lad. "That's torn it. What now, Baby?"

"Why, let's stop here, Pincher, right close up, till we frighten 'em off."

And very soon loud, smacking kisses, amatory pinches and ticklings, and skittish squeals of pleasure did their work. Silently the intruders rose and moved away.

But the boy stood gaping after them, open-mouthed.

"Well, I'm *damned!* If it wasn't just two hanged women!"

Retreating before a salvo of derisive laughter, the elder of the girls said: "We'll go out on the breakwater." She was tall and thin, and walked with a long stride.

Her companion, shorter than she by a bobbed head of straight flaxen hair, was hard to put to it to keep pace. As she pegged along she said doubtfully, as if in self-excuse: "Though I really ought to go home. It's getting late. Mother will be angry."

They walked with finger-tips lightly in contact; and at her words she felt what was like an attempt to get free, on the part of the fingers crooked in hers. But she was prepared for this, and held fast, gradually working her own up till she had a good half of the other hand in her grip.

For a moment neither spoke. Then, in a low, muffled voice, came the question: "Was she angry last night, too?"

The little fair girl's reply had an unlooked-for vehemence. "You know she wasn't!" And, mildly despairing: "But you never *will* understand. Oh, what's the good of . . . of anything!"

And on sitting down she let the prisoned hand go, even putting it from her with a kind of push. There it lay, palm upwards, the fingers still curved from her hold, looking like a thing with a separate life of its own; but a life that was ebbing.

On this remote seat, with their backs turned on lovers, lights, the town, the two girls sat and gazed wordlessly at the dark sea, over which great Jupiter was flinging a thin gold line. There was no sound but the lapping, sucking, sighing, of the ripples at the edge of the breakwater, and the occasional screech of an owl in the tall trees on the hillside.

But after a time, having stolen more than one side-glance at her companion, the younger seemed to take heart of grace. With a childish toss of the head that set her loose hair swaying, she said, in a tone of meaning emphasis: "I like Fred."

The only answer was a faint, contemptuous shrug.

"I tell you I *like* him!"

"Fred? Rats!"

"No it isn't . . . that's just where you're wrong, Betty. But you think you're so wise. Always."

"I know what I know."

"Or imagine you do! But it doesn't matter. Nothing you can say makes any difference. I like him, and always shall. In heaps of ways. He's so big and strong, for one thing: it gives you such a safe sort of feeling to be with him . . . as if nothing could happen while you were. Yes, it's . . . it's . . . well, I can't help it, Betty, there's something *comfy* in having a boy to go about with — like other girls do. One they'd eat their hats to get, too! I can see it in their eyes when we pass; Fred with his great long legs and broad shoulders — I don't nearly come up to them — and his blue eyes with the black lashes, and his shiny black hair. And I like his tweeds, the Harris smell of them, and his dirty old pipe, and the way he shows his teeth — he's got *topping* teeth — when he laughs and says 'ra-*ther!*' And other people, when they see us, look . . . well I don't quite know how to say it, but they look sort of pleased; and they make room for us and let us into the dark corner-seats at the pictures, just as if we'd a right to them.

And they never laugh. (Oh, I can't *stick* being laughed at! — and that's the truth.) Yes, it's so comfy, Betty darling .... such a warm cosy comfy feeling. Oh, *won't* you understand?"

"Gawd! why not make a song of it?" But a moment later, very fiercely: "And who is it's taught you to think all this? Who's hinted it and suggested it till you've come to believe it? ... believe it's what you really feel."

"She hasn't! Mother's never said a word ... about Fred."

"Words? — why waste words? ... when she can do it with a cock of the eye. For your Fred, that!" and the girl called Betty held her fingers aloft and snapped them viciously. "But your mother's a different proposition."

"I think you're simply horrid."

To this there was no reply.

"*Why* have you such a down on her? What's she ever done to you? ... except not get ratty when I stay out late with Fred. And I don't see how you can expect ... being what she is ... and with nobody but me — after all she *is* my mother ... you can't alter that. I know very well — and you know, too — I'm not *too* putrid-looking. But" — beseechingly — "I'm *nearly* twenty-five now, Betty. And other girls ... well, she sees them, every one of them, with a boy of their own, even though they're ugly, or fat, or have legs like sausages — they've only got to ogle them a bit — the girls, I mean ... and there they are. And Fred's a good sort — he is, really! — and he dances well, and doesn't drink, and so ... so why *shouldn't* I like him? ... and off my own bat ... without it having to be all Mother's fault, and me nothing but a parrot, and without any will of my own?"

"Why? Because I know her too well, my child! I can read her as you'd never dare to ... even if you could. She's sly, your mother is, so sly there's no coming to grips with her ... one might as well try to fill one's hand with cobwebs. But she's got a hold on you, a stranglehold, that nothing'll loosen. Oh! mothers aren't fair — I mean it's not fair of nature to weigh us down with them and yet expect us to be our own true selves. The handicap's too great. All those months, when the same blood's running through two sets of veins — there's no getting away from that, ever after. Take yours. As I say, does she need to open her mouth? Not she! She's only got to let it hang at the corners, and you reek, you drip with guilt."

Something in these words seemed to sting the younger girl. She hit back. "I know what it is, you're jealous, that's what you are! ... and you've no other way of letting it out. But I tell you this. If ever I marry — yes *marry!* — it'll be to please myself, and nobody else. Can you imagine me doing it to oblige her?"

Again silence.

"If I only think what it would be like to be fixed up and settled, and able to live in peace, without this eternal dragging two ways . . . just as if I was being torn in half. And see Mother smiling and happy again, like she used to be. Between the two of you I'm nothing but a punch-ball. Oh, I'm fed up with it! . . . fed up to the neck. As for you . . . And yet you can sit there as if you were made of stone! Why don't you *say* something? *Betty!* Why won't you speak?"

But no words came.

"I can *feel* you sneering. And when you sneer I hate you more than any one on earth. If only I'd never seen you!"

"Marry your Fred, and you'll never need to again."

"I will, too! I'll marry him, and have a proper wedding like other girls, with a veil and bridesmaids and bushels of flowers. And I'll live in a house of my own, where I can do as I like, and be left in peace, and there'll be no one to badger and bully me — Fred wouldn't . . . ever! Besides, he'll be away all day. And when he came back at night, he'd . . . I'd . . . I mean I'd —" But here the flying words gave out; there came a stormy breath and a cry of: "Oh, Betty, Betty! . . . I couldn't, no, I couldn't! It's when I think of *that* . . . Yes, it's quite true! I like him all right, I do indeed, but only as long as he doesn't come too near. If he even sits too close, I have to screw myself up to bear it" — and flinging herself down over her companion's lap, she hid her face. "And if he tries to touch me, Betty, or even takes my arm or puts his round me . . . And then his face . . . when it looks like it does sometimes . . . all wrong . . . as if it had gone all wrong — oh! then I feel I shall have to scream — out loud. I'm afraid of him . . . when he looks like that. Once . . . when he kissed me . . . I could have died with the horror of it. His breath . . . his breath . . . and his mouth — like fruit pulp — and the black hairs on his wrists . . . and the way he looked — and . . . and everything! No, I can't, I can't . . . nothing will make me . . . I'd rather die twice over. But what am I to do? Mother'll *never* understand. Oh, why has it got to be like this? I want to be happy, too . . . and everything's all wrong. You tell me, Betty darling, you help me, you're older . . . you *know* . . . and you can help me, if you will . . . if you only will!" And locking her arms round her friend she drove her face deeper into the warmth and darkness, as if, from the very fervour of her clasp, she could draw the aid and strength she needed.

Betty had sat silent, unyielding, her sole movement being to loosen her own arms from her sides and point her elbows outwards, to hinder them touching the arms that lay round her. But at this last appeal she melted; and gathering the young girl to her breast, she held her fast. — And so for long she continued to sit, her chin resting lightly on the fair hair, that was silky and downy as an infant's, and gazing with sombre eyes over the stealthily heaving sea.

SISTER ANN

"SISTER Ann, Sister Ann, do you see anyone coming?" — from poor cowering Fatima. And from the watcher on the look-out always the same monotonous reply: "Naught but the dust that blows before the wind!"

She was really Edith; but ever since as children they had acted the *Bluebeard* play, she had been Ann to them — Sister Ann. And the name fitted her like her own skin. For Ann quite literally spent her life on the watch — for the next disaster, she being the only one who might ward it off.

Of late, however, her vigilance had had a double aim.

Without counting her — and no one ever did, she was so different — there were six of them, six girls in a row. (Brother Stephen the lawyer came after Ann, and little Timothy, who still rode every day to school, right at the end of the line.)

While they were still young, being so many hadn't troubled them. But now that they were all but one of them grown up — and she fast coming on — the calamity of their number was self-evident. "Old O'Grady and his six gals" was the snigger that went the round. And though it stung, it was bearable. But what if, some day, the "old" was shifted from Papa, and "maids" took the place of "girls"? Merely to think of it made their respective bloods run cold, though at first each thought for herself; for even among sisters a fear of this magnitude was hard to broach. Time, however, shattered their delicacy and, nowadays, the likelihood (or unlikelihood) of their ever finding husbands was openly discussed.

No help was to be expected from Papa. Stephen's training and setting-up had cost *pots* of money; and of course the station didn't pay. When Papa bought it and carried them off from town, it was on the strength of a rumour that gold had been found there. Characteristically (and adorably) he had swallowed the yarn, prospecting, sinking shafts, and so on.

But not a trace of the colour showed; and the poorer by several thousands he had been forced to turn squatter — and of squatting he knew no more than a child. Things had gone from bad to worse with him; and ever since last winter's floods swept away his three precious bridges over the river, he seemed finally to have lost heart; and was now oftenest to be found sitting in the porch, his red beard sunk on his chest, a glass of rum and milk before him. Always just the least bit . . . well, fuzzy . . . so that if you spoke suddenly to him he had to look hard at you to make sure which you were.

It was Ann who had taken command: Ann, her skirts pinned up, in leggings or jack-boots, a battered old straw on her head, who stumped about from morning till night, seeing after hands, horses, stock. Her skin was the colour of a well-baked piecrust, her nose scaly, her hair always half down. While the sun-wrinkles round the corners of her eyes were fast running into her cheeks. But Ann didn't care a threepenny-bit how she looked. Or what she did. When an infuriated stallion broke loose from his paddock and came thundering up to the house, it was Ann who intrepidly led him back and replaced the slip-rail. Or when a new closet was needed, she went out and superintended the digging of the pit and the filling-in of the old old one.

Not that the rest of them were idle — Ann wouldn't allow that; each had her job, and grumbling didn't help. Car, next in age to Ann, was dressmaker to the family; and a good part of her day went at the treadle-machine. However, since her chief interest was dress and the fashions, it didn't come too hard on her. She was also a dab at cutting and fitting, and wore her own clothes with such an air that they might have been bought in Paris — helped, of course, by a marvellous, simply *marvellous* figure. Very tall, with a rich, full bust, Car possessed a waist so tiny that Gemma's seventeen-inch silver belt spanned it with ease.

The others, having no marked talents, fared worse. Deb toiled, till her feet throbbed, in the flagstoned dairy, amid great flat dishes of milk off which she skimmed cream wrinkled like parchment, and as yellow; or churned butter; or made cheese. Ell had charge of the fowls, the maddening fowls, for ever straying or laying out of the nest; and so it went on, down to young Flo, who ought to have been at boarding-school and wasn't, for lack of funds, and did her resentful bit by flipping a feather-whisk over surfaces on which you could have written your name in the gritty, white dust.

The single one of whom nothing was expected or asked was Gemma. For Gemma was delicate, and unfit for exertion. The beauty of the family, and Ann's darling, she was free to laze away her days thinking of her health or her looks; not getting up from the bed she shared with Ann (which Ann left at unearthly hours) till she felt inclined to, sometimes only just in time for dinner.

Papa, himself so given to "sitting around", could not tolerate idleness in others. He was for ever quoting the ant at Gemma, or making pointed allusions to drones. He had also an Irish impatience with "side" or vanity. And when poor Gemma, hungry for masculine admiration, was it only her father's, went up to him one morning and, with her chin in the air, showed off her newly-scrubbed and polished teeth, all she got was: "Teeth? Where? I see nothing but gums." And as he turned away: "My dear, they're not a patch on Ann's!" — at which there was a general burst of laughter. Really it took *Papa* to pretend he preferred Ann's teeth, large, white, even as these were, to Gemma's small pearls.

But Ann didn't laugh, she was furious.

"The old fool doesn't know what he's saying!" — And the horse she was driving came in for a cut over the head.

Once a week she got out the buggy and drove the ten miles to the neighbouring township, with a load of butter and eggs; or cheese; or fowls. These articles were her own peculiar perquisities; and she took no one with her to see what she made by them. The money was earmarked for a special purpose: to meet the expense of entertaining the guests she got together whenever possible. Young men only, of course; and from town, not township. For her sisters' qualms about their persistent maidenhood were slight compared with hers; and Papa, who had done the damage by burying his family alive, was now too inert to remedy it. For all he cared, these six girls — of whom even the plainest was comely — might wither unseen and unwed. And in a land, too, where women stood at a premium!

It was ludicrous, it was absurd; and since the poor things' own hands were tied, she herself had shouldered the job of finding them husbands. So far, without success. Indeed, everything that could go wrong had done so. Eligibles were rare, nor was she free to pick and choose, she had just to take what offered: with the result that Car, the stately, was philandering with a youth seven years her junior; Bab's making sheeps-eyes at a totally *in*eligible, while Gemma, the victim of a week of full moons and verandah hammocks, was shedding secret tears over a tall dark handsome fellow who, they had subsequently learned, was already bespoken. That must not, *must* not be.

On this particular day she, Ann, carried a more than usually heavy load. And the price she meant to ask for her goods was stiffer. For during the last visit paid them by the "ineligible", it had leaked out that he knew a wealthy squatter who was still a bachelor; and straightway he had been half-whipped, half-wheedled into a promise to bring this unicum with him, the next time he came. A splash had now to be made, Gemma got up to kill.

On Gemma her hopes were pinned: Gemma who, did she seriously lay herself out to please, was irresistible. — Which was one reason why Papa's aspersions on the girls' looks — Papa had gone on to say Gemma was getting fat, very soon she'd be able to boast a double chin (at twenty-five!) — had bitten so deep. For after all Papa *was* a man, and judged women with a man's eye. But there was more in it than this. The love Ann bore her younger sister had in the course of time grown to be a kind of passion; and it was with something of a mother's savagery that she thought of dimples running to lines, lovely lips thinning, the exquisite oval of the face losing its shape. — And as she bumped down and up the bed of a dry creek, breathed dust for air, fought the flies, she felt that she would cheerfully have given years of her own life to keep Gemma as she was.

He was short, thickset, sandy-haired — such hair as remained to him, it wasn't much — with pale, rather prominent blue eyes, which fled did they chance to meet yours, seeming to rest by preference on inanimate objects. Socially, too, he was a dead weight. He either sat mum, or barked out short, staccato sentences: the "and that's that!" style of thing which effectually put a stopper on conversation. And his name was MacNab.

Gemma's recoil was instant and instinctive (poor lamb, poor sacrificial lamb!). But feeling Ann's eyes glued sternly on her, she did her best, her *level* best, in the hour that followed. Her prettiest, too; making full play with her thickly-fringed lids and what was known among them as: her "Ellen Terry" mouth. She had him all to herself. Ann soon winked and grimaced and accompanied Papa from the room; Babs and the "ineligible" had been bundled off to gather mushrooms; while the remaining sisters — for fear of alarming by their numbers they had not been produced — kept religiously to the back of the house.

But "Gemma, what are you doing here?" from a dismayed Ann when, entering the bedroom, she found Gemma sitting limply on the side of the bed. "Where is he, child? What have you done with him?"

"*Done*? It's not me, it's Papa. He came back. And then he went over to talk to him," flamed Gemma, confusing her pronouns in her haste. "He *can* talk, too, if he wants to. He's not so dumb as he makes out to be."

"You silly child, it's only shyness. He's not used to a pretty woman's company. I saw that at a glance. Come now, darling," and Ann held outspread the dress, cut low in the neck, and sleeveless, to show the dimpled arms, in which Gemma should have continued her work of enchantment.

But the girl's lips were trembling, and she pushed the dress away.

"I'm *not* going to wear that thing. Oh, it's no use, Ann, I can't — I couldn't *ever* like him."

But Ann was obdurate. Petting and cajoling, she hooked and buttoned, and straightened the mass of chestnut hair. Then, taking firm hold of Gemma's arm, led the unwilling victim back to the forsaken guest. — "Or what will he think of you?"

But he wasn't thinking anything. Fortunately (or unfortunately) he seemed to be getting on quite well with Papa. At least, there the two of them sat pow-wowing, their glasses before them. Unfortunately again, and thanks to her own misguided caution, to-day that old fool Papa had all his wits about him, not a drop of liquor having crossed his lips till now. And when sober he *was* no fool. Even she saw how impossible it was for Gemma to chip in — on a talk more-over that turned entirely on sheep! And having stood for a moment, hat in hand as it were, Gemma gave her a flaming, what-did-I-tell-you look, and stalked out of the room.

At supper it was the same. Though she sat next him, he didn't even trouble to hand her the salt (after helping himself), but went on speaking to Papa across her. It was plain the man hadn't an idea in his head except business, and of business Gemma, alas! knew nothing. Her one effort, made in obedience to Ann's fierce eyes, merely exposed her ignorance. To cover it, Ann sprang in with a remark on the existing wool prices (about which she knew consderably more than Papa). And this led to a rather heated argument, in which she found herself siding with MacNab against Papa; for in all the former said there was a good deal of rough horse-sense.

That night (after giving Papa a wigging he wouldn't forget) she took the resentful girl in her arms and spoke long and earnestly. It wasn't only herself Gemma had to think of: it was everyone of them. Papa was literally on the rocks for money: if he couldn't contrive to get a loan the station might be sold over his head. In which case her sisters would have to turn out, go as governesses or even worse. It lay with Gemma to prevent this. As a married woman, with a substantial settlement and in a good position, she could give these unfortunates their chance: take them about with her, introduce them to the right people, see that they met likely men. About herself she, Ann, wouldn't speak: except to say she didn't know how much longer she'd be able to go on working as she did. She was nearing forty; and the most trying years of a woman's life were at hand.

Gemma's tears ran down her cheeks, trickling off her nose.

"I know, I know *all* that," she sobbed. "But, oh Ann, it's so . . . so humiliating. Besides, I've got *some* feelings of my own."

"Yes, and I know what they are, too, and why you're not putting your heart into this affair. It's because you can't or won't forget all that moonshine about young Spencer."

"It's *not* moonshine. He said . . . Howard said . . ."

"I don't want to hear. Nothing will alter *my* opinion of him. Now, darling, just you listen to me." — And patiently Ann set herself to begin again from the beginning.

She had the satisfaction next morning of seeing the pair go off together, Gemma having been cajoled into showing the visitor round. Never had Gem looked prettier: in a rose-besprinkled print, rose on white, a sort of Dolly Varden hat tied under her chin with rose-velvet strings. But from her spyhole Ann was concerned to see him halt at the pigsties; and not for a moment only: they continued to stand there in the sun, leaning over the wall. (Gemma! . . . who never went within coo-ee of the pigs without a handkerchief to her nose.) As was only to be expected, when at last they moved it was to make a bee-line back to the house, Gem feeling ill and needing to lie down. Not too ill though to say what she thought of him.

Ann clicked her tongue, and went away to scratch her head and ponder. The thing was plain: her schemes for Gemma's benefit were not coming off. Nor was it *only* Gemma's fault: the man seemed as little taken with her as she with him. Could it be that she was not his "style"? Himself so short and stumpy, might he not perhaps incline to women of more regal proportions? In that case, there was no lack of choice to hand. What about Car, Car, the tall and willowy, the superbly busted? The experiment was at least worth trying. And so Car was commanded to appear at dinner, introduced as if she had just come home. But it didn't work. For all the attention he paid her she might have been a broom-stick. He had evidently no more eye for a fine figure than for a pretty face.

That afternoon, Car having frostily withdrawn to make merry over him with the hidden sisters, Papa bottle-free and normally sodden, Gemma declining to get off her bed; that afternoon there was nothing for it, Ann saw, but herself to take him on. *She* had no feminine shrinking from sties; it didn't matter to her how long she stood over them, breathing in the odour of pig. No, *her* difficulty was to keep from smiling when she heard him say: "As I was telling your sister . . ." (Poor little Gemma!)

But soon she forgot to smile. For the man knew what he was talking about, having, it seemed, worked out the precise amount of artificial food required, in addition to household swill, to bring a pig to its prime. If what he said was true, she had been putting herself to unnecessary expense. The chance of saving so-and-so many shillings per week was too good to miss; and she asked methodical questions on weights and measurements.

The horses visited — there wasn't much about horse-flesh either he didn't know — she got into her breeches and rode with him to an outlying paddock where the hands were ring-barking. Here again she grew interested in spite of herself. For though, as one of them, he admitted the sheep-farmers' need for pasture, ever more pasture, he sighed over the havoc that was being wrought to attain it. Besides, it cut both ways. No grass without moisture; and the countries with abundant rainfalls were those that were richest in forests. How shortsighted then, to stip of its trees a land already so poor in rain! The present generation might wilfully shut its eyes to the folly of it; those to come would have theirs opened, and be the sufferers.

He loved trees, too, it seemed, for their own sake.

With a hand on the trunk of one they stood by, he said: "It goes to my heart to see a mighty specimen like this doomed to a lingering death."

Yes, he certainly gave one something to think about. — And that night Gemma was left in peace.

The following day the two of them went out together almost as a matter of course. ("Ann's Old Man of the Sea!" tittered the sisters.) And this time it was Ann who did most of the talking. As they climbed a boulder-strewn hill, their bridles over their arms, she found herself confessing to the struggle it was to keep the place going, bemoaned her own inexperience, Papa's fatal lassitude. And in doing so let slip, for the first time, the family's full size. He listened attentively and sympathetically; and in return gave her various useful tips how to cut down expenses and improve her control; for he, too, it now transpired, had once been poor, suffered hardship.

And so it went on. They walked, rode, talked together, for each of the five days he stayed with them.

On the last morning — he was travelling by the next day's coach — he turned to her, and abruptly, without a word of preamble, asked her to marry him.

They stood by one of Papa's make-shift bridges, which the oftener she saw them the surer Ann felt would be demolished by the first spring flood. Her thoughts were with her eyes, and she didn't grasp what he was saying till after she had been idiot enough to ask him to repeat it. Red to the ears with embarrassment and in a daze at what she heard, before she could stop herself she had blurted out: "*Me?* Marry *you?*"

It sounded terrible, cutting to a degree; and so, apparently, he took it, going even redder than she was, and saying equally bluntly: "I see. That settles it then."

"Oh no, it doesn't," spluttered Ann. — But this was even worse, for he might misconstrue it, and she rushed on: That is . . . I mean . . . Of *course* I can't marry you. But . . . but it's very nice of you to ask me."

Recovering from the snub he ventured: "But why not? What are your reasons?"

"*Reasons?* Why, I've never even thought of marrying — never! How could I? Desert all these poor things? . . . who depend on me for everything? Impossible!"

He ignored the family's claims on her. "Nor had I. Till I met you, Ann."

"Look here, I'm forty next birthday!"
"And I'm forty-five."

"That's different. No, please don't go on. It's not a bit of use."
"Then it's definitely 'no'?"
"Quite, quite definitely."

They made their way home in silence. Not till considerably later did Ann reflect that, of all the reasons she had urged on Gemma for marrying, not one had occurred to her.

The pair's reappearance, before the morning was half over, struck the sisters as odd, very odd. Car and Gemma also reported on Ann's extraordinary dumbness at dinner, and the clapping on of her hat directly after, MacNab being left to make the best of it with Papa. Could they have quarrelled? Or had Ann at last had enough of him?

Gemma was deputed to find out.

Ann was plaiting her hair for the night. She had taken off her bodice for comfort and stood in her corset, arms and shoulders bare, running her fingers nimbly down the first of the two long thick ropes that fell to below her waist. None of *them* had hair like Ann's — they, who would have known what to do with it! Whereas she just bundled it up anyhow — being of course long past vanity.

But one tail was finished, the other begun, it was now or never, for, once in bed, Ann went straight to sleep.

Gemma cleared her throat — she didn't much fancy the job, for Ann wasn't the sort of person you pumped — and her first words came a little tentatively. "I say, Ann, what's up? Between you and the octopus, I mean."

For a second Ann's busy fingers stopped their braiding. "*Up?*" she echoed. "I don't know what you're talking about."

"Oh, yes, you do," persuaded Gemma. "Why, at dinner anyone could see something was wrong; you hardly opened your mouth. And going off by yourself like that afterwards."

"Nonsense. Come, don't sit there half-undressed. I'm nearly ready."

"Oh, get on, Ann, you can't deceive me. Have the two of you had a row?"

"Mind your own business."

"I think it *is* mine!" said Gemma with some spirit. "Wasn't he brought here in the first place solely on my account?"

"I daresay."

"You daresay?"

"*Ah!* you should have played your cards better, my dear."

The covert sneer galled Gemma, and she retorted hotly: "I like that! Played my cards indeed! Who with! That dry old stick? — a person who's got no more guts in him than a ventriloquist's dummy?"

"Now it's you who don't know what you're talking about."

"Oh, don't I?"

"One might even say *you* were the dummy. And consequently failed to interest him."

"While you *have*, I suppose? No, really, Ann!" and Gemma broke into a low, but very offensive laugh.

Ann paused in the shedding of her clothing and glanced sharply up.

"My good girl, if I chose, I could make you laugh on the wrong side of your mouth. As it is . . . Now stop your silly chatter and get to bed."

"Silly chatter! But that's you all over. You never give anybody credit for an ounce of brains but yourself."

"Well, brains I'm afraid you must allow me. But attractions and so on, none worth mentioning, eh?"

"Naturally not. At your age!"

"Oh-o! Well it may amuse you still more to hear that everyone isn't of the same opinion. — I have had a proposal."

"You *what?*" exploded Gemma, shooting up from her seat at the bedside. But there it remained. Relapsing, she just sat and stared at her sister, open-mouthed, incredulous. And Ann had peeled off both stockings and hung them up to air before Gemma came to sufficiently to put the natural but superfluous question: "Who from?"

"Who do you think?"

"You don't mean to say . . . want to tell me that man's asked *you* to marry him? *You!*"

The tone bit. Ann flushed. "And why not? I'm neither a chimpanzee, I suppose, nor do I yet hobble about on sticks!"

But Gemma could only sit and mutter to herself: "Well, I'm *damned! Damned*, that's what I am!" Ann had poised her long white nightgown above her head and wriggled into it before Gemma asked faintly: "And . . . and what did you say?"

"Never you mind," said Ann. "That's my business." And puffing out the candle she got into bed and pulled the sheet up over her head. — Gemma had to finish undressing in the dark.

She couldn't sleep. And as soon as Ann's breaths began to come heavily and regularly, she sidled out and padded barefoot to the room where Car and Deb lay.

"Girls, wake up!" she hissed. "Hush! don't make a noise," for Car, a light sleeper, was at once on the spot. "But I simply must tell you. That . . . that creature has asked Ann to marry him!"

"*Ann? Ann*, do you say? Good *God!*" from Car, sitting bolt upright.

"That's just what I said. And wasn't she in a paddy!"

Here Deb raised herself on one elbow. "Does she mean to take him?"

"How do I know? She's huffed, and wouldn't say."

"*Well* . . . of all the — God, what a scream!" And Car laughed so immoderately that she had to retire under the bedclothes.

"What the dickens'll happen if she does?"

"Lord knows!"

"Well, he mayn't, but I do," said Deb. "If Ann goes, I'll never set foot in the darned old dairy again!"

On coming in next morning from her early round, Ann was confronted by a battery of eyes: eyes big and bold with curiosity, or stealing furtive peeps from under their lids, but all alike greedy for information. Better just take the bull by the horns and be done with it.

Summoning the six to the bedroom and firmly closing the door, she turned to them and, in what was privately known as her "public-speaker" voice, "addressed the meeting".

"I see Gemma has told you. And I suppose it had to come out. Though I didn't intend it till later . . . after the person concerned had gone."

"Then —?"

"Then he *is* going?"

"Of course he is."

"So you refused him?"

"Of course I did!" said Ann again, this time with considerable emphasis, and a sharp glance round. (Was it fancy, or *did* she surprise a queer expression on more than one of these prying faces?)

"But —" ventured Car.

"But why?" Deb asked out-right.

"*Why?*" echoed Ann, seemingly unable to believe her ears. "Well, of all the idiotical questions . . . Are you daft? What in the name of fortune do you suppose would become of this place — Papa and the whole lot of you? — if *I* weren't here to look after things?" — To which, naturally, there was and could be no reply.

But, though tongues were held, the silence was an uneasy one. And presently it was broken by Gemma, the privileged, who murmured as if to herself: "When I think of the dozens of reasons for taking him that were rammed down *my* throat!"

At this Ann opened her eyes, opened them very wide indeed. "What's that got to do with me? You're surely not trying to compare us, are you?"

"Lord forbid! I hope I know my place. Still, *some* people might say what's sauce for the goose can also be sauce for the ganderess."

"Don't be impertinent."

"Impertinent? Just because for once I venture to say what I think?"

"I've no wish to hear it."

"Of course not! You never want to hear anybody but yourself. Only what you think or say or do matters. You must always be cock of the walk."

"Well, well, well!" said Ann in a low descending scale, and with an appreciatory nod to each word. "So *that's* your opinion of me, is it? That's your thanks for all I've done for you? Cock of the walk!" And swinging round on her heel, to get the whole pack under her eye: "Are any of you labouring under the delusion that I enjoy being forced to slave as I do? To toil from morning till night solely to keep the place together and a roof over your heads? That I wouldn't rather have had a life of my own — like any other woman? If so, you're even greater numb-skulls than I thought! Fools — who ought to be thanking God on your knees that I saw where my duty lay. Without me to look after you, you'd all end in the gutter!"

"Gutter or no gutter, I'd be jolly glad *not* to be looked after for a bit," from Deb, who sat with her feet on a chair.

Ann laughed contemptuously.

"Well do I know it! If I weren't here you'd every one of you be lolling round — just like Papa. Eternally resting from something you hadn't done!"

"What we'd like is a rest from *your* eternal bullying and badgering — *In*cluding the dairy!"

"*And* the sewing-machine!"

"And those beats of fowls!"

And dusting rooms and working in the kitchen, said the eyes of the two youngest, whose tongues lacked the courage to speak out.

This time the pause that followed had something ominous in it. No one, nothing stirred: except Ann's eyes, which travelled cold as ice from one to other of the rebel faces.

"Well, upon my word! — And may I ask if that's all? Are there any more insults, any more names you'd like to call me?

I may as well know exactly where I stand."

"It's *in* you, I suppose, to make slaves of people."

"Or it's grown on you. I don't believe you *could* stop now, even if you tried."

"Papa says so, too."

"Says you won't even let us call our souls our own."

Ann's cheeks burnt a brick-red.

"Oh, he does, does he? So Papa's in it too, is he? Well, that makes it *quite* plain — plain as my nose — what's at the bottom of all this. It's just the dirty Irish blood in you coming out!"

"You've got it, too!"

"I'm damned if I have!" And with a shattering bang of the door, Ann flung not only from the room but the house.

At breakfast her chair stood empty. — And an uncomfortable meal it was. Papa asking fatuous questions, where she could be, what doing; MacNab sitting stolid as a lump of wood; themselves suffering from a severe attack of cold feet the aftermath of their daring.

By this time Ann was miles away, having walked her hardest and without a stop, to put distance between herself and the house — the house that held them. In all her life she'd never been so angry, felt so outraged. And fresh spasms of wrath kept gripping her at each fresh memory of the things she had had to listen to. How dare they, how *dare* they! The ingratitude, the vile ingratitude, of their conduct was bad enough, but ten times worse the impudence of it. These underlings — creatures who had sat at her feet, eaten out of her hand ever since the youngest of them came into the world. Whom she had washed and dressed and dosed and punished. To whom her lightest word had been law. Why, it was just as if a flock of tame domestic animals should suddenly go berserk and tear the hand that fed them. — But she'd make them pay! A bully, was she? . . . a slave-driver? Well, from now on they should learn the real meaning of these words. No more excusing, no more favouritism; all alike should work the clock round; Deb, the ringleader, answer for every ounce of butter she failed to produce, Gemma be hauled out of bed at her, Ann's, own hours. — And as she plunged forward, over stick and stone, her lips curled with malice at the separate forms of revenge devised for each single sister.

But, little by little, pace and distance told; and hurt got the better of anger. For the wound to her self-love had been a cruel one. Her own picture of herself — the pleasing, private image nursed by each of us — was that of a superior being: able business-woman, expert manager, sole brains and hence rightful head of the family, looked up to in admiration by every one who came in contact with her — and especially by her sisters, for the masterly manner in which, Papa having failed them, she had leapt to the rescue. Whereas it now turned out that they had given her as small credit as thanks for the feat. Instead of prizing her, priding themselves on having her, they had all the time been secretly resenting her authority, thinking mean, underhand things of her, poking fun at her behind her back. The sting of it, the humiliation, was so harsh a mouthful that, like an overdose of mustard, it brought tears hot as mustard to her eyes.

MacNab waylaid her trudging home, grim of face.

He attached himself to her, turned back with her, remarking as he did: "I noticed you weren't at breakfast, Miss Ann."

These harmless words gave Ann just the peg she needed. She laughed loudly and sarcastically.

"You don't say so. Now fancy that!"

He winced, and made an apologetic sound. "Is . . . er . . . is anything the matter?"

Her only answer was to quicken her steps, in an attempt to shake him off.

"I wondered . . . merely wondered . . . if *I* could be of any use?"

"When I need help I'll ask for it."

"Miss Ann —"

"Oh, for God's sake, hold your tongue and let me be!" And with that her face wrinkled and contracted, she began to cry in earnest. (Devil take the man, with his poking and prying.)

Undeterred, he kept on at her side, suiting his pace to hers, now quick, now slow.

Till she rounded on him: "If you can't take a hint . . . if you *must* know . . . well, to-day I've made the pleasurable discovery what my sisters really think of me . . . and feel about me."

If she thought to surprise him she was mistaken.

"Yes?" he said unmoved. Adding in the next breath: "I saw that from the first."

In her own surprise, Ann lowered her handkerchief to exclaim: "*You?* How?"

"Oh, one has one's ways. One's not as big a fool as one looks."

"You're no fool," she said warmly. "It's me. I'm the fool

and always have been. Blind as a bat. Hugging the belief that they needed me, and . . . were glad of me. When all they want is to get rid of me, to be left to their own devices."

"And don't you think it might perhaps be quite a good thing, for them?" A question so inept, so inane, that it did not seem to Ann worth answering.

However she raised no objection when, on coming to the pigsties, he seemed to wish to pause there. For, with her face in the state it was, she couldn't show herself at the house. Rigorously she mopped her eyes, wiped her cheeks, blew a resounding peal on her nose.

He gave her time, himself standing in an easy attitude, his arms crossed on the top rung of the gate, one foot on the lowest, looking down as if absorbed in the tumbling mass of piglets. But when she ceased to sniff and had put her handkerchief away, he turned.

"There's something I'd like to say to you, Miss Ann, and I do hope you won't take it amiss. First, I'm exceedingly sorry for what has happened — in a way I'm afraid I've been the innocent cause of it — and sorrier still for the pain it has given you. But it's like this . . . or at least this is how I look at it," he corrected himself. "Your sisters — these *very* charming young ladies — are all grown women now and you . . . well, of course one sees how hard it must be for you to realise it, who have had them in your care since they were children. But don't you think you are perhaps holding the reins a little too tight? Keeping the curb on a little overlong?"

"But, but —" spluttered Ann, incensed anew by this busybody interference.

He raised his hand. "I think I know what you're going to say. That if you did not treat them as you do —"

"Nothing of the sort! If every one of them didn't pull her weight, take a fair share of the work —"

Again he broke in. "Where would you be, eh? Or, rather, where would they be? To which my answer is: very much poorer no doubt, but also very much happier. As happy as you are."

"*Me?* I, happy?"

"Why certainly. Though you won't admit it. Believe me, Miss Ann, you're one of the born workers, belonging by nature and bent to the busy bees of this world. Were you forced to sit idle, you would droop and pine. But every mortal has his own idea of happiness, and yours is plainly not theirs. Now why not leave them to themselves for a bit? Give them a taste of freedom? Frankly I don't think you would regret it. They'd soon find their feet."

"Not if *I* know them."

"You're too hard on them."

Ann was pale with anger.

"Does this mean you're siding with them? Standing up for *them* — against me? I've never heard anything so unfair! Or such nonsense either! All this twaddle about happiness. Why, Papa would go smash in six months and they'd be dragged down with him! You've seen for yourself what he is."

He nodded. "But I've seen something else, too. That *you* have washed your hands of him! He at least is free to follow his 'own devices'."

"I think you're a thoroughly unprincipled person. Happy — and bankrupt!"

"Not necessarily. If I could only persuade you, Miss Ann, to give my plan a trial, I'd see to it that your father got a substantial loan."

"A loan? A loan to Papa? Oh no you *don't!*" — as crushingly as if he were out to borrow rather than lend. "Why, you might just as well pour your money down the sink! You'd never see a penny of it again."

"I called it a loan but . . . Come, come, Ann, be reasonable, show yourself the sensible woman you are, and — and change your mind."

For a moment she could do no more than echo his last words. Then, however, their full significance dawned on her. "Look here — is this an attempt to buy me off?" she plumped out, at the same time rounding on him with a look that was meant to kill. But it failed. For the small, pale eyes that met hers were so full of kindliness, of understanding, and, yes, of a sort of mischievous twinkle, that she hurriedly dropped her own. And even felt something of a fool for her heroics. So *he* didn't take her seriously either. Like the rest of them had probably all along been smirking behind his hand at her expense. This discovery ought to have been equally mortifying, but, strange to say, it wasn't. And as she stood there, fumbly and unsure, she became conscious that offence and anger alike were petering out. The goodwill that shone from these eyes, after what she had gone through that morning, was so grateful that it had a queer effect on her, making her feel soft and silly. If he didn't stop looking at her like this, she'd end by having to fish for her handkerchief again.

"Oh, the whole thing's so absurd . . . so utterly absurd," she mumbled, with a hearty sniff to relieve her need.

"On the contrary it's the most sensible proposition — business proposition — I've ever made. To anyone."

"A business proposition? That I should desert them, leave them in the lurch. Let Gemma — *Gemma!* — make what hash she likes of her life?"

"But, my dear woman, it's her life. You can't live it for her. And she's quite old enough to know what she wants. Now just you let them choose their own sweethearts" — this with so much meaning that Ann squirmed. "A beauty like Miss Gemma" (so he had thought her pretty, had he? It sounded almost funny now) "will never lack suitors. No doubt she already has a favourite up her sleeve."

"Oh, is there anything you *don't* know?" sighed Ann in despair. "I declare you're enough to provoke a saint."

But he felt her weakening, and steadily pressed his advantage home. Until she found herself reduced to the flimsy objection: "But how can you be sure I shouldn't bully and slave-drive you, too?"

"No chance of that, my dear, between people who're labouring for the same end. And to whom work's a sort of gospel. Your sisters now, you'll never feel safe or happy with them again. A scene like this morning's — from which if I mistake not you're quoting — will always stand between you. — See here, Ann: the very first time I saw you I said to myself, there's the woman I've been looking for, that's the wife for me!" And covering with his the hand that lay on the wall, he fell to in earnest to raze her last defences.

Round the spyhole from which, a few days previously, Ann had stalked him and Gemma, were congregated the sisters, armed with an old field-glass through which, by turns, they followed the couple's every movement.

Minute by minute the excitement grew.

"*Lordy!* He's put his arm round her shoulders."

"Oh, *let* me see!"

"No, me! I'm next."

"Heavens! I do believe she's going to take him," from Car, holding tight to the glasses and warding off the pushful with her elbows.

"I believe she *has* taken him," said Deb solemnly, after a further prolonged scrutiny, and freed her eyes to drink in the effect of her announcement on the staggered group.

But not for long were they mum. And amid the self-congratulatory hugs, the hoorays and polka-steps in which they let off their feelings, Gemma's absence was noticed.

"Gem! I say Gem, where *are* you? Oh, come here, do! You're missing all the fun."

But Gemma did not budge. Stretched in a hammock, her hands clasped behind her head, her eyes fixed and distant, she was already deep in her own problem. How, without loss of dignity, to lure back the tall dark handsome lover so boorishly shown the door by Sister Ann.

PART TWO

TWO TALES OF OLD STRASBOURG

Life and Death of Peterle Luthy
The Professor's Experiment

LIFE AND DEATH OF PETERLE LUTHY

PETERLE was born in hospital. — The first hiccuppy breaths drawn, his little body washed and swathed, he was wheeled, together with his mother, down the corridor to another ward, and put to sleep under a feather-bed in a blue-and-white checked covering. Seven beds stood in this ward, with seven cots beside them, and five were in use when Peterle came to his. The seventh was taken possession of before sunset. Again the doors of the ward opened, to admit two attendants pushing a truckle-bed. The new arrival was a sturdy fellow, who had all but been the death of the young girl his mother: she lay white as chalk, her eyes closed, her auburn hair tumbled loose on the pillow. — Meanwhile Peterle, bottle to mouth, was engaged in learning to suck; and the imbibing of a smooth sweet fluid, that lulled and sated, was the first good joy he knew.

Peterle was very puny: emotional visitors clasped their hands and turned up their eyes at the sight of him. But he was of a contented humour, and would occupy himself for minutes on end, making worm-like movements of his fingers before his face, in a vain attempt to guide them to his mouth. If a sunbeam tickled his nose he sneezed, and then his tiny wizened face puckered into a thousand fresh crinkles and creases — like the hands of a laundress on Monday evening. Every day a square of sunshine took a journey across him, his bed standing next one of the high windows that opened on the garden. It travelled over his mother, too, who, to begin with, so weak was she, could hardly raise her arm to pat him when he cried; she lay and dozed in the warmth, a delicate-looking girl, with fine princess hands, which years of scouring and scrubbing had not disfigured.

On the third day, pulling herself up in bed, she moistened her handkerchief and cleaned out the corners of the infant's mouth and nose. In the afternoon came visitors. Peterle had just emptied a bottle, and, exhausted with the labour of drinking, had fallen asleep. On being handled he wakened, was sick, and uttered shrill cries.

His grandmother shook her head.

"Well, well!" was her heaved sigh of comment on him, as she put him back in his cot, where he fretted himself to sleep again. — She was a pale, thin, tidy woman, with a face which, in its ineffectual flatness, resembled a mask of scantly worked clay. The grinding years, instead of deepening the charactery, had blurred . . . erased.

With her were the babe's two brothers. Gustave, who had arrived at breeches, neither felt nor feigned an interest in the newcomer. Thumb in mouth, noisily shuffling his feet, he strayed round the ward, staring with a child's audacious curiosity at the bedridden women, and dragging a sticky finger unrebuked over tables and chairs. But Willi, who had seen only three summers, gurgled with joy on discovering his mother, and made for her outstretched arms with all the speed his infirmity permitted: his legs were so bandy that, when he walked, he staggered, like an old salt taking land. And Peterle's mother forgot Peterle over him; for Willi was the apple of her eye. In briefly responding to the elder woman's brief questions, it was Willi's butter-coloured hair she smoothed, Willi's eyes she looked into — two limpid, black-fringed pools, that had caught and kept a glint of the May blueness on which they, too, had opened.

A bell rang; the handful of strangers retired; the ward resumed its everyday air. Sinking as into downy depths, the weary childbearers surrendered themselves anew to a dreamless repose; and the hush was broken only by the quickly stilled wail of an infant, or the flip-flop of a nurse's bast shoes. For days Peterle lay at peace in his generous bed: he slept, sucked, and stared into the sunshine: and, except when raised to be stripped of his swaddling, found life a very pleasant state of being.

On the morning when he was nine days old, his mother threw off her coverings, and having reached a chair, dressed first herself, then Peterle, whom she bound to a pillow. Downstairs in the tesselated corridor, where lilac rapped and beckoned at the windows, the perambulator was in waiting — a big-bellied clothes-basket on wheels. Peterle, placed in it, was topped by a feather-bed, and trundled out on his homeward journey.

It was May, and a dazzling morning; streets and houses lay as if new-scoured in the strong, pure light. The steep roofs shone gaily red; their dormer windows flashed and twinkled. In old walled gardens, snowy masses of fruit-blossom seemed to focus the sunlight and give it back intensified. On the banks of the river ancient wood-encrusted buildings, square bridge-towers, the prim, delicate lines of a chateau, all lived again, to their tenderest details, in the water at their feet. Distances were marvellously clear. To the north a chain of mountains drew its bold profile against the sky; behind the town, a second chain rose a little more nearly, a little less boldly: a ridge of infinitely blue hills, deeper in tint where a cloud's shadow hovered or a valley narrowed — two natural walls to the fertile, Rhine-washed plain. Peterle's mother had not far to go, but she covered the ground painfully: the roads were cobbled, and her unused feet burned. Her way led her through the old inner town, where the winding streets were narrowest; the electric tramcars, which came bounding along in a series of jerks, were so incongruously big that they called to mind unnatural stage proportions. Twelve o'clock had not yet rung out from the many steeples, but in shops and offices the midday rest had already been called, and the pavements were black with people. In the roadway companies of soldiers, in various uniforms, were returning to barracks from drill on the military grounds outside the city gates: at their head rode or strode their lieutenant, dusty and begrimed as they. Peterle's mother paused, with a quickened interest, to watch a handful of sappers salute a general: he pranced by, proud and gaudy, and the parade-step hammered the stones. On a bridge spanning the river she drew up anew, to look over at the fishers who dotted the paved footpath that ran level with the water: they stood vacant yet absorbed, lost in ponderous expectation of the fish that never bit. Farther downstream were moored the floating wash-houses — shallow, roofed barges, in which women knelt to scrub, and rinse, and wring. Alongside of the tramway lines, sturdy dogs strained at their harness in milk and ice-carts; vegetablemongers cried their wares; yellow post-vans, manned by blue-coated officials, lumbered heavily. Over all this noise and colour, over toiling women, fishermen and soldiers, over a congeries of gabled housetops, hooded chimneys, storks' nests, rose the slender solitary tower of the immortal Minster, a landmark on the plain for many a mile round — from afar off, when the rest of the town still lay level with the horizon, this spire rose like a giant finger pointing skywards — and, in wandering about the place, did one by chance turn into a certain little narrow street, the vast pile itself, all the red-brown glories of portal and facade, broke upon the sight with a splendour that took the breath away. Seen thus, by one standing midgelike in the shade of its mighty walls, the lacework of the tapering spire pierced so far into the sky, was so little more than a streak of filigree against the blue, that it was hard to believe it the work of human hands: the ancient houses, six and seven storeys high, that ringed in the square, reached but to the foot of the great rose-window. And when storms were abroad, the clouds raced and flew, it was possible to fancy one saw, with the naked eye, the yielding swing of the frail apex to the wind.

In his wheeled bed, Peterle blinked and averted his face from the too vivid light. Before the open stall of an arcade he made a long halt, his bald head bare to the sun, while his mother, over some trivial purchase, drank in the gossip of the saleswoman, the immense black bow of whose head-dress filled the narrow opening like the outspread wings of a bat. Crossing a leafy square, the two entered a side street. In this, Peterle's home to be, the pavement formed a mere edging to the houses, from the overhanging upper storeys of which the inmates could talk across in everyday tones.

At a doorway two men were standing. One had a long black cigar between his lips.

"Boschur, Mamsell Henriette!" he greeted affably, steadying the cigar with his hand: it was an itinerant vegetable-hawker, who lodged in the family attic. "Welcome home! But you bring back more luggage than you started with, I see!"

A binder's apprentice from the ground floor capped the pleasantry; and both laughed.

Peterle's mother did not turn colour. *"Boschur bisamme!"* she gave back politiely and impassively. Then, since it was beyond her strength to get the perambulator, with Peterle in it, up the two high steps leading to the front door, she first carried in the child, whom she laid on the wooden lid of the pump, just over the threshold; then, returning, dragged, bumped and coaxed the unwieldy carriage after.

It was a very old house, of generous proportions. In earlier times, before the town had burst its girdle of river and canal, this alley had been an aristocratic dwelling-place; and the heavily brassed door, which now swung to and fro on its leather pad, had remained shut to the street, in proud reserve. Both flights of stairs ended in landings the size of a goodly room. On the first of these, the walls were composed of enormous presses, built in, and faced with mirrors — or what had once been mirrors; for the glass had long since disappeared: great cupboards, in which a man would stand upright. On the second storey they were wanting: but, in the low, spacious rooms themselves, the fireplaces, supplanted now for a score or more of years by unlovely iron stoves, were equally ornate with those of the *bel-etage*: oil-paintings and small looking-glasses were inserted in their woodwork, which was carved by hand, and had once been white.

This upper landing, which Peterle's mother reached panting for breath, was sand-strewn, and two oleanders grew in tubs. In a dark little kitchen overlooking the courtyard, a man with his arm in a sling sat smoking, an empty wine-carafe on the table before him. His chin was sunk on his breast, and he did not glance up at the ascending step; nor did Peterle's mother pause to greet him. She went past, into the front room where she housed with her children, and, in default of the perambulator, laid her infant on one of the great feather beds, in a nest burrowed out by Willi and still warm.

On entering the kitchen she found her stepfather in the same dejected attitude.

"No better, Father?"

He shook his head, without speaking. He was down on his luck at present. A stone mason, earning his six marks a day, he had had the misfortune to break his arm: it had been set crooked by a quack in the neighbourhood; and when he went, under protest, to the hospital, the doctors had held it necessary to re-break and re-set the limb. — In person, he was a small, blond, sallow man, with a pair of ethereal blue eyes.

Peterle's mother, while waiting for a pan of milk to boil, drew a chair to the table.

He eyed her lackadaisically. "Where's the child?"

She pointed with her thumb over her shoulder, wasting no words. She was reckoning up the days that must elapse before she could go out to work again. — Not that there was any very pressing need for her to do so. Besides what Mother earned by charring, they had three of their rooms let; and this was enough to keep them; for they were thrifty folk. Still, Father as a good German, liked his chunk of beef in the pot at midday — liked a genuine meat soup, not a sham one, such as was sometimes served in even the best houses — and his keg of red wine in the cellar. The children ran through boots and clothes; there was now an extra mouth to feed; while she, too, if she was to dance this summer, must have a new blouse, a neckerchief, a pair of pointed shoes. — And, as she sat there, her hands open in her lap, her body as limp as though some of the bones had been withdrawn from it, Henriette let her thoughts stray to one of her partners of the year before: a merry, black-eyed Italian overseer this, who had brought a gang of navvies up over the Gotthard, and, on leaving, had more than half-promised to return. In fancy she talked hot nothings with him at *Fuchs am Buckel*, or tripped it at the *Messti* Ruprechtsau . . .

Meanwhile, though, such dreams were idle: there was Peterle to watch and tend. And this, and much more, she did, with the mute and stoic patience that was in her. Unaided, too. For, regularly at seven of the clock, Peterle's grandmother pinned on shawl and apron, took her big covered basket, and went forth to char. She was in constant demand, being the pink of cleanliness, and honesty itself; and never of her own free will did she spend a day at home. This setting out of a morning was her panacea, *her* method of surmounting the dullness of existence. She savoured the excitement of seeing below the surface of strange households; forgot herself and her home troubles in sipping at the overflow of other people's fates. And so Henriette, left to herself, washed, dressed and fed her children; cooked the family meals; held the house spotless; and for a time her sole outing was to the market, whence she would come back bearing, on top of the necessaries, such dainties as half a pound of frogs' hind legs, delicate and juicy, a bowl of green gherkins, or red cranberries, or blue bilberries; or, greatest titbit of any, a lump of jellied eel.

In the sunny front room, Peterle, a tiny prisoner to life, lay stretched and bound in his carriage bed. Between sunrise and sunset a variety of things happened to him. Fairly early he was washed; and thereby he learned to know the taste of yellow soap, and to writhe under its cruel bite in the eye. Then, his top having been coated, his naked legs were seized and thrust into a kind of pillow-case, in which they were tied up. Only when a fresh loincloth became necessary were they free to kick and sprawl — two diminutive sticks, lean as the bare wishbones of a chicken. His feeding-bottle was his first love; and its appearance had power to throw him into transports of delight, long before he was able to recognise her who held it: as if mounted on wires, his tiny arms would work towards it, his hampered legs feebly trying to imitate the motion. Next in favour stood his "comforter" — though with this he could, on occasion, pick a quarrel. But just awake, his judgment still cloudy with sleep, he would start, did he find this friend at his lips, to suck with tremendous energy, believing it to be the mouthpiece of his adored bottle; and then, instead of the soft thick flow of milk, empty air-bubbles would drive down his little gullet. — Gradually, there emerged from chaos the gracious author of bottle and comforter, and he learned to know the touch of the kind hands that caressed his body. His brothers, on the contrary, were early objects of fear to him. Gustave pinched him on the quiet, and made ugly faces at him, once, too, dropping into the perambulator something slimy and ice-cold, which hopped on to Peterle's face, and caused him to make agonised protest. Willi was less to be dreaded. Willi snuggled down beside him, slobbered over him, and indulged in wild bouts of tickling him in the stomach. He practically never went out. His world was the big old square wicker perambulator, the dark walls of which hemmed him in on three sides, the fourth consisting of his featherbed, beneath which, throughout the summer, he lay unresistant. For sky he had the dingy ceiling of the room, on which the flies walked upside down. These flies were his enemies: they descended by the dozen to investigate his sticky little lids, to feed on his succulent dribblings. And his blind strokes fought them in vain, or dismayed them only for an instant: they retired, rubbed their probosces clean, and came back to tickle and bite anew.

Thus the first tender weeks slipped away, added themselves to a month, then to two, and to three. In the life around the perambulator certain changes took place. Even twice-broken arms heal at last; and, sooner or later after childbirth, the colour comes back to the cheek, springiness to the step. Henriette's slim form looked as girlish as of old. On her meek and placid face alone was the stamp of her maternity visible; and even in this, which time would surely hammer into a replica of her lifeworn mother's, the blue eyes could still flash with pleasure, the pupils darken and dilate.

That was a hot summer. Day for day, the sun beat on the hard-baked ground. At five o'clock of an afternoon, stone steps were still too hot to be touched by the bare hand. The roads that led countrywards from the several gates of the city were inches deep in a dust that powdered white, trees, vehicles and people.

With the dusk, the river vanished beneath a pall of white mist; mists hung over the woody swamps at its edge. Above these danced, in millions, the giant Rhine-mosquitoes. At nightfall they raided the town, where those sweating inhabitants, whom experience had not rendered artful, became their prey. In Peterle's home no extraordinary care was exercised; and the babe's bald head, his soft face and hands, were soon a mass of sores.

Still, the young life made headway: the blue eyes learnt to turn corners, to follow people about the room, to linger with approval on the mother form. Then, however, a week broke that was big with consequence for every one.

Now, it was midsummer: the tubbed oleanders, everywhere set out, were masses of intolerable red sweetness. In the town park, the green knobs that dotted the orange-trees were turning yellow; the hanging-gardens on roofs and balconies shrivelled for want of water, or ran wild. Dwelling-houses were deserted, given over to easygoing caretakers. The German residents had fled, exasperated: even the sun-loving Alsatian, rejoiced though he was by their absence, thought it time to make a move: and were it only to a hired cottage outside the walls of the town. Here might be seen little black-eyed boys in barred stockings and without coats; here were dolly little girls, and thin, natty women in black, or masterful, high-bosomed business women, who had come out from the counting-house of some *magasin de commerce*, some *epicerie* or *patisserie*, to sit about in overgrown vegetable-gardens, and inhale the rarer air. The inhabitants of the most ancient quarters — the *Bungaverts*, or *Klein Frankreich* — frequented the pavement-cafes, and made excursions of a Sunday.

About this time Peterle's mother went out to dance. It was not quite a novelty: more than once of late Henriette had rebelled against the confinement of the long, sultry evenings, and Peterle had wept for her ministrations in vain. But now came a certain Sunday when even the blindest might have seen that something was in the wind. Henriette, having gone about all the morning in petticoat and bedjacket, began to prepare herself festally directly the midday-meal was over. Taking off her bodice, and exposing her grey cotton corset, above which showed the unbleached linen of her shift, she let down her black hair and combed it. Like that of most aspiring merrymakers, her temper was none of the best; she grew short even with Willi, when he clung to her skirts and hindered her: she shook and slapped him: and both babies piped in unison. Her arms and neck lathered and dried, she drew on her best blouse and laid her shawl in readiness, moving about the room in her stocking-soles; for the new pointed shoes, which she had just freed from tissue-paper, were tight, and she spared herself their nips and pinches till the last. Meanwhile her stepfather went in and out, in a white dickey and a black suit, of which only the coat had still to be donned: this hung brushed and folded over a chair. At three o'clock the pair set off. Henriette was very cross indeed when it came to leaving the children, and many were the reproaches heaped on the absent grandmother's head. For Grandmother, after promising to stay at home and mind them, had, in the end, let herself be seduced by a wedding engagement; and, since none of the three adults was willing to forgo a pleasure: skat, a wedding, and the dance respectively: there was nothing for it but to shut the door on the little ones, and trust to luck that they would come to no harm.

But the six-year-old Gustave was also bent on holiday-making; and having watched his elders turn the corner, he straightway reached for the milk, being resolved to get the nourishing of the infants, with which he had been entrusted, over once and for all. In this, he was unlucky enough to upset the jug: he fled the consequences, and played truant in the streets till evening. As feeding-time drew near, Peterle and Willi became as restless as caged animals in a Zoo; but their protests went unheard; and finally Peterle, a baffled, empty, outraged babe, cried himself to sleep, and slept till he was awakened by his grandmother's hands.

To her cares ensued a period of sated repose. Then again he was disturbed.

It was the middle of the night. High, angry voices, broken by sobs, filled the room. The grandmother it was who wept; Henriette, like a statue come to life, was talking, talking, in a passionate, threatening way. Her stepfather sat at the table, his head between his hands, sullen and malignant; a kitchen lamp, backed by a round tin radiator, shed its blinding glare on his eyes, heavy with wine. When Peterle woke and cried, Henriette snatched him from his bed and cuddled him to her. The mother-arms soothed his wailing; and over his head the bandying of taunts and accusations went on, punctuated by the grandmother's lament of: "Ah! it's me that ought to go. Yes, if *I* were out of the way!"

Henriette's black brows drooped over her wrathful blue eyes, which glowered at her stepfather. "Mother had two when you took her!"

"Two . . . yes!"

"What! You'd throw this up at me, would you?" — and she jerked Peterle forward.

He pshawed. "But here you'd be off down over the Alps with this blackamoor!"

"Blackamoor yourself! He's willing to marry me."

"And you'd go? . . . leave us all? . . . never come back? Henriette! *Mädele!*"

He pleaded with her, in a low voice, talking volubly. And Henriette let herself be moved; she ceased to be angry, lost her readiness of tongue, and drooped her head till it touched the head of the child, fallen into a light sleep on her heart.

Suddenly the relative calm was broken by a rude hubbub without. This proved to be the vegetable-hawker who lived in the attic: he was mounting the stairs, plainly neither sober nor alone. An indignant family met him on the landing and barred his way, Grandmother even coming out of her bed, to which she had retired; and the candle she held aloft illumined her wispy grey hair, her night-costume of jacket and shift, her thin naked legs. All three were justly irate: theirs was a respectable and orderly house, and no *Wackes* should carry on in it with promiscuous *Frauenzimmer*, if they could help it! The hawker, too drunk to argue, leaned against the wall and stuttered irrelevancies. But the good-looking piece his companion was only mildly tipsy, and did not shrink from parley. The rough dialect flew. At length she was got downstairs and locked out into the street, where her abuse died away; and the other inhabitants, who had been peeping curiously from their doors, closed them and withdrew. The hawker was half cajoled, half bullied up the third flight to his attic; after which two nervous women, one with a fretful babe at her breast, sat in the dark on the bottom stair, till the drunkard's light went out, and snores told of his physical collapse.

In the further course of that night Henriette, having unwisely drunk a glass of beer after eating stone fruit, was taken very unwell. Time and again she started up from feverish dreams, in which the dapper Italian, his languishing eyes, his milk-white teeth and coal-black moustachios played the leading part — was wakened by spasms of knifelike pain.

Next morning she was limp and distracted; and

hasty-handed with two peevish little children. She had a hard day's work before her, too. In addition to her ordinary job, the main item of which was "doing" the room of the second lodger, who, a late sleeper, rose at the last possible moment, threw on her clothing and fled for the shop in which she was employed, carrying her *brioche* half-eaten in her hand, and leaving everything, even to the freeing of her comb from its fluff of dead hair, to Henriette: in addition to this, which always took a considerable time, to-day was the day on which the big front room had to be turned out and set in order.

For twenty-nine or thirty days in the month, the family had free use of this room: and they availed themselves of it, with due respect for its contents. For here were gathered the handsomest strip of carpet, a console-pedestal and mirror, a suite of furniture, an embroidered tablecover, bunches of dried grasses and artificial flowers. The room had two large windows, flanked by scarlet geraniums, which blossomed furiously in the fierce sun; and the bed stood in a curtained alcove. The tenant, an elegant and formidable Councillor of Justice, "in the best years", paid them rent to the amount of twenty marks a month. — In person he was tall, dark and colourless; and wore a shiny black pointed beard, gold spectacles, buttoned patent-leather boots, and lemon-coloured kid gloves.

So, throughout the morning, Henriette swept and scrubbed and polished, sometimes heaving a sigh, sometimes rebuking her children, but for the most part silent as a songless bird.

After dinner, when Gustave had gone back to school, when everything was clean and shining, and she herself washed and dressed, she lingered by the flower-box to snip off the withered leaves from the overgrown geraniums. The window in the mansard opposite was open, and the man who was dying of consumption behind it had pushed a sickly india-rubber-plant out into the guttering. No sun fell on that side of the street, and the plant looked as unwholesome as himself. On seeing Henriette, he pulled his blue lips back over his gums, in what was meant to be a smile, and addressed her in the stringy voice that made her think of a cracked guitar.

"You look pale to-day."

Henriette heard the malice in his tone — the satisfaction with which he verified the decrease of colour in another's cheeks — and the attitude of defiance she instinctively assumed was that of the living towards the dead.

She nodded vengefully. "I was dancing last night."

"In this heat? I thank God it wasn't me!"

"And now I'm going out."

"Why not? I — I, too shall go out next week!" he gave back, devoured by hatred, well knowing that he would never set foot in the sunlit streets again.

Henriette turned contemptuously away. The liar! . . . thinking he could befool a person like that — And she made a great show, knowing he watched her, of pinning on her neckerchief and dressing the children.

The idea of going out had been invented only to annoy him. Now, however, she asked herself why not. Why should she not take the afternoon off, and join father for the *Vierebrot*, at his work on the banks of the Little Rhine?

With the aid of a neighbour she got the perambulator down the stairs, and laid Peterle in it. At his feet she put his bottle, a cake for Willi, and a surprise for Father in the shape of a big white beer-radish. Above this came the feather-bed, and on top of all perched Willi, his legs dangling over the side of the carriage.

Henriette pushed this load through the summer streets, in bent and muscle-less fashion. While in the crowded inner town, she walked mainly in the middle of the roadway; for in places the footpath was not much more than a glorified doorstep. But having crossed a bridge, she came into the modern quarter, where the streets were wide, and tree-lined. Arrived at the east gate, she followed a narrow canal that linked the two rivers. High poplars edged the path: she rested for a time on a shady seat. Barges, so heavily laden that their rims were level with the water, moved forward inch by inch; women sat at their helms and steered, or dandled infants, or hung out washing; their little chimneys smoked, noisy dogs raced yapping from stern to prow. These barges were towed by men, three abreast, yoked like oxen and bronzed to blackness, who crawled laboriously along the towing-path, head and neck bent, eyes fixed on the ground. Beyond the canal was a sprinkling of old French villas, painted in delicate pinks and lavender-greys, one and all furnished with heavy green shutters, and surrounded by damp, overgrown gardens. Stiff rows of poplars led up to them. On some steps that ran down to the water, washer-women were at work: they knelt and scrubbed garments with brushes on the wooden steps. Now and then one of them would sit back on her haunches, and hold up for scrutiny some gaudy red or blue rag; after which, bending forward, she plunged it afresh into the water. The swing-bridge was in motion when Henriette got to it, and she made one of a group that watched, with idle interest, a bigger barge than usual glide through. Crossing it, she shuffled through the dust of the road. The bicycles that dashed to and fro left long, slowly subsiding trails, as of smoke, in their wake. By a weir stood the last little inn, in the garden of which workmen and bargemen sat at *Vesperbrot*. But Henriette went further, went round the corner and out among the sandbank cones, where she found her stepfather smoking in sight of his work — the repairing of the stone embankment that protected the low-lying, wooded ground from the inroads of the swift and shifty Rhine.

Here they ate their meal. Not many words passed between them. Willi had to be kept from under the wheels of the bicycles that spun along to the end of the parapet: had to be dabbed with spittle for the relief of gnat and mosquito bites. Peterle gave trouble, too. For the first time in his life, after lustily crying for food, he refused his bottle, averting his head when it was offered to him, pushing the mouthpiece away with protruded lips. Henriette felt the milk anxiously: it was still warm, as how could it fail to be, considering it had been sat on by Willi, and used as a footwarmer by the babe himself? She tried it, but could taste nothing wrong; so, following her stepfather's advice, she dropped in several lumps of sugar, begged from the inn. Having shaken the bottle till these dissolved, she forced the teat between Peterle's lips; and now he drank, though not with his usual gusto.

Until both children slept, she caused the carriage to move gentle to and fro. Then, she felt herself nudged.

"Look here, my girl, would you like a new neckerchief?"

She shook her head. "I've got one."

"Aye, but a handsomer than that?"

"*Ne*, it's good enough."

"One with roses on it."

"Roses?" Her eyes ceased their straying; the pupils grew.

"Aye, great roses, and forget-me-nots, and madonna lilies! On a yellow ground."

"Lilies? Where'ud *you* get it from?"

"Where d'you think? *Mädelle, schau her!*" and from an inner pocket the man drew forth a slim packet, folded in tissue paper. Opening it, he disclosed the lovely cloth.

Henriette gasped.

"Makes you open our eyes, lass, what? Put it on!"

Dazzled, Henriette removed her own drab little cape, and

laid the new finery round her shoulders. Her eye hung reverently on the silky texture; her fingers followed it. "How pretty! . . . oh, how pretty!"

"What did I tell you?" He spat, well content. "Cost me the inside of a five-mark piece. And now just you remember it was me that bought it — me, *Mädele* . . . for you!"

Long after her stepfather had gone back to work, she sat with it still about her; and more than one of his fellow-workmen sent a glance at the girl in her grandeur, which set off, by vivid contrast, her raven black hair, lake-blue eyes, and pale, oval face.

Then, however, suddenly waking from her reverie, she saw that a great army of stormclouds had come up and was resting on the mountains, which in their turn had drawn perceptibly nearer. Hastily removing the neckcloth and tucking it into the perambulator, she straightened out her children and pushed off on her homeward journey. It was none too soon: as she entered the house the first raindrops fell, the size of florins, and simultaneously came a loud clap of thunder.

Not many minutes later a messenger handed in the fruit, flowers and sweetmeats which the *Justizrat* never failed to provide; and, shortly after, Mamsell Mimi herself arrived in person to decorate and arrange.

These were gala evenings. Grandmother left her job early; Father came straight home from work. For they all adored Mamsell Mimi, who, when she had finished what she came to do, usually stayed for supper with the family, bringing lollipops to the children, and to their elders a goodly supply of piquant gossip. For Mamsell Mimi knew life; she had also frank and cynical opinions about it, and a sprightly, overcharged tongue. She was a big, handsome woman, with golden hair, and a figure that swept in and out in astonishing curves — like those of the letter S. In observing her, the wonder grew that it was possible exactly to control such a surplusage of flesh. And indeed, after she had eaten, and was sitting at ease on the sofa, she herself offered scant apology for loosening both bodice and corset.

"Or I shall explode with the heat, good people! . . . go off pop, like a child's balloon. Heavens! The struggle it is to keep one's figure!"

For figure was the *sine qua non* of her profession — that of *Büffetdame* in a popular restaurant — and the wasp waist and monstrous billowing of the bosom were as necessary to success in it as a good head for arithmetic and a pretty wit.

She looked longingly forward, she told them — between ear-splitting crashes of thunder — to the day when, casting constraint and care for appearance behind her, she would be able to live wholly in *negligee*. That would come to pass when she retired from business and settled down, it might be with a good, complaisant husband, it might also be without. For herself, she would prefer to be free. Men were too great a nuisance; one had always to be dancing to their tune. Now in a village not far over the borders of Baden she had an old motherkin, and there, too, lived her heart's darling, her little cabbage, her *p'tit Tonerl*, a strapping youngster some five years old; and, if she pleased herself, she would take up her abode with these two, and never again have to do with anything more troublesome than pigs or hens. Of course, though, that would not be for many a year yet; and Mamsell Mimi heaved a great boom of a sigh that resembled a soundless laugh; then drew a rapid sketch of herself in the faded years, and laughed in earnest. Well, well! when the day did come, she would at least be able to drink her fill of beer. Now, if they would believe her, she was prohibited a drop. Oh! she did not want to say a word against a certain person: he was very generous to her, and in every respect *ein anstandiger Mensch;* but they would not misunderstand her if she called him exacting. Only two months ago it had almost come to a rupture between them; he had accused her of letting herself go, of growing fat, of enjoying her *Munchener* on the sly: and — would they believe it? — next time he had actually brought a yard-measure in his pocket, to see if his suspicions were justified. Fortunately, she had been able to persuade him that the extra inch was due to a bulkier petticoat; but it had given her, all the same, a shock, and the very next day she had purchased new corsets, of the rigour of iron — yes, truly! an iron bandage, in which she had ever since been encased. Except at night: that she could not bring herself to. Some did, who were more ambitious than she; but she — *ach Herrje!* — she loved her ease too well. One night she had made the effort, and in the morning had been obliged, on rising, to part with the cheese and cucumber of which she had partaken for supper. Such a thing had never happened to her before. No, there was no doubt the skinny and bony — though she did not envy them! — had the best of it. It was simple enough for *them* to imitate nature; and her followed several merry tales of the ruses "the scrags" resorted to. But even they ran a constant risk — that of discovery. *Ach, du mein Gottele!*

women truly did not have an easy time of it in this difficult world.

Thus talked Mamsell Mimi; and, of her three hearers, the smoking man smiled cynically and nodded, while the two pale, packhorse women drank in, open-mouthed, their guest's gay wisdom. All the time she talked, she dandled Peterle, who was restless and would not sleep: it was the thunder had unsettled his stomach, said Grandmother, and gave him her horny, work-seamed finger to suck. Mamsell Mimi adored children: her dream would have been, she vowed, to have a dozen of them round her, one always small enough to fill her arms. But *Gott bewahre!* such joys were not for the like of her: her single one, her Tonikin, had added a whole stone to her weight. Love them, though, that she could! — and she hugged Peterle to her great bosom, which — *nicht wahr, meine Lieben?* — they would have judged able to nourish the dozen of which she dreamed; whereas, if they could credit it, for her treasure, her well-beloved little cockchafer, it had yielded not so much as a mouthful. And so she fondled Peterle, drawing him to her, then holding him away again to look at him, many times in succession, always with loud smacks of kisses in between. — In the course of which Peterle hiccupped, and was very sick.

He was sick again after Mamsell Mimi's great deep laugh had died away on the stairs, leaving its echo on the different floors, and a pleased content in the hearts of all who heard it that something so big and handsome and jolly as this woman should exist. He was sick also several times later on; Henriette was in and out of bed with him during the night. And next day the sickness continued; he could not keep his milk down, and, unless she paced the floor with him, cried unceasingly. She hardly dared to let him out of her arms, for fear his wailing might disturb the inmates of the front room. In the afternoon, as other violent symptoms set in, and he had twice turned from milk altogether and was tossing as if in pain, she bore him to a wise woman who lived in the neighbourhood.

This person who, in the intervals of her profession as midwife, carried on a kind of surreptitious practice, poohpoohed Henriette's fears. It was merely an attack of indigestion: a "spoilt stomach". She prescribed doses of camomile-tea; but, more especially, cognac.

"A dash in each bottle, *Fraulein* — that's all that's needed. He'll take to it, you see, like a cat to fish."

But this was not the case: Peterle continued to avert his face when his bottle was presented to him, to wail, and to slobber a watery fluid. Next morning, as he looked pinched about mouth and nose, and did not seem able to wake up properly, his mother put him in the perambulator and wheeled him through the sunshine to a free dispensary for children, in the new quarter of the town: among the stratum of the population to which Henriette belonged, they were held to know "double as much about children" as at the real hospitals.

After waiting half an hour she was called into a room built wholly of white tiles. The doctor was in a white overall, flanked by a Sister, also in stiff, white starch. Henriette felt that she and Peterle, well washed as their garments were, formed drab blots on the snowiness of the room. Otherwise the doctor, a youngish man, gave principally an impression of squareness: his yellow beard was cut square, as was also his brushlike hair; he had a square forehead, and large square hands. But he was not ungentle, and had, besides, the shortsighted man's ingratiating habit of pushing up his glasses while he talked, and smoothing out a tired eye with a band three fingers broad. He examined Peterle — far too cursorily to please Henriette — touched him here and there with a big white forefinger, and looked inside his mouth.

Her lengthy explanations were cut short. "You've been careless."

This charge she could honestly rebut.

"Haven't troubled to boil the milk, eh?"

Henriette denied this, but less surely; she remembered how, on the afternoon excursion, she had been in a hurry to set off, and had though the milk would "do" — was hot enough, the day being so hot — without waiting for it to spin and bubble.

The doctor made an entry in his notebook. "Well, leave him here. We'll see what we can do for him."

But at this Henriette hugged Peterle to her. "I'd rather look after him myself."

"At your own risk then!"

She nodded.

The doctor shrugged his shoulders: he had no time to argue and persuade; other mothers hushed sickly wailings in the outer room. So, giving her some instructions, he bade her come back with the child next day. But as she disappeared he could not refrain from saying hotly to the Sister at his side: "You women are not fit even to look after your own children.

They should be taken from you at birth." — At which the woman who, being young, and radiant with health, thought him the most wonderful man in the world, merely smiled.

Henriette did not return: a wild fear gripped her lest they should have some power policeman-like to wrest Peterle from her. As, however, next morning the babe was perceptibly worse, she carried him to one of the hospitals. Here, the doctor was less gentle. He turned back Peterle's eyelid as carelessly as though it had been a dead leaf, and said gruffly: "Why come here only when the child is dying?" Still, he gave her the medicine she had been counting on: you could always reckon on getting that at a proper hospital: and the very size of the bottle, and the redness of the fluid it contained, reassured her for the time being.

Next day, in despair, she fetched the wise woman. But now the latter, too, only shrugged her shoulders, attributing the change for the worse in Peterle's condition to want of faith in her treatment.

"Take my advice, *Fraulein*, and stick to milk. Children don't never thrive on them barley messes."

But Peterle's day for milk was over. Inserted now dropwise between his lips, it dribbled idly out again. He could not swallow: his little mouth and throat were a bed of ulcers. All through the long, hot afternoon, Henriette, unconscious of fatigue, paced the floor with him, his head, hardly strewn yet with a light down, lolling helplessly from side to side. And whenever she turned at the door, to make the length of the narrow room again, she saw fixed on her, at the opposite window, the glittering eye of the living skeleton behind it — an eye alight with malignant pleasure that it was no longer he only, who was to be called on to leave daylight and the sun.

Towards evening her strength gave out: she laid the babe back in the perambulator. Here, beneath a square of mosquito-netting, the mountain of feather-bed sloping steeply up over him, Peterle, alone and unaided, fought his tiny, blind, unknowing way towards the great dark . . .

The *Madame* for whom Henriette had worked before her confinement, hearing of his plight, came to see him. She, being tender-hearted, could not listen unmoved to his puny moans, and shed tears of pity as, lifting the net, she peered down at the waste bit of humanity beneath it.

"Give him air. Take off the feather-bed," she pleaded. But Henriette shook her head: Peterle had had his comforts while he was well; they should not be withdrawn from him now.

Towards evening his moans grew fainter, his little feet turned cold. And just as dusk was settling definitely into night, he heaved a sigh and died.

Henriette went out at once to fetch a doctor; and a young man in the neighbourhood, who had a small, working-class practice, was found to certify that Peterle Luthy, a male, of the Protestant religion, aged four and a half months, had just, by reason of infant cholera, ceased to breathe. As it was late, and his work over for the day, the doctor was in no hurry to be gone. He sat and enjoyed with Father a glass of red wine and a slice of bilberry-tart, over which, having discovered in each other "good *Sozis*", they cracked the obligatory jokes concerning "Siegfried Meyer's" latest dodge with regard to Morocco.

Next morning there was much to be done. Father set off earlier than usual for work, that he might register the decease by the way. Grandmother stayed at home from her job, without even troubling to send word of her intention, "a death in the family" being a fact of sufficient importance to allow a break with precedent. Henriette walked to the cemetery, to arrange about the grave; and, on her road there, ordered the coffin. This was to be made by a joiner who lived a few doors down the street, and was promised for that evening; for, in such hot weather, and considering the nature of the illness . . .

All day Peterle lay in state on the top of a chest of drawers. He had several visitors — an ugly, shrivelled little yellow doll, in a dress fantastically bunched up with blue ribbons. Two real wax candles burnt at his head and feet. These were a present from Mamsell Mimi, and had been brought by special messenger. There was also a magnificent wreath of painted tin immortelles. The kind-hearted *Madame*, on the news being carried to her, had given Henriette three marks for a wreath. The latter chose, not living flowers, which would be dead by the morning, but this solid and enduring symbol, which would last for weeks, even months, to come; which would still be there, still existent, when all that remained of little Peterle had become a thing unspeakable, from which thought shrank away . . .

His coffin, a small deal box, painted a light and vivid green, was a misfit balcony flower-box, which the joiner seized this opportunity to get rid of.

"For such a little man as him one must have something bright and cheerful," he said chattily, while he inserted the body. Adding piously, as he noted Henriette's downcast air:

"And give thanks, *Fraulein*, that it has pleased the Lord to put an end to his pain."

Next morning the perambulator, with the green box inside it, was carried down the stairs once more. There was no need to-day for the feather-bed. Henriette spread a shawl across the foot-end of the box, and upon this perched Willi, his legs dangling over the side of the carriage.

The cemetery was a long way off — was out beyond the octroi-house and the city walls. The dusty road wound slightly uphill, and Henriette had to exert all her strength. In the vicinity of a barracks she passed many idle, lolling soldiers, and heard expressions of curiosity about the contents of her box, only one or two catching sight of the wreath and baring their heads. At the grave there was no time for ceremony: Peterle was lowered and covered over almost before you could count twenty, Henriette's chief concern being to prevent Willi from falling in and getting buried, too. The mound raised, she laid the tin wreath on it: by this she would know in future where Peterle lay.

Her load was lighter now. But now, too, for the first time, she felt how tired she was. And on the way home, Willi having fallen asleep, she sat down at the table of a pavement-cafe to drink a glass of beer. Her arms felt, and no doubt for a day or two would feel, strangely empty. Still, it was better so. Two were enough, more than enough. And she would take care — oh! such care . . .

Her thoughts swam to a mist. She fell into a doze as she sat, under the stainless violet-blue of the summer sky. Then, however, waking with a start, she sprang to her feet with a guilty sense of work undone; and laying the money for the beer on the table, pushed with fresh zeal for home.

And before the sun went down that night, it was almost as though Peterle had never been.

THE PROFESSOR'S EXPERIMENT

I

THE dusty sunlight of a June afternoon slanted in under the iron shutters, which were lowered and thrust outwards, upon the Professor and his sister, who sat at tea. The table was small, and covered with a waxed cloth, the floor was laid with waxed linoleum, and a tall, white, tiled stove stood like a gravestone in one corner. The cups and saucers were Delft, and did not match.

For some moments the Professor was silent, twiddling the cord of his eyeglasses between finger and thumb. Then, waking with a start, he said: "Annemarie! . . . I will thank you to give me another cup of tea."

For years he had, with these words, at this same hour of day, passed his cup to be refilled. On the present occasion, however, Annemarie, instead of taking it, jerked up her chin, gazed at him, and ejaculated: "*Another?* But, Paulchen, you have already had two!"

The Professor shot back his extended arm, and put his cup down as though it had bitten him. "Indeed?" he said in confusion. "I . . . that is, my thoughts must have been elsewhere."

"I think so, too," said Annemarie.

Raising the stocking she had on her pins to knitting level, she became absorbed in the arithmetic of the heel. She was a tall, angular woman, with large hands, a flat figure, and iron-grey hair. Her speech had something of the drill-sergeant's bark; and it was clear she was used to being obeyed, when, at the stroke of a clock, she said shortly: "Five o'clock, Paulchen!"

"Thank you, Annemarie. I heard it strike."

But, in place of rising to leave the room, the Professor remained sitting, still fidgeting nervously with his cord. Annemarie bore with this for a further second or two; then, letting her knitting sink to her lap, she asked in a tone of stupefaction: "But, Paulchen, is anything the matter? Is it possible you do not intend to take your walk to-day?"

For the first time in his life the Professor felt that Annemarie's emphasis was excessive, her regulation of his habits overdone. Nevertheless, he at once got up, replacing his chair at the table.

At which Annemarie added: "Besides, Marthe is waiting to clear away the tea-things."

"Surely five minutes' delay will not seriously inconvenience her, Annemarie?"

The protest was made in a tone of extreme diffidence, not to say weakness; nonetheless, his attitude was so unheard-of that again his sister sat dumbfounded. Worse still, he went out of the room in the middle of her reply, leaving her with her words only half uttered. Now, what in the world! ... Something must be seriously amiss. Either Paulchen was going to be ill; or else some hitch had occurred in connection with his *magnum opus*, the "Oscan Declension", on which he had been at work for the past fifteen years. It had happened more than once, during this time, that some nimbler colleague had filched a valuable discovery from under his very nose: Paulchen always cut his learned journals with a trembling hand. Also, awkward crises had sometimes arisen when the facts refused to fit into his theory of them. Being only a woman, Annemarie understood little of learned details. But she knew that these were black moments indeed, in her good Paulchen's life. Then must all voices sink to a whisper, the felt-shod servant creep on tip-toe past the study door; behind which Paulchen wrestled with these devils of his own conjuring, and sought to bend them to his will.

During the time it took Annemarie to meditate these things, in picking her teeth with her spare needle, the Professor was dawdling in the corridor — dawdling deliberately — for as long as he dared. With his hat and umbrella laid in readiness, he made as though he searched for his gloves — though these were snug in his pocket — going into his bedroom on a pretended hunt for them, and returning, openly bearing but one, while he smacked his pockets for its fellow. The moment, however, a step on the stair was heard, he snatched up hat and gamp, and in two-twos was outside the door of the flat. Going down, he met the postman coming up, and wordlessly held out his hand. The man, having once more peered solemnly through his spectacles at a letter, handed it over, and the Professor, after one hasty glance at the superscription, as hastily thrust it into his pocket.

On emerging from the house, he opened a large grey cotton umbrella, which he carried in a wrinkled grey cotton hand. It shaded a grey felt hat, broad of brim and shapeless with age, which would have suited a stage bandit. His blue-grey clothes, built for ease rather than show, were so much too big for his short, thick figure that the seat of the trousers hung far below that portion of the body it was designed to fit; while the legs of the garment descended in corkscrew folds over his elastic-sided boots. These boots, shaped like spades, had as little pretence to form as the rest of him, and continued a series of transverse lines which, in their prodigality, would have delighted a Durer. But the eyes that beamed from behind the double spectacles — cross-lined these, too — were kindly, and the face, when pleased, had a childlike candour and glow.

His way led him past small white villas, towered and turreted like baronial halls; across shadeless, unfenced fields where vegetables grew. It was very hot; and, on reaching the shade of an avenue of poplars, the Professor sighed with relief. Entering the town park and leaving a Gothic restaurant behind him, he crossed an artificial lake, spanned by rustic bridges and dotted with manufactured islets, and climbed a sham mountain path that wound round an imitation precipice and led to a new plantation, where he would be safe from interruption. Seating himself, the Professor laid hat and umbrella at his side, and rubbed his spectacles free of dust. His glasses on his nose again, however, he still let several minutes go by before he drew from an inner pocket the letter he had come out to read. He seemed timid of opening it. He scrutinised it back and front, took in the size of the envelope, the hour of posting, the wording of the address. At length, heaving another sigh, he inserted his penknife and neatly slit it. It was not a long letter, did not quite fill a page; and it was written in a copperplate hand, minute as the strokes of an etching, regular as print, the capitals alone opulent and handsome with their prescribed loops and bows. In it the Professor could spy but two errors: a redundant comma, and a slight tendency in the lines to slant upward at the end. Perhaps, too . . . yes, perhaps the upper strokes might have been a trifle lighter, the down a shade thicker. That they failed in symmetry was no doubt due to the fact that, while on the school-bench, the writer had let her mind wander — had not kept perfect time with the teacher's beat, according to which the whole class wrote in unison: a lift of the baton for the upstrokes, a drop for the down. The little rogue! The bewitching young lazy-bones! He could imagine her titivating at a bow, or throwing sly glances at the spring buds that enticed through the schoolroom windows. It was even possible that her thoughts had strayed to this supreme moment of a female's existence, of which none other than he was the begetter. Meanwhile, his brain had swiftly taken in the contents of the letter. It was what he had expected. There was mention in it of the great honour done, of the happiness felt, of sincerest gratitude; and it bore the signature "Elsa Braun". The Professor let the hand that held it fall to his knee, and sat gazing at the arrangement of shrubs and ferns on the rockery before him: they seemed suddenly to have grown very lush and green. For the first time, too, he noticed that the nightingales were uproarious in the surrounding bushes; while the roses, trailing in festoons from post to post of the central avenue, were a hot and scented mass of bloom.

The Professor was about to take the great step in life.

He had turned seven and forty, and it could not be said of him that he was young for his age. Life had been something of a struggle for him. For he had not been brought up to a profession, but had spent his green years on the stool of a merchant's office. He was well past the middle of the twenties before, finding himself his own master, he had given the rein to his ambition, and begun to equip himself for a learned career. Annemarie had joined her slender means to his, both while he went through his course as a student, and afterwards when he lived as unsalaried lecturer at the university of his native town. Until he was ready to publish the earliest results of his research — mere crumbs and droppings, such as would not damage the appearance of his *magnum opus* — brother and sister had scraped and pinched as one. Shortly after the publication of his pamphlet, however, success had come, and in a truly gratifying way. From *Privatdozent* he had been made *Extraordinarius;* and, not six years later, an invitation had reached him to fill the Chair of Comparative Philology in his present place of abode.

Up till now, the Professor had lived absorbed in his work, as blind to the visible world around him as the mole in its ebony burrowings: roots, derivatives, and their subterranean branchings, had been the world in which he was at home, a failure to trace a radix his profoundest grief, success in this his most piquant joy. But, having attained material prosperity

— his income was the princely one of six thousand marks a year; never again would he feel the nip of poverty — he had grown conscious of a change in himself. He was invaded by a set of soft, pushful feelings and wishes, such as he had not dreamed were in him. He caught himself remembering that he was, after all, only in middle age, with at least fifteen years of energy and activity before him. And his eye *would* range round the circle of his colleagues, whom he saw one and all comfortably housed, with plump, devoted wives at their elbows, their wives' furniture in their rooms, and knots of thriving children at their heels. The comparison made his own home seem the more cheerless. Annemarie's ideas of comfort had never altered — were Spartan in their simplicity. And the wish rose in him to line his own nest: to have at his side one to whom *his* word would be law; to see his youth renewed in sons who would look up to him and obey him.

These sensations were still chaotic in him when, as if in answer to them, a suitable person crossed his path. First met on the annual excursion of the Faculty to the mountains, in which Annemarie did not join, owing to a corn on her foot, the young woman in question, who was there under the wing of a friend, had at once favourably impressed him, not only by her retiring, womanly bearing, but also, it must be confessed, by a pleasing plumpness, an air of only half-concealed drollery. He had had her as his companion on the climb through a pine forest to a celebrated nunnery; and later on, with a peculiar pleasure, had found himself picking out her voice in the part-songs to which the moonshine stirred the ladies. As he walked home from the railway station, he hummed what he believed to be these airs, while at the same time his thoughts played round the mysterious charm of a woman's form. Almost he forgot to enter the house quietly, so as not to disturb Annemarie. In the weeks that followed he set a few private inquiries on foot; engineered — with all caution, and so that they committed to nothing — a couple of meetings with the lady at the friend's house, and, finally resolved, with a great heart-thump, with the sudden forcible-feeble courage of the weak, to take the chance Fate offered, had, the day previously, made by letter his proposal of marriage.

Things had gone smoothly with him; he had every reason to feel satisfied; and he did — so long as he kept his mind off Annemarie. At thought of her, the gooseflesh rose along his thighs. How in all the world should he break the news to her, who had no more suspicion of the truth than a babe unborn?

As far back as he could remember, Annemarie had lived for him and domineered over him: she was eight years older than he, and her word had always been law. In earlier life, he had accepted her attitude as a matter of course. After entering on his present post, however, it had begun to gall him; and now, with this momentous step before him, it seemed sheerly unbearable. He was a person of authority everywhere but in his own home. There, Annemarie held sway; it was she who handled his salary, who prescribed his expenditure: in spite of her pride in his learning, she was never able to forget the days when she had cuffed him and cuddled him.

The Professor was rebel against this yoke.

As he walked home — he had never in his life been late for a meal — he told himself, for the dozenth time, that reason was on his side; that the step he proposed to take was a natural one; that he had neither selfishness nor unkindness with which to reproach himself. That might be; but the seventeen years for which Annemarie had gone through hardship and privation with him rose like a century before his mind's eye. And, admit it or not, he knew that he had acted in an underhand fashion. He had fixed the whole matter before approaching her, making it firm, irremediable, an instinct warning him that only in this way could he hope to bring it off. The moisture broke out on his forehead; and the nearer he drew to home, the more impossible did it seem that he could ever tell her, in plain language, what he was about to do.

Annemarie was in the kitchen, slicing potatoes for a salad — he saw her through a chink in the door — and before he had been in his room for more than a couple of minutes came the tinkle of the little hand-bell that called him to meals. A drop of perspiration emerged from his hair, crossed his neck, and, gathering momentum as it ran, trickled rapidly down his spine.

They sat opposite each other at table, and Annemarie prepared to apportion the food. But the neat white heaps of cold potato shining in oil, the red circlets of fat-flecked sausage were not fated to be disturbed on their dishes. The guilty flurry, the red confusion of the Professor's manner betrayed him; and, laying down spoon and fork before these had touched the eatables, Annemarie demanded to know what the matter was. His behaviour at tea-time had been peculiar; Marthe had espied him receiving a letter, which he had seemed to wish to hide — even the postman had made a joke about it, on a later round — and she was resolved not to touch bite or sup till she learnt what this meant. Had he come into conflict with the university authorities? — he, her sober-minded, order-loving brother? Or had the bank failed, that held their scanty savings? Either of these would have been earthquake events in her life; but they were as nothing to the truth. When, at length, from the Professor's stammerings, as from his last brutal outburst, in which, despairing, he flung the truth like a ball at her head: when Annemarie learnt the worst, she was paralysed. She sat with her two hands pressed against the table and stared at him, without uttering a word, till the poor little Professor shrivelled in his seat, under sensations not unlike those he had felt when, as a child, he had ripped a rent in the seat of new trousers, or, out of curiosity to see if anything would happen to him, had swallowed his cherry-stones, instead of obediently parting with them as ordered by Annemarie.

Then, she found her tongue, found words for her anger, her contemptuous, unbounded amaze. Under their lash, the Professor drank a hasty gulp of half-cold tea, wiped his forehead with his table-napkin, and rose to pace the room. For now all manner of unpleasant things came to light. He heard, for the first time, her true opinion of him, heard of his weakness, his want of character. It was very unpleasant, very unpleasant indeed.

But when she passed to herself, it was worse still.

"Have I failed in any way in my duty? Have I left anything undone?"

"Annemarie! I assure you . . . On the contrary!"

"Then why have you served me this trick?"

"Annemarie, if . . . if . . . I — I . . ."

"I . . . I! If . . . if! Oh! that such a thing should happen . . . at your age . . . an old man like you! . . . and after all I have done for you."

"Annemarie!" said the Professor distractedly, and wrung his hands. "Since you take it thus I will break off the match. I will write to-night, and say it was a mistake — yes, all a mistake!"

"What? — and make yourself the laughing-stock of the town? Have the person bring an action against you? — you? — at your age? Is there no dignity in you? I knew it wasn't much, but so little as this I never suspected it to be," cried his sister shrilly. Oh, how painful was this scratching-up of the surface!

"Control yourself, Annemarie!" he implored her. "What if

Marthe should hear what you say?"

"What matters Marthe, when every one of our acquaintances must soon know of your disgrace?"

Then she wept.

Her tears were the last straw. The Professor had never seen the gaunt, manly woman cry, and, at the sight, was reduced to tears himself. He outdid himself in expostulation and supplication, knowing all the shame an erring son knows, when he sees his mother's tears flow for his misdoing.

But she would not listen to him. "You've gone mad — mad!" she cried, and, leaving him vainly reiterating: "My home will always be yours," disappeared into her own room, and locked the door.

The Professor spent a distracted night, and the letter he wrote to his "bride" was stiff and cold. Annemarie's wrathful grief numbed his faculties; now, he saw his action through her eyes, and himself believed that he had not been far from madness when he undertook it: reasons and excuses fell to pieces like burning paper. All that beforehand had seemed to him natural and right took on blackest shapes of folly and ingratitude.

Manlike, he had never thought out clearly what was to become of his sister after his marriage; he had only said vaguely to himself that she should never want. Now, the fatal promise that she should continue to live with him given, he was chained to her as securely as before. This had indeed not been a part of his scheme, and he emitted sigh on sigh. Then, however, he shook himself, vowing that nothing would be too much to atone to Annemarie for what she was suffering: life comprised duty, not pleasure alone; and, after all, blood-ties came before any other.

But this was not the end. Annemarie's tears dried, but her tongue retained its sting; and in the days that followed she drove home his crime to her brother, with wordy force: his ingratitude, his cowardice, his age, the poltroonish figure he was going to cut: till the Professor felt as if she had been saying these things to him all his life. And, again and again, she put the unanswerable question: "*How* did I fail to satisfy you? — I! who would have given the skin off my bones to serve you."

Explanation was useless: it would also have been no easy matter so much as to hint at the spring-like sensations that had got into his blood. Annemarie was a woman; such feelings were a closed book to her. Repentant, galled, humiliated, he could only reiterate: "There shall be no change — no difference. It will be the business of our lives to make you happy."

But his use of the plural cut Annemarie to the heart. It also stiffened her determination not to yield her place. For she was of those who can suffer on behalf of another only so long as the object of their devotion remains wholly theirs, their thing, the ivy to their tree. To endure without reward, or under neglect, was beyond her.

And of the stuff of which human sacrifices are made, she essentially was not.

II

THE bride-elect dutifully repeated her betrothed's assurances, on that red-letter day when Annemarie so far manned herself as to tie on her bonnet and pay the visit custom required of her. Arm in arm brother and sister covered the intervening streets, Annemarie looking straight before her with unseeing eyes. For, as they walked, the matchless harmony of their steps brought home to her, once more, their lifelong unity. Never should interloping stranger come between!

Before his hardest of tests, Elsa Braun was fluttered and ill at ease. She reddened to the ears had she to accost the Professor; deferred meekly, in word and look, to her "dear sister-in-law"; hung on Annemarie's lips, her own parted in a thin, ingratiating smile that should beg for favour; and finally, her various little arts failing of effect, found it as much as she could do to keep from crying. All of which gave her manner something childishly unformed.

Annemarie sat stubbon as a stone image on the plush sofa, responding in dry monosyllables to the amiable efforts of Elsa and her father. She took but a single sip at her wineglass; left her aniseed biscuit unbroken. And the ten minutes prescribed by convention at an end, she pushed wine and biscuit from her, and rose to her feet. The Professor followed suit with alacrity. He had sat on thorns, lest anything should be said to wound Annemarie's sensibility. He was, besides, consumed with curiosity to hear her opinion of his choice: after having all his life walked by her judgment, he could not now suddenly dispense with it. And so, farewell embraces having been exchanged, the rites and formalities of passage and front-door were rapidly got over, to the grand relief of all parties. Hardly had the sound of steps on the wooden stair died away, before Elsa was dissolved in tears. At the same time, she could not control a spasm of hysterical laughter at the epithets which her father, who was free of speech, heaped on Annemarie's head.

Elsa Braun was no longer young; she had passed her four-and-twentieth year. She was plump, a little too plump now for an unmarried girl, and tall, with a bright, cherry complexion, which with the years had grown a shade too marked. Her eyes had once been of the radiant, glancing kind, which leap to every sally; and though time had tamed them, they could still twinkle merrily when she laughed. And laugh she did, readily as a child; for little things amused her, and the ridiculous was for ever popping up. In few, she was one of those beings who are intended by nature to advance joyously though life, to the tune of happiness; and who, baulked in this, still retain a suppleness, a willowy grace of movement, to be seen in those slim, fleet, dancing figures on vase or frieze, in which has been caught and fixed the joy of motion. Against her, as she went, a many-folded drapery should have flattened or swayed.

There was a good reason why she had not married, at marrying-time. Just turned eighteen, she had been indiscreet enough openly to betray her feelings for a handsome young lieutenant. His mess-room comments on her behaviour having got abroad, a buzz of scandal ensued; and, for long after, Elsa had been asked nowhere. Now, however, the tale of her indiscretion was of such old date as to be a mere legend, and, assuredly, it had not reached the Professor's ears. She lived alone with her father, who was retired from business — a genial, red-faced, white-haired man, fond of good living, of a racy story, and not at all displeased to be widowed of his spouse, who had been thin and a grumbler.

So jubilant was he, over Elsa's late-found good fortune, that the marriage settlements fell out better than the Professor had dared to hope.

"Dear son-in-law, you have made me a proud and happy man!"

The bridal stock of household linen was large enough to satisfy even Annemarie: Elsa had stitched at it since their earliest schooldays, tatting and crotcheting the laces that trimmed it, drawing threads and embroidering monograms, her lips growing yearly more pinched at the thought that she might never need it. Now, all was changed; and she bloomed anew in the weeks that followed — uplifting weeks of congratulatory visits, of the sending of betrothal cards, the exchange of rings. She was not in love with the Professor, and, with the best will in the world, could not find him handsome: he was small and thick-set; hair and beard were of a sandy red; his broad, flat nose had a crest of little hairs feathering from the tip. But the blue eyes behind the spectacles were mild and fatherly, and on this benignant gaze, which was now often bent on her, Elsa set great store. She felt passionately grateful to him for having singled her out from among so many; and, when her feelings were drowsiest, would rehearse to herself the several ways in which she might repay him: they ranged from airing his house-jacket to tidying his writing-table, and even, in moments of ecstasy, soared to copying his manuscripts. Such a firing of her affection was most needful on coming in from one of the bi-weekly walks which she now took on his arm, under the chaperonage of Annemarie. Conversation drooped on such excursions; for Elsa was tongue-tied, Annemarie adamant; while the Professor had for so long been accustomed to think out the morrow's work as he walked, that he could not at once break himself of the habit. And so there often fell a silence between the three. Then, on reaching home, Elsa would fling her arms round her father's neck and hug and kiss him.

"There, there, snailkin!" said Herr Braun, and laughed, and laughed. "Practising on poor old pa, what? Well, well! he must take what he can get, while he can get it."

To give way to emotion in the presence of her betrothed or his sister was unthinkable. Manlike, the Professor might have looked with leniency on her lack of restraint; but the stern eye of Annemarie would have blighted any fit of girlish expansiveness at its core. And so it was with everything. In Annemarie's presence, Elsa never lost the sense of being an unfinished child. Had she to speak, her words came haltingly; to use her hands, they seemed all thumbs; while the consciousness of her ignorance, her shallowness, her utter incapacity, in short, was magnified tenfold. Humbly she consulted Annemarie at every turn; and, what was more, took the advice given — even in matters of dress. And this called for considerable self-denial, her own tastes leaning to the airy and bright, not to say gaudy; while Annemarie poured scorn on flimsiness and colour, and looked only to the number of years a stuff would wear. Elsa also sat meekly by while, with practised hands, Annemarie disposed on the Professor's shelves the lavendered dozens of sheets and cloths into which she, Elsa, had sewn so many hopes. She would, too, dearly have liked a say in the arrangement of the handsome furniture she brought with her, in the rooms that would also be hers; but a timid hint to the Professor called forth a mild, yet peremptory: "True, my love. But think of the occupation it will afford Annemarie during our absence." To which there was nothing to be said.

Her father was the only one of the party who did not sing placebo. For him, the tall angular spinster stood for the epitome of all a woman ought not to be. Blind to her sterling qualities, he never tired of mimicking her, thereby sadly embarrassing his daughter, who, having entered the Professor's family, feared to impinge on her loyalty did she so much as smile at her father's antics. To himself, Herr Braun called Annemarie "a dry-nurse", "an old he-goat", and wished an apoplexy might carry her off soon after the wedding ceremony. All said and done though, she formed but a trifling drawback to the match. At heart, the old man was as proud as Punch at Elsa's rise in life; and, in frequenting his Ninepin Club, played fast and loose with the phrase: "My son-in-law, the Professor." Another thing: he no longer needed to worry his poor old head over what was to become of Elsa when he was gone. And he grew rounder and ruddier than before.

And society was in league with him, helping to forge the coming fetters with a unanimity that smacked of malice. Annemarie's raven prophecy was not fulfilled: no one rose up to find that the Professor, by reason of his years, and his ancient bachelordom, cut a sorry figure. On the contrary, he was greeted on every hand like an overdue vessel that at long last makes harbour.

Met in Aula or Vestibule, those of his colleagues who already wore the yoke wrung his hand with a new warmth; on their lips the set patter of congratulation stood for his entry into a mystic brotherhood. The unmarried were also well content with him; did not his example light them along a road they were only too pressed to follow?

But if the men looked more than they said, their womenfolk made up for this restraint. They buzzed and hummed round Elsa, a very Greek chorus of approbation. Her decision was applauded to the echo. Especially by the matrons. These deep-bosomed, wide-hipped women of forty-odd were never weary of stressing the advantages that would accrue to her from the match. Position and title came first in order. After which, they sang the praises of her betrothed's steady-going habits; and, in this connection, hinted at dark dangers, the shoals and currents of the married state, which she might count herself fortunate in escaping. Out of the depths of their experience, they fished up dire tales of previous attachments, of early entanglements, errant fancies — on the part of these light-o'-loves, men — and though it was no more than an infidelity of the eye. Ah, yes, she was a thrice lucky girl. — They even made the best of Annemarie. What a prop, said they, for a young wife to have at her side. What a mine of wisdom to draw on, till she should be thoroughly schooled in all her husband's wants, ways and wishes. Thus led, she, in her ignorance, would run small risk of failing to please.

Wives of a briefer standing frankly envied her the title. But, gossiping over their needlework, one and all agreed they would choose to have no old maid interfering in *their* homes. As for the shoals and shallows Elsa was to avoid, did not these give the relish to marriage of mustard to meat? A husband with no little excesses to make up for — a flirtation, a beer-journey, an overlong seance at the skat-table — would, thought his wife, prove but a dull and stingy partner; while the cream of wifehood, that of comparing notes over the coffee-table, would be lost. In short, none was exactly averse, at heart, to having a mild Lothario for spouse.

The young girls of the circle made game, among themselves, of the Professor's appearance — though, like Elsa, any of them would have learned to overlook this, had his choice fallen upon her — and went on nursing their secret girlish passions for shapely lieutenants. However, they accepted Elsa's invitations to coffee, and, in viewing and discussing the trousseau, ate enormous quantities of cakes, pastry, and whipped cream; and Elsa, who had begun to stand uncomfortably alone, too old for the unmarried, yet shut out by her spinsterhood from the society of matrons, was again re-admitted to the fold.

Thus, Annemarie alone stood for revolution, for a violent break with tradition.

And the engagement was as short as decency permitted, there being nothing to wait for, and the Professor falling every day more deeply in love. The wedding — a very quiet affair — took place early one morning in September. The Professor's hands and feet were ice-cold, both at the civil marriage and afterwards in the church. Elsa did not know whether to laugh or to cry, and did a little of each. But Annemarie was neither nervous nor in doubt of her feelings; and face and air, as she stood gauntly erect in her brown silk dress, would better have befitted a funeral.

III

THE Professor could not take his eyes off Elsa as they stood on the railway platform, waiting for the train to bear them south: Elsa, in a drab-coloured dustcoat, a grey hat with a brown gossamer veil flying from it, and yellow boots; with a little travelling-bag slung across her shoulders, and carrying a handbox and a brown-holland hold-all, on which, in red cotton, with many a flourish, was embroidered: "A pleasant journey!" The charming sight so worked on the Professor that, disregarding her protests, he gallantly relieved her of the handbox; and, alone with her in a compartment of the train, shut the door leading to the corridor, sat down beside her, and took her hand in his. "My sweet little wife!"

The honeymoon was planned to last six weeks; but a bare four had elapsed when the postman delivered a letter announcing the pair's return; and a couple of evenings later Annemarie stood waiting at the front door, which was green-begarlanded, and topped by a large "Welcome!" Then the travellers appeared from the dark well of the staircase, Marthe toiling up with the baggage in their rear. The Professor was in high feather at getting home; he rubbed his hands, cracked jokes, and, as soon as Elsa had removed hat and mantle, offered her his arm for a tour of inspection. They went from room to room, while the Professor appraised the new wallpapers, the placing of the new furniture, the rows on rows of shining crockery and skyblue saucepans that decorated the kitchen shelves; winding up with the study, where accumulated letters and papers so engrossed him that, forgetting the ladies, he took root there, and had to be rung to supper.

At table, his satisfaction with the world continued.

"All said and done, my loves, there is no place like home," he declared, the while he helped himself to sausage and the little golden potato-balls that accompanied it. "Home, home, sweet home! Annemarie, my felicitations! We have not tasted so delicately prepared a potato since our departure."

"I knew before you went, Paulchen, that foreign travel would not agree with you," was Annemarie's retort as she diluted the tea.

"True, Annemarie, true! Still, it is a well-known fact that to see other countries than one's own enlarges the mind. But now, my dears, I must leave you," said the Professor, and therewith untied his table-napkin, which he had worn knotted round his neck after the fashion of a child's bib. "So vast a quantity of work awaits me that it will take many a long day to make up for lost time. Well, well, we know who is to blame for that!" And leaning over, he mischievously tweaked his wife's ear.

Finding Annemarie's eye on him, however, he abruptly desisted. "I hope we are not to have any nonsense of that kind here!" it seemed to say. Aloud, Annemarie remarked drily: "I think, Paulchen, you are not aware that you are still wearing your best coat."

"Dear me, so I am," ejaculated the Professor, and made this an excuse to hurry from the room.

Elsa had sat silent, with far-away eyes; she jumped when spoken to, then smiled, in a hasty, apologetic kind of way. The journey had greatly fatigued her; and as soon as she had unpacked her trunk she went to bed. When, towards midnight, the Professor tore himself from his desk and tiptoed into the bedroom, she lay rosy and relaxed, fast asleep. And as he moved warily to and fro, shaking out and folding up his coat, and hanging up his socks to air, his heart warmed, as on the first day, towards this gracious creature who had come to adorn his home.

The following morning Elsa paid a visit to her father; and, sitting on the old man's knee, enlarged on her travels as she had not yet had a chance of doing: in face of the Professor's measured sentences, she had shrunk from stuttering out her delight; and her letters had been of a pathetic poverty of expression. Now, with neither pen nor husband to disconcert her, she gave full play to her enthusiasm; and Herr Braun listened with admirable patience, considering this kind of thing was not at all in his line. At length, however, he cut her raptures short with a hearty kiss, and set her down; for she was heavy, and made his old bones ache.

"Little Frau Professor!" said he, and patted her cheek; the while he indulged anew the comfortable reflection that the responsibility for her welfare now lay on some one else's shoulders.

The first duty of the newly-wed was to pay a series of formal calls on the Professor's colleagues; Annemarie drew up a list in order of precedence. And thereafter, for many a week to come, between twelve and one of a Sunday morning, Elsa in her best dress, the Professor in voluminous frock-coat and curly-brimmed silk hat, hurried from house to house, and up and down stairs of varying quality: from shallow flights, richly carpeted, to steep and bare stone steps. Over the breakfast-table frank calculations were made how many visits could, with decency, be got through in a morning. Elsa and he became virtuosi in the art of greeting their hosts, sustaining an animated conversation for the fewest possible moments, and then adroitly taking their leave, bringing it up, despite distances, to the incredible figure of six visits per hour. From so business-like a proceeding little pleasure was to be got. And before many Sundays were over, Elsa had no feeling for anything but the scandalous fleetness with which quarters-of-an-hour escaped them.

"Tch, tch, tch!" the Professor would mutter, consulting his watch as they padded down a stair. "We stayed there five minutes too long. I *must* beg of you, Elsa, not to forget yourself in conversation. At this rate, we shall hardly reach the Spiegelbergs' before they go to table."

Sometimes, too, the callers were kept waiting, sat listening to the seconds ticking by, while the lady of the house, busy in her kitchen with the boiling of her Sunday roast, or the basting of a vinegared hare, scrambled into her Sunday silk; so that when she did appear, scarlet and soap-glazed, they had either to offer their adieux with her apologies hardly cold on the air, or to break into the quarter allotted to the recipient next on their list. And setbacks of this kind grew commoner as they sank in the scale, descending from the Ordinaries to the Extraordinaries and *Privatdozents*.

Then came the return visits, when Elsa ceremoniously led each lady to the sófa; and the Professor, at the first tinkle of the door-bell exchanging his working-jacket for the black coat that hung in readiness behind the study-door, emerged to give voice to his pleasure and surprise. The receiving of calls did not make so criminal an incursion on his time as the paying of them. All the same, Elsa breathed more freely as the whole business drew to a close, and ceased to provide the main topic of the dinner-table, in the shape of endless grumbles from her husband, and comments of the: "I knew it! I told you so!" order from Annemarie.

However, finally the day came when the last pair of callers pressed the springs of the furniture; and therewith the long formality was over. It constituted the sole concession the Professor was willed to make to the claims of society. Before marriage he had laid before Elsa, in detail, the manner of life she would be expected to lead at his side — just as one instructs the incoming domestic in his or her particular duties — and Elsa had agreed and been content. So that now there was nothing in the way of them taking up their regular routine.

Punctually at half-past six of a morning, a match was applied to the wood-fire laid overnight in the stove of the Professor's dressing-room. Breakfast was at half-past seven: by eight o'clock, all trace of the meal had been cleared away. At this hour, the Professor, carrying his newspaper under his arm — for he liked to be first of his household to learn what had happened in the world — but not unfolding it, for fear of distracting his mind: at eight o'clock, the Professor withdrew to his study and was seen no more till midday. Elsa watered the flowers, did a few light jobs about the house, and answered the door-bell while Annemarie and Marthe were at market. Did they return, she herself went out to walk, or to do a little shopping, or to visit her father. After dinner, which was served on the stroke of half-past twelve, the Professor read his newspaper, informed his ladies of any news he thought would interest them, and took a nap; during which not a pin might fall. Annemarie, letting her knitting sink to her lap, nodded in unison; and Elsa, her hands condemned to idleness, sat looking at the two of them across her embroidery-frame. On those afternoons when the Professor was on duty, she walked down the street with him to the University, and met him again when the lecture was over. On other days, he continued his habit of walking alone. After supper, before retiring to his desk for the evening, he would read aloud to them — preferably a French or an English book, for the sake of the language — and this was the pleasantest hour of the day.

Their programme never varied; was repeated week after week, month after month, till it began to seem to Elsa that the three of them were mere clockwork figures, wound up to perform a series of mechanical actions. With words that fitted these, and appropriate doll-like gestures.

She had no enterprise; and consequently never succeeded in getting even a tithe of the housekeeping into her own hands. The earliest arrangement, which was that of Annemarie continuing to hold the keys while she gradually initiated Elsa into the Professor's ways, remained the abiding one, except that, after a very short time, the initiation ceased. The fond girlish dreams of ministering to her husband's comfort, which she had nursed before marriage, came to nothing; he did not care for her cooking, or her schemes for variety: he was dyspeptic, and kept a rigid dietary, his stomach warming only to Annemarie's familiar dishes. And so it was with everything. If she aired his slippers or his house-jacket for him, she saw, in spite of his attempt to look pleased, that he was vexed not to find them in their accustomed places. For, at heart, the Professor abhorred change — he called it disorder — and, after one forcible-feeble effort to escape from his crusted shell, he sank back into it with what was almost a sigh of thanks-giving. For he, too, made a discovery in these early months; and that was, that he prized above all else the peace and tranquillity necessary to mental production. And fortune was on his side. Elsa gave no trouble; put up no fight for self-assertion. On the contrary, so faithfully did she obliterate herself that, his first ardours over, the Professor began to take her presence in his house as a matter of course, and, lost in the deeps of the Oscan Declension, to forget all about her.

For company she was thrown wholly on Annemarie. From the first, her own friends were not very welcome guests here: they ate too many cakes and sweets to suit Annemarie's purse; brought too loud a buzz of chat and laughter into the ordered stillness. Besides, they could only be comfortably entertained during the Professor's brief absences. No sooner was his key heard in the lock than Elsa fell into a nervous twitter, and could think only of politely getting rid of them. Otherwise, supper would be one long jeremiad. Nor was it any better with the regulation coffee-parties given by the wives of other Professors. Did she, Elsa, attend these, it meant entertaining in return — and still worse grumbles. She soon learnt her lesson, and became an adept at excusing herself.

It was Annemarie or no one. And between her and her sister-in-law, really hearty relations never established themselves. The two just rubbed along. Oddly enough, when it came to the point, Elsa's very submissiveness and anxiety to please formed the chief stumbling-block to their intimacy. For all her martinet airs, Annemarie would have preferred to see her brother's wife showing more spirit; venturing here and there to stand up for her rights. As Elsa, however, only waxed more and more listless, she despised her for her want of backbone as roundly as, at bottom, she would have resented any show of independence.

Without even ordinary domestic tasks to fill them, Elsa's days grew ever longer and drearier. She had already spent a third of her life at her needle; and every bit of her was a-scream for a little harmless variety — the variety she had fondly expected marriage would bring her. Whereas life in the Professor's house was whittled down to a monotony, a dead level of dullness, that passed belief. She had known dull enough days at home, and the disgrace of a prolonged spinsterhood had begun to weigh heavy on her. But life there had had a bright side. Her father had always been ready to crack his jokes; and had liked nothing better than to hear her laugh and see her merry. Nor had things ever needed to be up to time — time, whose bondslave she now was — but had gone as they listed, in a haphazard, chancy kind of way. There had also been an abundance of talk, and gossip, and loving raillery. Here, the primness, the soulless exactitude, the undeviating punctuality she was called on to exercise ground her down; and before a year was out the Professor seemed to her a mere dry little pedant, without a single human stirring under his hard-baked surface. As for Annemarie — well, enough to say, Elsa never dared to carry out even the one little breach of discipline she was always contemplating: that of some day coming in late for a meal. Before Annemarie, she stood the eternal schoolgirl in face of her mistress. And the heckling and pruning she had to submit to lent body to this feeling. She knew she was untidy, and gave herself all pains to cure the fault; but it went beyond her; for she simply did not know what Annemarie would call untidy next. If a curl caught by the wind strayed on to her forehead; if a string slipped and her petticoat showed beneath her skirt . . . oh, it did not matter what . . . she was hauled up as for a crime. She could not open a book unrebuked: they must always be commenting on what she read. Annemarie disapproved of poetry; the Professor was sarcastic over the light literature which, before marriage, had been her chief fare. Music disturbed him; she might not play the piano save in his short absences; she might not run, or sing, or even laugh too loudly. And the fine inborn gaiety of her nature declined from day to day.

She grew uncertain in temper: sulked, would not speak when spoken to. Annemarie put up with this for some time, then complained to her brother, and the Professor, grieved and surprised, laid down his pen to point out the selfishness of giving way to moods and whimsies. Elsa burst out crying, and locked herself in the bedroom. Altogether, at this time, she cried easily: sometimes of a morning, as she walked along the banks of the canal, where barges swam and women washed linen, she could hardly see to put one foot in front of the other, for the sudden mist of tears that blurred her eyes. "Why did he marry me? Oh, why did he marry me?" And the thoughts that darted through her brain in answer were dark and unwifely.

But the day came when she ceased to question; when doubts and frets were swallowed up in a vast satisfaction; and the Professor, as father of the child that was to be, took on a new significance in her eyes. She had been unjust to him, she saw it now: he was as pleased at the prospect as she herself — if in a sedater way. For now she had to sing: there was no keeping back the tunes that rose to her lips. At last, too, she had found an occupation: with Annemarie's help she cut out and stitched the many little garments needed; and over this work she glimpsed unsuspected qualities in even her stern old sister-in-law.

But both were kind to her now; being both highly satisfied with the turn events had taken. Thought the Professor: it was the duty of every woman to bear children; they were as exactly the complement of her existence as work was of a man's; and would put an end to all dumps and doldrums. Annemarie's reflections were of the same nature — with a fine shade of difference. It was, of course, proper that her brother's union should be blessed with offspring; a family would, in her eyes, form its only justification. Otherwise, she was tempted to wonder what had been the object of bringing this weak, moping, untidy girl into their well-regulated home. Poor dear Paulchen! . . . unless at his desk, delving roots and their derivatives, he was as blind as a bat; and quite unversed in the difficult task of appraising women. Manlike, he had let himself be captivated by an agreeable exterior. What a different choice she would have made for him! However, much would now be forgiven Elsa if she did her part in a sensible and healthy manner; by no flightiness or carelessness endangering the precious young life that had been given into her keeping. For, towards the unborn child, her brother's child, Annemarie's heart was already tender.

All the same, she would not have been a woman if she had not felt a slight malicious satisfaction. She did not begrudge Paulchen his pride at becoming a father; but he had, she knew, as little idea what it cost to bring a human being into the world, as the unconscious arrival itself. Now, if a man would persist in marrying, he must face the music; and she saw no reason why Paulchen should have the experience softened for him. So she impressed on him the necessity of making Elsa's welfare and Elsa's wishes — no matter how strained and far-fetched these seemed — the hub round which all else turned. And for the first time in his life, the Professor found himself a person of secondary importance.

Elsa held first place. And it did not offend her that this new dignity was only, as it were, a kind of reflection cast by the coming child. She had never had any morbid, modern sense of her own individuality; had never, in fact, been conscious of it at all; and she was, besides, already much more engrossed with the new arrival than either of the others could be. In addition, she had two thoughts for company which uplifted her far above petty considerations. She said to herself: this little one that is coming will be all mine, belong to me alone; for, young-motherlike, she forgot in her way, just as Annemarie in hers, that two go to the parenting of a child. Again when she felt most crushed by her sister-in-law's superior airs, she would remind herself: soon, now, there will be something about which I shall know more than she does. Which was a prop to sustain her.

She enjoyed, with her whole heart, the regime of do-as-you-please idleness, to which by doctor's orders she was now condemned: she might get up late in the morning, stay at home if she did not feel moved to go out, spend several hours of each day on the sofa. Her father came to see her every afternoon. The fat, rubicund little man would tiptoe into the room, finger on lip, half in order to amuse Elsa, half from a very genuine fear of disturbing or calling forth his learned son-in-law, with whom he found it impossible to fraternise. And Elsa never failed to laugh at the threadbare joke, and pulled the joker down by his long, white beard, to kiss him. He brought her sweets, which were not allowed her; and the light and foolish novels she loved. And though these might now have passed unscathed, she kept them tucked away under the sewing in her work-basket.

Father and daughter shared a secret; and when, in their hearing, Annemarie, whose say neither dared dispute, magisterially wished the expected infant to be a boy, Elsa would look slyly across at her father, and lift her embroidery to her lips to hide the smile that played there. For her part, she hoped otherwise. In a boy the other two would claim too large a share; while a mere girl she could have for her very own.

Now, the baking heat of summer was upon them; and Elsa seldom left the house. Never a day passed, however, but what Herr Braun toiled up the steep stairs to visit her. He panted more loudly each time; his face was red as a boiled lobster; and so stout had he grown that his beard stood out from his chest at right angles. The doctor was uneasy, he said, because he did not transpire properly; but he snapped his fingers at such a trifle.

Annemarie eyed his retreating figure with disapproval. "Your father is letting himself go," she said severely: he had puffed into the room that afternoon like a veritable grampus. Annemarie could feel no respect for Herr Braun, because of the many shortcomings of Elsa's up-bringing.

"But so long as he is happy?" gave back Elsa lightly, without thinking what she said — as she often dared nowadays to answer.

"Happy? Pray, what has that to do with it? You talk as if happiness was the sole aim of existence!" snorted Annemarie, out of patience with such soft, indulgent notions.

Elsa flushed an apology. She had never seriously reflected on life or life's meaning. Now, in face of Annemarie's sterner standards, the laxity of her ideas came painfully home to her.

Weeks passed, and all was going well, when one day Herr Braun dropped dead in the street of an apoplexy. A foolish servant carried the news hotfoot, and the grief to which Elsa yielded was so immoderate that days of acutest anxiety followed. By doctor's orders she was put to bed in a darkened room, and kept there; was forbidden to move hand or foot, Annemarie sitting over her to enforce obedience. And by the time the danger was over, and she permitted to rise, Herr Braun lay, stiff-stretched and decorous, under his new mound of earth, and would never be seen by mortal eyes again.

Looking very wan in her new black dress, Elsa sat and moped and fretted. The doctor recommended a thorough change of scene; and as July was now well advanced, it was arranged that she and Annemarie should set out forthwith for a watering-place in the mountains. There, when the academic term ended, the Professor would join them.

In their absence he was left to the mercy of the servant — a thing that had not happened to him within living memory — and he tasted all the many, petty discomforts of bachelorhood.

His meals were unpunctually served, indifferently cooked; and he, who had never wanted for anything, might now tinkle his hand-bell or raise his voice in vain. Marthe was never where she should be: escape from the unwinking control of Annemarie, she did what she chose, went where she listed. Once, late in the evening when he believed her to be in bed, the Professor came upon her at the house-door, gallivanting with a soldier; and once, he was sure of it, he heard not two but four feet ascending to the servants' quarters at the top of the house. Listening on the landing in his nightclothes, he could have sworn to apprehending a male snore. He did not, however, dare to tackle Marthe outright; she took even a mild reproof for dawdling, in saucy fashion. He was afraid of her, and the traps he laid for her were underhand traps; but, try as he would, he could not catch her. The chase assumed a morbid interest for him; and the composure necessary to scientific literary production went to pieces over it.

When, however, he joined his ladies, he found so marked an improvement in Elsa that he forgave and forgot his tribulations as a housekeeper. Her bloom took him back to the early days of his courtship, and made him feel wondrous kind.

He playfully pulled her ear: "My pretty little wife once more!"

The three of them, Elsa leaning on his arm, promenaded the flat, pleasant roads, shaded by fruit-trees; and, now, brother and sister suited their steps to hers. When the band played they drank coffee in the *Kurpark*, while Annemarie knitted and the Professor read; and Elsa, who had never been much from home, found occupation enough in watching the crowd of summer visitors. If they went farther afield, she rode in a bath-chair, which was pushed by an old, one-eyed man.

Thus the summer passed.

IV

ON their return — it was the end of September, and the evenings were beginning to strike chill — returning, Annemarie found dirt and disorder everywhere, and plunged them into a belated house-cleaning. Even the Professor saw the need of this; but, none the less, it was a time of forlorn discomfort. He had never before been present at a thoroughpaced cleaning; and mournfully he picked his steps over the dust and shavings of scraped parquet, or avoided, with a sigh that was deep enough for an oath, pails of steaming, strong-smelling water. The whacking of beds and furniture, the scraping of floors, trampling feet and loud voices murdered thought; and only his confidence in Annemarie's sound judgement sustained him. He had had a further proof of her acumen: her hawk eye had at once detected Marthe's backsliding; and, the house in order again, you could hardly say Jack Robinson before the miscreant's box was packed, and a new brawny-armed maidservant dumped down the soup-tureen. Yes, some women were born to general-ship. Had it been Elsa now ... Elsa? ... *some* women, he said.

After the many sacrifices they had made on her behalf, Elsa was behaving poorly again. Pressed, she declared that the sight of the house brought her loss back to her anew: it was here she had seen her father last — now who would have thought she had so doted on him? Annemarie did not mince her words; the Professor reasoned and expostulated. As, however, nothing they could say took effect, and she was twice found in tears, they called in the doctor.

"Try cheerful society," said he. "Your wife is too much alone."

But out of Elsa's hearing he was more explicit, and even hinted darkly at a constitutional weakness. Upon which, the eyes of brother and sister met in a wordless flash. What! ... this, too? In trying to pick up the scattered threads of his work, the Professor was mastered by a very human irritation: had he been the dupe of a mere surface rosiness and plumpness? While Annemarie's big-boned hands trembled, as she dished up potatoes in their jackets for dinner. Was the last stroke to be put to Elsa's wishwashy shallowness by her inability to bear a healthy child?

Well! they would do their duty, no matter at what cost. Grimly Annemarie issued invitations for a coffee-party; the Professor as grimly retired, with an armful of books, to the seclusion of a sunless attic; and a round dozen of ladies, armed with workbags and satchels, arrived to sit in circle about the waxcloth of the dinner-table. But, cakes and coffee disposed of, the infant trousseau duly examined and admired, an air of flatness settled on the party. Elsa, who should have been its life, sat vacant and aloof, taking no share in the gossipy talk. Thus the entertainment planned to distract her proved a failure; and the Professor resumed possession of his study with a sigh of relief, and the clearest of husbandly consciences.

Had it only ended here! This, however, was but the first of a series of derangements and discomforts, the like of which he could never have believed possible. His home was no longer his own; his day's routine was broken into, he himself pushed to one side, the last person in the house to be considered or initiated. Annemarie went about rapt in mystery and importance; the very maidservant was more in the swim than he. He seemed merely in the way: a tripper over unlooked-for baskets and cradles; an unwilling trespasser on private conversations, which, at his entry, crashed into silence.

There was, for example, that unfortunate afternoon when, going to the bedroom to wash his hands, he found that he had blundered in on a confabulation with the midwife, come to pay her visit of ceremony: a burly, big-bosomed female, of a type hitherto unknown to him, her top crowned by a vast, flower-laden hat. She sat with her knees apart, a pudgy hand on each, and turned, at the opening of the door, to fix the intruder with two beady, inquisitive little eyes.

"Aha! Der Herr Papa!"

The Professor fled.

Again, the whole thing could not have happened, for him, at a more inconvenient time. He was just prepared to issue, in pamphlet form, a further slice of his life-work — the second in ten years — and for this momentous undertaking he needed not only the utmost tranquillity of mind, but the peace of the grave about him. The deliberatings, the weighings of the fors and againsts, that preceded his decision to publish, were a labour in themselves. For the Professor suffered from so deep-seated a lack of self-confidence that it amounted almost to mental paralysis; causing him to sift and re-sift his findings till scarcely anything of them remained. He had also to look to it that, whilst whetting the appetite of his brother-philologists, he did not make them all too free of his main issue: that master theory of the "Oscan Declension," which was some day to settle the vexed question for good and all. Yes! a thousand subtle doubts and inhibitions had to be battled with and overthrown, ere the fruits of his learning could come to birth.

Now, however, all preliminaries were behind him; and, as he walked home one late November afternoon, under an avenue of maples still richly hung with rosy-yellow leaves, he, too, felt as if bathed in a sunset glow. On his desk the first proofs of his booklet lay awaiting him. They had come by the morning post, but he had resisted even stealing a peep at them, till his work in the lecture-room was over. Proofs! Most seductive form of printed matter! In fancy the Professor tasted the good things that lay before him. First, he would drink a cup of tea, savouring to the full the fine flavour of Annemarie's brew. Then, going into his study and shutting the door on the world, he would change his coat, seat himself at his desk, and let the galley-slips unroll: as it were to see himself, see the very essence of him materialise, in the black and white of the printed page. Oh! life held no purer joy than this. Afterwards came the exquisite pleasure of correction. Not the smallest inaccuracy escaped his eye; never yet had malicious printer got the better of him! And, had a note to be made, it trickled scroll-like, microscopic, a decoration in itself, a-down the clean, white margin of the page.

Of things such as these did the Professor dream, hastening towards them as another to the arms of his lover.

But they were fated to remain a dream. For, on entering the house, he found himself in a scene of wild confusion. Elsa's hour had come, and Annemarie and Mathilde were scuttling about, banking up the stoves, disarranging the furniture, rearranging the beds. Not even the kettle had been put on for his tea; and, dry-throated and unrefreshed, he had to sally forth again to fetch doctor and midwife.

For three nights he did not take his clothes off. His meals were cold scraps, served at odd times; his bed remained unmade, his boots uncleaned. When, at dawn on the third day, the surgeon's forceps brought a puny infant into the world, and Elsa's cries ceased, the Professor himself felt on the verge of collapse. The strain on his nerves had been too great. He had also discovered in himself an unsuspected tender-heartedness. Again and again, in waiting, in listening, his eyes had filled and overflowed. None the less, deep down in him, there housed a bitter resentment. Other women bore children without this merciless ado. Why not his wife? Why must all this happen just to him, who loved peace and tranquillity more than anything? ... yes, verily, above *anything* on earth.

Now, however, a divine quiet restored, he manned himself, and went bravely through with his day's work. But he returned towards evening feeling more dead than alive; and there being no change in the sickroom, where Elsa lay in a heavy sleep, he retired to his shakedown, losing consciousness as his head touched the pillow.

He seemed hardly to have closed his eyes when he found himself sitting up in bed, trembling violently. What was it? ... what had happened? He listened into the darkness, straining his ears. Nothing ... nothing ... and he was just on the point of sinking back into a heavenly oblivion, when a shrill scream jerked him up again and brought the sweat out on his forehead. So that was it! ... Elsa! — God in Heaven! she was beginning anew.

His first feeling was one of utter rebellion. Impossible! ... he could not, no, he could not ... every nerve in his body rose in arms at the prospect of being racked afresh. Between the second and the third cry, there was almost time to fall asleep again. The fourth roused him to a mood of murderous fury, as, utterly without shame, it shrilled through the house.

Now someone was battering at his door.

"Paulchen! — get up, get up! The doctor! Something terrible has happened." It was Annemarie's voice, choked, unrecognisable.

"Yes, yes! I'm coming."

Throwing back the feather coverlet, he dropped his legs over the side of the bed and groped on the floor for his socks. And so dizzy with sleep was he that for some seconds it did not occur to him to light the candle. Again and again his lids fell to; and the effort of putting on each single piece of clothing was enormous. But one breath of the cold night air roused him.

This was at midnight; and so it went on till dawn, when Elsa died without regaining consciousness.

For a fortnight after, the wailing of a sick child made the days and nights a torture. Then, despite their care, the babe, too, died; and he and Annemarie drove a second time to the cemetery, a miniature coffin before them on the seat of the *droschke*. When they reached home, black as crows in their stiff, heavy mourning, the house itself, sepulchrally dark, sepulchrally silent, felt like a tomb. Annemarie went round drawing up the shutters. Mathilde was bidden to prepare the tea.

While this was being done, the Professor retired to his study. As he went, he drew a black-edged handkerchief from his tail-pocket, and, for the dozenth time, blew his nose and wiped his eyes. He was still deeply moved; it would be many a day before his heart healed of its wounds. To lose wife and child thus, at one stroke ... the mere thought of his widowed state so touched him that it was again necessary to fumble for his handkerchief.

This time, however, he did not find it — neither it nor the pocket that hid it. For, following the habit of a lifetime, on entering his room he had automatically exchanged his tail-coat for the familiar grey working-jacket that hung behind the door. So he had now to content himself with sniffing. For at the selfsame moment he espied a bundle of letters lying on his desk. Not one had yet been replied to. Crossing to the table he sat down. And then it was, in handling the letters, that the forgotten proofs caught his eye. They lay just as on the day Elsa was taken ill, virgin-pure of ink-mark or correction. Putting out his hand, he drew them to him. He read a sentence; he skimmed a paragraph. Whereafter, as always for reading, he removed his spectacles and peered at the print with a naked eye. A magic stillness reigned. He read on. Suddenly to give vent to a click of the tongue. A wrong fount had been used. And again: a ridiculous misspelling! Tch! the carelessness of printers. Mechanically he reached for his pen.

When, a little later, Annemarie opened the door by a hand's-breadth to peep in, he was too engrossed to hear her. Noiselessly she withdrew.

Back in the sitting room, she, too, looked about her for an occupation. Her work-basket stood in a corner; taking from it a half-finished sock, untouched now for weeks, she began to knit. The table was spread; in a little while she would tinkle the handbell that summoned Paulchen to tea.

Click-click, click-a-click, went the busy pins. And except that her dress was black and crepe-laden, Annemarie sat as she had sat for the past twenty years, and as she might be expected from now on again to sit, day in, day out, waiting for the same meal, at the same hour, turning the heels and narrowing the toes of Paulchen's socks. But appearances deceived: for all her seeming placidity, her brain was a whirl of new, queer thoughts. And soon this inner commotion grew so strong that hands and pins fell to her lap, and she sat idle, staring straight before her.

It began with her catching herself listening for an infant's cry. And when the silence remained unbroken, and she reminded herself that never again need she hope to hear that thin, fluty wail, she felt a sudden stab of ... of what was almost fear. Yes, let her confess it, she was afraid: afraid of the stillness, the vacancy, the deadness that had closed down again upon the house. And on those in it. For a year past, she had had at her side some one to parley with, to manage, to whip up. She had also learnt what it meant to care for a little child. Now, the days to come yawned empty as untenanted space. What should she do with them? ... how endure the creeping of the hours? For what had once satisfied her was no longer enough. Never again could she sink back into the automaton, the figurehead, who existed solely to smooth another's path, smothering meanwhile every personal wish or want, to receive, in return, hardly a thank-you for her pains.

Since last she had sat here knitting, knitting, knitting for Paulchen, hanging on Paulchen's words, awaiting his pleasure, she had passed through a great, a vital experience. The mysteries of birth and death had been enacted before her: the coming of a new soul, the going forth of one with whom you had shared your daily bread. This was life — what it really meant to be alive — not the humdrum monotony that had always fallen to her lot, which she had put up with only because she knew no better. Advantage had been taken of her ignorance. And by whom? By Paulchen. — Paulchen? Who *was* Paulchen that he should demand such a sacrifice? Was his life of so much more worth than hers? She turned her eyes on him, and, as she looked, the scales fell, and she saw him as she had never yet dared to see him; as a mouldy little bookworm, a narrow blear-eyed little delver in abstruse symbols, who lived wrapped up in himself, and for himself alone, without thought or care for the well-being of those around him. As long as he was ministered to, his comfort assured, nothing else mattered. Even at this moment, with wife and child barely cold in the grave, he found it possible to take up his old routine. And no doubt confidently expected her to do the same. At this thought, the suppressed, unconscious resentment of years came to the surface in Annemarie, and she felt that she almost hated him. He and his Oscan Declension! Was it worth a rap to anybody but himself? Did it do anyone good? ... help the sick and needy? ... or those in travail? What had it ever done for her, but rob her? ... of all life might have held for her as a woman. Had it not been for this fetish, this Moloch, she, too, might have joined the ranks of happy wives, have fulfilled her woman's mission, borne children. In a flash she saw them, these lost children of hers, a whole row of them, rising step by step from the toddlers up: *she* would not have died in giving them birth, not she! And, in their stead, all that had been offered her was the right to stand by and watch Paulchen work, for his own honour and glory, at this bloodless abstraction. Oh! her scorn, her bitterness, knew no bounds. His mole-like absorption; his inflated self-importance; his pitiable worthlessness as a human being — "Mouldy . . . mouldy . . . mouldy . . . and *I* am to moulder, too!"

Mathilde, carrying in tea, nearly dropped the pot at sight of her mistress sitting stormily weeping, and not even troubling to hide her face. Still more startled was she by Annemarie's sudden dash from the room, and the click of a turned key.

"Now who'd ever have thought the old stick had so much feeling in her!" was the girl's comment, in retailing the juicy incident to the maid in the flat above.

And the Professor, in place of the peace and serenity he craved, having knocked till his knuckles were sore and got but an angry bidding to let her be, had not only for the first time in his life to pour out his own tea, but to drink it in a solitude peopled by gloomiest forebodings.

The while, behind her locked door, Annemarie continued to indulge thoughts and hatch plans of the kind that herald revolutions.

THE COAT

SUCCEDANEUM

MARY CHRISTINA

THE COAT

THE train was late, and she shifted uneasily from foot to foot as she stood, the coat clinging and dragging like the water-logged clothes on a drowning man. For the weather had done one of its perverse changes, the November morning broken sunny and mild. Just her luck: yesterday she could have worn the wretched thing in comfort. Now, the mere thought of what lay before her — the traipsing to and fro, the crowded buses, the overheated shops — exhausted her.

But there, thank goodness, came the train, slithering round the bend like a sly brown serpent. And before it fairly stopped the windows were black with heads, carriage-doors flew open, porters shouted and were shouted for, bags and cases tumbled out. She had posted herself much too far down; had to trudge almost the length of the platform before she found Margaret, standing stolid and composed amid the racket. Just the same old sobersides. The same old face, too: nature unadorned, not a touch of make-up: country from hat to shoes. One felt very chic and towny by comparison; and as the two of them moved to join the tail of the crowd at the gates, she saw to it that the skirts of the coat swayed becomingly.

More than once she thought she felt Margaret eyeing her, but: "So good of you, Katherine, to undertake to pilot me round," was all that was said. Or (ridiculously): "Even to crunch the London soot underfoot is a treat." And when they were out of the station, through the arch and on their way to the bus, there was nothing for it but herself to focus the other's wandering attention.

"What do you think of my coat?"

"Oh, er . . . very nice, very nice indeed. But isn't it rather heavy for such a warm day?"

"Oh dear, no. Fur of *this* quality is never heavy." And as Margaret's sole response was an agreeable smile: "It was a present from Harry, you see. On my last birthday. He paid a ruinous price for it — he's a regular spendthrift where I'm concerned."

"Really? And so it has been a great success — your marriage?"

This time she, too, contented herself with smiling.

"I hope I'm to be allowed to meet him?"

"Yes, he has promised to join us for lunch."

Glibly she brought out the falsehood. But, a strenuous morning's shopping over — the sums she had to sit by and see spent! For the plainer and dowdier the clothes, the more it seemed they cost. And only the best of everything was good enough. The "ruinous price" attributed to Harry began to give her qualms. And in the shoe-shop she took care to keep her own feet out of sight — no Harry met them.

At midday, then, they sat alone at their table in the restaurant of a great store.

"It looks as if he hadn't been able to get off. He's quite an important person in the office nowadays, you know."

"Splendid. Perhaps he'll rise to the head of it before he's done. There's nothing like a steady climb, is there? So much the most satisfactory way."

Oh, this harping on Harry. And even here, where the air was thick with heat and food, she dared do no more than loosen a button at her throat, while she sat and listened to Margaret poke and pry. An inquisitive old maid, that was what the past three years had turned *her* into.

"No children?"

What next! "Good Lord, no! Harry's much too considerate. You've no *idea* what an old silly he is about me. When I scolded him for buying such a coat, all he said was: 'It ought to have been mink'." And with a forced smile over the choke of the collar: "Next year I'm to have a car. One of the best on the road."

Was she laying it on too thick? (*Could* her shoes have been spotted?) Or did she only imagine the dryness, the lack of acceptance, in Margaret's steady gaze? Anyhow, real or not, the suspicion was enough to give her pause. In a flurry she snatched up bag and gloves.

"I think . . . if you've quite finished? For it looks to me as if it's going to turn foggy. That's the danger of such fine mornings at this time of year." (The danger, too, that trains might not run, and she be forced to take Margaret home with her. Oh, *anything* but that! The "charming bungalow", the "spacious garden".)

Outside, they had to cross the road; and at once there was a muddle. Still rattled, she stepped off the pavement just as the lights changed; and Margaret wasn't sharp enough. (You had to be a Londoner to take chances.) To see what the fool was doing she turned her head, and a bus chose just that moment to swing round the corner and come charging down on her. Anything more appalling than the nearness of this scarlet monster . . . like a house got loose, a moving mountain . . . She had to jump for her life, blindly, desperately: but jump she did, with a nimbleness that amazed her, clogged as she was: and the next instant found herself safe on the opposite pavement. But someone hadn't been so lucky: there was a hideous shriek, a chorus of grinding brakes, shouts, cries, wildest confusion. God! where was Margaret? That hat, she would have known it anywhere. But not a trace, not a speck of its ludicrous cock's-plume, in the crowd that ran together like fowls after food. She tried to call out; but no voice came. And even if it *was* Margaret, she couldn't go back. Accidents terrified her; the sight of blood turned her sick. And so, palsied with fear, her heart pounding fit to split her chest, she stood and watched the traffic pile up, policemen spring from the earth, the crush thicken, everyone pushing and shoving to catch a glimpse of what lay in the road. Then, the bell of an ambulance, which, still walled in by people, loaded its fearful burden and drove off. Whereupon the crowd thinned and melted. But still no Margaret beckoned to her or came over to join her. Finding her voice, she turned to a man who stood by and asked if he could tell her who had been hurt. But he didn't seem to hear her. A kind-faced woman, however, gave her an odd look and a smile in passing, and, without being asked, said gently: "It's all over. Don't be frightened."

Frightened? Fright was the least of it. For what now? — now that, thanks to another's imbecility, she had been landed in this hole. (Oh, that she had never set eyes on Margaret!) Now, she would need to go to a policeman, allege faintness, say she missed her friend; hear to which hospital the ambulance had driven, make her way there, listen to gruesome details, perhaps even see and identify the body. Horrible indeed: but it wasn't this that made her shiver and quake. And, while she put a hand to her jaw, to stop its chattering, her brain fumbled with thoughts of escape. Nobody here had known she was to meet Margaret; at this end she was safe. But down in the country, at Margaret's home, a letter might be found bearing her name. If she did not come forward she would probably be broadcast or advertised for . . . oh God, oh God!

Insensibly, however, she had begun to walk away: to follow, as if drawn, in the direction of the ambulance. And here she was in Portland Place. Or so she supposed. For sure enough fog *had* come down, filling the eyes, throwing a haze over streets and people, muffling the tall buildings till you couldn't tell one from another. Still, she plodded on, in growing bewilderment: the coat alone remaining true to itself and making a labour of each step.

A seat! . . . a seat. She hailed it with a relief that went up like a prayer of thanks. Never had anything come so opportunely. Alone, too, and fog-screened, she could at last unbutton the coat. And this she did, throwing it wide from neck to hem, drinking in deep, luscious breaths of air; if air it could be called.

But not for long was she alone. A figure took shape in the murk, and turned to a man, who sat down beside her. She edged away; for he didn't look much, and she had her fur to think of.

Now, he was actually speaking, asking if she had lost herself.

Of him she made short work. "Certainly not. I'm just taking a rest."

"And the fog will gradually lift."

"Let us hope so." She meant to leave it at that, but found herself adding: "What I *have* lost is the friend I came out with."

"Can I help you?"

"You? How, I'd like to know!"

"Well, if you would perhaps remove your coat . . ."

Aha! so that was what he was: a coat thief. She had read of such things happening under cover of fog. Hurriedly she re-did her fastenings. If he was after the coat he'd have to take her too. And she was tall and strong.

But he made no move to attack her. And again some inner urge forced her to go on speaking.

"The very idea of me sitting here without it! I should be much too . . ." — "bare" was the word that presented itself, but she choked it back, it sounded so odd, and said "cold" instead, though she was perspiring freely.

"As you will," said the man. And evidently took the hint; for when she looked round next he had gone.

Fool, oh, fool, she with her suspicions. After all he might have known, have been able to tell her what it would be best to do. She raised her handkerchief to her smarting eyes; and as she lowered it saw another figure growing as it were out of the mist: a woman this time, so no cause for alarm. But the be-stringed bonnet, the antiquated mantle *could* only belong to a charwoman or some such person; and again she made to edge away. But was brought up by the end of the seat. And the new-comer plumped down almost on top of her.

Thus wedged in she had to listen to the same fatuous question.

"Can I help you?"

What the hell did they mean by it, all of them? (The next one that came along she'd be beforehand with.) And her reply was as crushing as she knew how to make it.

But a glance shot sideways, to see how the creature took the snubbing, froze the words on her tongue. Round-eyed, open-mouthed, she wrenched herself loose, to turn, to make sure.

"*Mother!* — you? What on earth are *you* doing here? In this fog, with your rheumatism? You'll be ill again, you'll be laid up!"

"Don't worry about me, my dear. It's you we have to think of."

Which was Mother to the life. Always ready to belittle herself and her ailments.

"Well, I must say. But oh, it seems too good to be true. For you're just the person I need. I'm in such trouble, Mother, such terrible trouble!" And breathlessly she poured out her tale: the accident, her own lucky escape, her fears for Margaret, her laming uncertainty.

Except for a gentle click or two of the tongue, she was listened to in silence. But when she stopped speaking, in place of the expected sympathy, the sound, motherly advice, all she heard was: "But first take off your coat."

And that was like the stab of the drill on an inflamed nerve.

"Oh, *curse* the coat! Can't you any of you leave it alone? Besides, I never heard such nonsense. How can I possibly take it off? I should be much too —" Again she had to fight an impulse to say something she didn't want to, or mean.

"You needn't mind being bare before me, little Katie."

There! — the word was out, and said not by her but another.

Though staggered, she managed a mocking laugh. "Bare? It

sounds as if I had nothing on underneath. But 'little Katie' — how good that sounds! No one has called me Katie since . . . *since* —'' The fraction of a second in which her heart stood still, and she was on her feet, her balled fists digging into her cheeks, her eyes wild with fear, all the blood in her body galloping back to her heart.

"*Mother! You?* But — but how *can* it be? For you're dead, Mother — *dead!* — and have been for years and years."

"I will explain."

"Explain? Explain *that?* Oh Christ, what does it mean? Am I going mad?" Her legs abruptly failing her, she fell face downward on the seat, crying and sobbing.

"Quiet, child, quiet. But come now." And by some means or other the coat was undone, loosened, pulled off her: bringing to light, in all its meanness, the shabby, out-of-date dress that was her sole wear. She shivered into herself as though she had been stripped naked. And yet . . . rid of the coat's intolerable drag, the fug of it, the stickiness . . . Now, she could move, sit up with ease, turn her head, look about her. For the man had been right; the fog *was* lifting, had shrunk to mere whiffs and puffs of mist in the upper air. But — this was not Portland Place. No old Lister with his sideboards, no rows of cars and taxis. Nor houses either: just a wide, open, desolate space, with a single seat planked down in the middle of it.

Stupefied she stared round.

"Where am I? What am I doing here?"

"Safe with me, little Katie."

"With you? How can I be? — Mother! You don't — you can't . . . It was Margaret, I tell you, *Margaret*, not me! That bus never touched me, I swear it didn't! Do you think I wouldn't *know?*"

Again she was on her feet, went raging up and down, her bunched hands shaking convulsively, in defiance, in despair.

"I won't, I won't be dead, I tell you, I *won't!* — Besides, it's preposterous, it's insane. Never have I felt so alive! Oh, there's some awful mistake somewhere. Why, I've got years and years of life before me: I'm only thirty-six: I mean to live to be an old, old woman. Oh, do something, say something! Can't you see I'm going mad?" And flinging herself on her knees she hid her face in her mother's lap.

Now, her hat too was off; and she felt the touch of hands on her hair.

"Talk on, my child. You have many things to say to me."

"You're wrong, I haven't, not one! Except that it's all a mistake. Or else I'm dreaming. Yes, that's what it is: just a hideous dream. The shock of seeing Margaret killed was too much for me. I shall wake up, I know I shall — I *will!* — and be able to laugh at myself."

In her ears there was now a kind of singing, or humming, which added to her confusion. (But which was also a proof that she dreamed.)

"Oh, *why* couldn't the woman have stopped where she was? Why did she need to come to London? I never asked her to, I didn't want her. And this, this is all I get for being kind to her."

"Was kindness your only motive, Katie?"

"What else?" And with a bitter laugh: "Do you think I enjoyed dragging at her heels like a dog on a lead? Watching her fling about with pounds as if they were shillings — *I*, who am so poor, so poor? Don't you call that kind?"

To this there was no answer; except from the humming, which seemed to grow momentarily louder. She shook her head as if to chase off a winged pest, stopped her ears with her fingers; but neither helped. To drown it she was compelled to go on speaking.

"In every single shop we went to, her one thought was, to get the best of everything. More money than she knew what to do with, and no one but herself to spend it on. When she bought shoes, Mother, I had to hide mine under the chair. And so . . . when the bus got her and I knew I'd never have to see that smug, self-satisfied face of hers again — oh, wasn't it only natural I couldn't feel sorry? You must understand that, you must, you must!"

Here, the humming rose to a wail, like the whine of a high, thin wind among the chimney-pots on an autumn night. (A sound that had always got her down.)

"And you, you're trying to make out it wasn't her but me — *me!* Oh, what shall I do?"

"Talk on, my child. Only your mother hears you."

"Haven't I said enough? That I hated her — yes, *hated!* — and was glad she was run over?" But it seemed not, for once more she listened in vain for a response. Her face hardened. "Very well then, if it's not her, if it's me, and I'm dead, then I'll stop dead. And the dead don't talk."

For these words she paid dear. The whining swelled to a

screech, a chorus of screeches, like the fierce cawing and quacking of a swarm of rooks about to pounce. Bitterly she rued her bravado; tried to atone for it by carrying on, in a voice raised to all but a shout against the din.

"The one single thing I had better than her was my coat. She couldn't touch *that*. Oh, how thankful I was I'd worn it! Though it nearly did for me. You were right, every one of you, when you told me to take it off. This is the first time to-day I'm able to breathe."

"Good, child, good. But go on, make haste."

"Why? What's the hurry?"

But even as she put the question, she too began to feel that time was flying. To let it escape unused was somehow to court disaster.

Yet still she fenced and hedged.

"Yes, there — the coat, I mean — I had her. And — and Harry. For she'd never managed to get a husband; nobody ever asked *her* to marry them. She's one of your born old maids. *And* envious! When I told her about Harry, how fond he is of me and the fuss he makes over me, she went green with envy. But — Oh, Mother, Mother, what *is* the awful noise inside my head? Is this what it means to die? I'm frightened, I'm frightened. Oh, help me, for you can, you know how, if only you will!"

"No one can help you but yourself, child. But be quick, your chance is passing."

In the knees she leant on she thought she felt a movement as if to rise, and panic seized her.

"For God's *sake*, don't go, don't leave me! . . . alone in this fog."

For the mist was gathering again; had come as low as the face above her, blurring its outlines. More: even as she looked these seemed to change their shape, to be growing fluid. Terror at the sight broke down her last defences. Taking the other's dress in both hands, bringing it up round her face for a screen, she began to speak, so fast, in so little above a whisper that, to any mortal ear, what now came would have been inaudible.

"Stay with me, only stay, and I'll tell you everything. Oh, I've been a wicked woman, Mother. I'm a liar and — and a thief, yes, rotten through and through. Nothing I told Margaret was true. Harry never gave me this coat. He never gives me anything. He doesn't care a hang for me. Nor I for him. I hate him and despise him. I only took him because there was no one else. And ever since I married him I've tricked him and done him. The money I got for the house, I've always kept back part of it. It didn't hurt him, for he didn't know. He's the sort of man who never knows anything; what he eats or what things cost. Or sees how shabby I go. And anyhow he wouldn't care, he's got no pride *in* him. For months and months I've been saving up to buy a coat. But it was never enough. And when I heard Margaret was coming — *she* to see what I had sunk to! — I couldn't bear it, Mother, I simply couldn't."

The tears were streaming now, splashing hot on cheeks, hands, dress.

"And so . . . I got a bunch of keys at the ironmonger's, and found one that fitted the drawer where he keeps his money, for rates and things, and took it and went out and bought this coat. But surely as much for *his* sake as mine? That Margaret shouldn't know how mean, how despicably mean he is? No, wait, stop, that's not true. But at least I meant to sell it again after she went, and put the money back. Or didn't I? Oh God, I don't know, don't know any more what's true and what isn't. Perhaps I meant to keep it — he's never at home by day to see what I wear. And it was going to be quite easy to invent a burglary, turn the rooms upside down, say the house had been broken into while I was out. But *now* he'll open the drawer and find the money gone and see the coat and know me for what I am — a common thief. Oh, just one day more, *only* one, to put things right! You can do it, you can save me . . . Mother!"

Humming, wailing, cawing alike had ceased. In her and about her lay a stillness that was as precious as balm to a wound, or the sudden lull in a griping, gutting pain. But her joy in it was short-lived, for now, past question, her mother was making ready to go. She widened her hold, clung for dear life: but to what? To a form which, from flesh and blood, was growing intangible as air. And which, in thinning, was receding, fading back into the mists from which it had sprung. She staggered up to follow, and, as she did, caught her foot in the coat, lying on the ground. And some impulse made her stoop to this, pick it up and drag it after her, by one sleeve.

Too late. Now, all that remained to her was a voice: so faint, so far, that it had no more body to it than the echo of an echo, heard from the high hills.

"I shall be waiting for you . . . be waiting."

"Tch! I do believe she's coming to," said the nurse in the

Casualty Ward, and threw a troubled glance at the house-surgeon, who, his job done, had turned aside. "Look! . . . actually trying to speak."

With a swab of cotton-wool she wiped the blood and foam from monstrously distorted lips, all that was now to be seen for bandages of the dying face and, stooping, put her ear to them.

"I'm afraid she's gone, your friend," she said a few minutes later, to the shocked, benumbed woman who kept vigil in the corridor. "But believe me it's better so. Though we haven't managed to get hold of her husband yet."

Here she hesitated. And, with an eye to stuff, cut and cost of the other's clothing, asked a little diffidently: "Is your . . . are you by chance 'Margaret'? Oh yes? So it *was* you she was thinking of. She seemed to be trying to tell you something. It was all very jumbled and confused, I only got a word here and there. Something about a coat — the one she had on when she was brought in, I suppose — and a thief. Perhaps she was afraid it had been stolen. Though," very apologetically, "it did seem once as if she was calling herself a thief. Still, they often talk nonsense at the end. Well, sorry I couldn't make much of it. I'm afraid you won't, either."

But, on coming face to face with the shabby, careworn little man, of the sloping shoulders and limp, uncertain movements, that was Harry, Margaret, deeply pitying, believed she understood.

SUCCEDANEUM

1

WITH the brim of his wideawake turned down, the collar of his overcoat up to his ears, Jerome Mocs stepped into the street. It was late afternoon, and the air smelt of coming rain; the sky was spread with cloud as evenly as with mortar from a trowel. The young man shot a single glance of distaste round him; then, hunching his shoulders, made for a narrow street that led to the centre of the town. He walked listlessly, dragging his feet. Yet rather than chance brushing up against a passer-by, he went to the trouble of stepping off the pavement into the road.

In his present mood the very sight of his fellowmen was odious to him. For he was that most distracted of mortals, the creative artist whose inspiration has failed him. The rich flow of musical ideas, the power to bend these rhythmically to his will, to compress them in the chosen form, everything alike had deserted him, and as abruptly as once it had descended. He was left hollow as a clock emptied of its works; left flat, cold, purposeless; a *cui bono* in the flesh. — For, without this power that was mine a moment back, who am I, what am I? A straw driven before the wind; a null; a parasite at life's board. — And, on top of this, the envy, the murderous envy, of those who were still masters of their genius. No! envy was not the word: it was at once too much and too little. What he felt was more like the hurt and bewilderment of a child who has been shut out, for no conscious fault, from a lamplit festivity, at which all but him make merry. Sven Arped preached patience ... but Sven was old in comparison: his early fires had burned low. And he, Jerome Mocs, was still so young. Beard in hand, Arped taught that these blanks, these breaks in one's continuity, served an end: they obliged the artist to come to grips with life in the raw, from which he might distil further sublimates; had, in short, a reproductive value. Sven himself at such times sought the company of women; found, in women's simple, unsophisticated minds, a wholesome contrast to the subtleties of art, to the eternal and damnable preoccupation with colour and line. And, then, so wild were his extravagances that his name burned on men's lips. But he, Mocs, had still no use for women as a surrogate. His attitude to them was one either of contempt or of exaggerated awe. — Again, there was Gregor Muthesius, the poet. Gregor drowned suspense in alcohol, went blind and deaf to his barrenness, till he could rise once more full of pristine vigour for his task of beating out a super-reality in words. (But then Gregor had the physique of a lion-hunter, and could permit himself the luxury of debauch.) And so it was with all the rest: each had his peculiar trick of surmounting these breaks in his artistic being, when impulse died at the spring. He, Jerome Mocs, alone had not learned wisdom. And this time the loss hit him harder than ever before. For he had been on the edge of completing what he believed to be his masterpiece, a free symphonic rhapsody that should carry his name far beyond the select inner circle — had not the great Ricchi himself promised it a hearing? And he had swept forward, gaily, audaciously, prodigal of his riches, never doubting that they would last him to the end. Then, the block had come, and he had risen one morning to find his verve gone, his grip loosened, his mind dry as a drained keg. Angry, incredulous, he had fought like one possessed to recapture the flow: in vain. Worse still, he began to be invaded by doubts, to look critically at his beloved work; and gradually a feeling of aversion for it grew up in him that fell not far short of hatred. — Oh! surely no other anguish could compare with this? ... Just as no other human joy touched the joys of creation: this acme of lightness, this sense of walking on rainbows, this supreme surrender to a force outside oneself! Some, he knew, went on doing hodman's work in place of a creator's; claiming that a skill born of long practice carried you over the bare patches. But Arped was not one of them, nor yet Gregor, nor, by God, he, Jerome Mocs! He was still jealous as a girl of his immaculateness. There was no room for compromise in him. Rather, and savagely, he descended into hell. And in hell he remained.

At moments on this particular afternoon, when he touched bottom, he threw back his head and swept the sky with a look that resembled a shaken fist, or a dog's bared teeth. Put into words it would have run: Oh, You up there! ... You, Who have granted us artists but a single faculty — that of aping You, of playing the Creator — and Who then freakishly and thievishly rob us of the power to do it ...

At one such moment his sullen eyes, in falling, met those of a girl who had paused on the kerb to decipher a scrap of writing. She had glanced up unthinkingly as he drew near; but she did not look away again — he saw to that! It pleased him suddenly to fix her eyes with his, to pin them fast, paying out his own evil mood in the look, till his victim reddened and made off. And he did not so much as turn his head after her, though she had been both young and winsome.

But the little encounter diverted him, and on the next likely object he tried the trick anew. And again a woman started, and shrank, and quickened her pace. The third, on the other hand, held out his look and paid it back in kind. After this the thing became a game, a means of killing time; and gradually he fell to classing the eyes he caught. There were those that met his frankly, and as frankly fled. Those that fell like smitten doves, only to flutter up again a second later. Some peeped demurely from behind their curtain of lash; others — the few — pretended to be outraged, indignant. But there also met him the flattered eyes of little work-girls, which fawned shyly, or laughed an arch response; as well as those of riper women, which hung on his with the scantly veiled allure of a Mona Lisa. Oh, these women's eyes.

Till, all at once, the biter was bit, the fisher tangled in his own net. Suddenly he found himself gazing into two eyes which neither fled, nor beckoned, nor repelled; which gave back his look with the ingenuous freedom of a child's, and yet were very woman's in their depth and knowledge. He had never seen eyes like them: he could not tear his away. And so dreamlike was the state he had fallen into, that it needed a push from a passer-by to wake him to the fact that they were the eyes of no living person. What he stood staring at was but the drawing of a woman's face, life-sized, and traced by a master-hand. — With a laugh at his own folly he turned on his heel.

Then, however, curiosity pricked him, and he stooped to see whose was the face that had duped him. The picture was here used as an advertisement, other posters surrounded it; but it was now some days old, and of the lettering that had originally accompanied it, not a trace remained. So he was none the wiser. Stepping back, with his head tilted slightly to one side, he took another long look. Then, since a fine rain had begun to fall, and his game for the day was spoilt, he went to seek shelter.

But that night, when he fought by means of any trifle to ban the thought of his impotence, of all the eyes whose secrets he had filched, these counterfeits alone came back with any clearness. Again he sank his own in them. And now he saw that they held a vital spark, a kind of spiritual promise, which none of the living had possessed: as if the unknown artist had condensed and compressed in them a sum of human experience. And gradually it began to seem that their message was aimed specially at him; as if these eyes were striving to make some wordless revelation to him, of mysteries in his art, in life, to which he had not yet attained. — And this idea grew till it became a certainty.

Next morning, for the first time since the break, he did not sit with his head between his hands, despairing. His coffee gulped down, he went out and back on his steps of the day before. Walking more and more swiftly as he drew near the place where the picture had stood. For a sudden fear seized him lest it should have vanished overnight, have been pasted over or torn off. And so it was. In its stead he now faced the announcement of a *bal pare*. Then the hunt began. He scoured the streets, head down before a biting wind, running from one quarter of the town to another, gyrating round advertisement columns, without success. Not till late in the day was his search crowned. Then, once again, the mysterious eyes met his. And this time, too, beneath the portrait, he was able to make out the half-torn lettering of a name. Bianca Josefa del S. ... Bianca Josefa del S. ...

Who was she? Where was she to be found?

II

JEROME MOCS gave chase. Overnight, without a word even to Arped, he vanished from his friends' midst, a prey to one of those ungovernable impulses that have their breeding-place in empty, worked-out brains, and exasperated nerves.

Himself he felt as if, by yielding to the urge, he was escaping from a world peopled by bloodless shades. Of which his art was as chimerical as any. And at first the novelty of his journeyings — until now he had travelled only in tones, with an eye everlastingly bent on notes and staves — helped him to the belief that he was in touch with reality at last. His way, too, led him through many lovely places, the time of the year was spring, and he but two-and-twenty.

But the clues he followed continued of the slightest — a word here, a line of print there, a glimpse caught in passing of a tattered paper face. And very soon they failed him altogether. A little care-chantant artist seemed to enter a great city only to be lost in the crowd; the prints of hundreds of other feet closed over hers. Once again he was baffled; and, at this new check, the same fiery anger ran through him as at the failure of his inspiration. Now, though, it was directed against the unknown woman who, by her witch-hold on him, was eating up his life. Woe to her when he found her!

Thus, savage and despairing, he hawked from place to place.

Then a queer thing happened.

From the noisy streets of a city in central Europe, he turned one night into a cafe for his evening meal. It was early, a mere sprinkling of guests was present, and the waitresses loitered in a group, idly gossiping. They seemed very merry. The one who came to take his order was giggling; giggling when she planked his *Krug* down on its mat. She had a fat, foolish face, on which the one-time dimples had run to lines.

Mocs raised misanthropic eyebrows. "Pray, what's the matter with you?"

The girl sniffed apologetically, drawing her knuckles across her mouth. "Oh, nothing. It's just that Salli there. She mimics people that it's a scream. — The little dark one ... with her back to us."

Having been the last customer to enter, Mocs cocked the apprehensive eye of a very young man at the quizzing group of girls. Two were just the ordinary plump pigeons. The third still presented her back to him — a sturdy, broadish back, topped by a small dark head. But, as he looked, she turned and faced him ... and then, at the hard, stony, disbelieving stare to which he subjected her, her smile died out as if a sponge had been passed over it, leaving her round-eyed, open-mouthed.

To the waitress, who was turning away, he cried: "Here, you! ... Berthe, Mizi, Trudl, or whatever your name is ... send that girl Salli to me!"

"But 'tisn't her table! She serves the row by the wall."

"Hers or not, she's to come here."

"My goodness me! — But you won't get far with Salli, young sir. She's not that sort."

"That's my affair!"

With a perk and a toss, she rejoined her mates; Mocs saw the four deep in confab. The pigeons eyed him with a spiteful curiosity. But the little dark girl shook her head, and vanished through the swing-doors leading to the kitchen.

Fat-face strolled back to him, wearing a thin, malicious smile.

"Now then! ... is she coming?"

"I guess not! Or not till you say what 'tis you want."

"Well and good then!" And picking up his glass, Mocs stalked across the room to re-seat himself at a table by the wall.

"*Jesses!* ... aren't you a one?" murmured the waitress behind his retreating form, and pettishly swished the table with her cloth.

Mocs sat with his eyes glued to the door. Now, she could not escape him! And no sooner did she reappear than he raised a customer's crooked finger and beckoned her to him. There was nothing for it; she had to obey. Sulkily, unwillingly, she crossed to his side.

He had not been mistaken. Before him, in this ordinary little serving-girl, he had one of those staggering resemblances occasionally to be met with between two mortals who are yet unlinked by any ties of blood. It was, indeed, more of a replica than a resemblance, though both features and outline gave the impression of being slightly blurred, and though the whole face was triter and commoner, entirely lacking in the wilfully heightened charactery of the unknown artist's brush. But the eyes were the very eyes of his haunting. Here, in this vulgar setting, shone the twin stars that had robbed him of his peace.

Dazed, dumbfounded, he sat with the bill-of-fare in his hand, meandering a finger down the list of meats without knowing what he read. His one thought was, how to detain this image, how so to arrange things that he might keep the face before him. He had made a bad start; his cheeks still tingled from it. For, at first sight of her, and almost against his will, the foolish words had leapt from him: "What are *you* doing here?" At which she had turned a fiery red, and with a puzzled: "Me? ... doing here?" had pointed to her chest like a child counting out in a game. Not in this way should he go to work.

First, though, to give an order. He named a dish at random, and, she having stiffly and dumbly retired, gripped his head with his hands and sat with closed eyes, trying to plumb the sensations this apparition had stirred in him. He felt strangely angry; words like: "How dare she ... how dare she!" went round and round in his brain. For this flagrant, fantastic resemblance affected him like a theft — like something filched, purloined, stolen. And by such a one! ... from the woman of his dreams. It was a desecration — a crime. And yet ... as he sat nursing his anger, he gradually became aware that the presence of even this reflection of his eidolon was sending small thrills through him, of excitement and anticipation. And a growing desire to look again mastered him; along with a fear lest he had offended her, and she should send one of the other girls to wait on him in her stead.

But she herself returned, carrying a tray: and her reappearance was the signal for a fresh shock ... of recognition, of satisfaction. Swiftly his mind was made up. Leaning forward and calling her by her name, he said in a low, urgent voice: "Salli, there are things ... see, I *must* speak to you! When do you get off? What time does this place close?" At the queer look she threw him, however, he again turned uneasy; what if she was expecting something else, something more personal? Spurred by the thought, he tried to take her hand as it moved over the table.

But she jerked it away. "Don't! I won't have it!" And then, aggrieved and bewildered: "What is it you want? Can't you let me be?" She had a dry throaty voice that grated on his ear.

Both that night and the next, and the next again, he waylaid her. The moon, three-parts full to start with, waxed at each meeting, and their shadows grew nightly denser and stumpier. There she stood, the typical little working-girl, in a round black-straw hat, the brim of which cut off half her face, a prim little black cape hanging from her shoulders. But, say what he would, he could make no headway. She did not thaw — just stood and let him talk, in watching the toe of her shoe draw circles on the pavement.

Not until their third meeting would she agree to him walking home with her: to the little wooden house by the river where she lived with her mother, a "fancy ironer." And it took him over a week to persuade her to throw up her job and go away with him. She was "not that sort." Nor did the conventional "I love you," with which he backed up and, as it were, decked out his persuasions, deceive her. But in the course of this week he paid a private visit to the mother, whom he found easy-going and compliant. So that in the end, public opinion, voiced by this mother and the girl's fellow-workers, who were loud in envy of her luck: "*Such* a pretty boy!" "Money, too, or I'll be eat!" "Fool, you, if you don't get all you can out of him!" wore her resistance down. — And Mocs carried her off.

III

He christened her Bianca; and she came to the name as humbly as a dog to any that his master chooses to bestow on him. It *is* so: hence it must be so. A more spirited creature might at least have shown some curiosity. Not so she: she had not a grain of spirit in her. Altogether there was something doglike about her: her dumbness, her servileness, her ... her stupidity. Yes, that word fitted her best: stupid she was, and stupid she remained. Thus, at the end of a day or two, he summed her up.

In this dullness, which warped their intercourse and made all but the crude physical side of it a cumbrous and a laboured thing, her eyes alone had no share. These continued to burn with a strange inner light, and lost none of their power to move him. He still felt, when she turned them on him, that in them some ancient wisdom lay hid, which it was imperative he should make his own. *When* she looked! The trouble was, she remained as mutinous as ever about facing him: just in this, most crucial way denied herself: casting none by sly, sloping glances, that fled even as they touched him.

Hence, his original scheme, of snatching what he wanted and letting her go, came to nothing. With a nature such as this he did not know how to deal. None of his strokes told. Hitting at her was like hitting into a lump of dough. Though that there *was* another side to her he very well knew, remembering his first sight of her. Again, one hot afternoon when she believed him sleeping, he heard her chattering away in the wash-house below, where she was bearing their landlady company. — For, in this semi-alpine village, where the mountains tapered off into hills and the hills ran down to the plains, they had found a lodging with the chief laundress of the place, Frau Rosi, who stumped about her tubs the livelong day, her bare feet thrust into clogs, her vast, unbound figure a-swing. The soapy, steamy air of the wash-house was no doubt a homely odour, to a girl used to the hot air of the ironing-room. At any rate it served to loose her tongue. While as far as he was concerned, she might have been born without one.

He had approached her too roughly and precipitately in the beginning ... he saw that now. So, grown warier, he did his best to hide from her how personally unattractive she was to him. (And, he being her first lover, and she very young, it was not hard, he flattered himself, to bluff her.) The plain truth was, nothing about her pleased him. Her way of walking, for instance. Short and thick-set, she advanced with a roll from side to side that was little less than a waddle. Speedily he rid her of her intolerable "Sunday best," now her daily wear, by buying her a peasant-dress, which hid the worst points of her figure. Her hands were not so easily got rid of — these short, fat, work-seamed hands, with deeply bitten nails. He put one from him once, in a moment of disgust; and simultaneously felt the shift of her lowered gaze from it to his own slim, well-tended musician's hands. After that, she carried hers tucked under the voluminous black apron, or doubled up behind her back. And one day she capped the climax by appearing with a pair of huge, clownlike, white-cotton gloves dangling from the ends of her plump little arms. He was convulsed with inward laughter, but made no comment; and together they walked paths strewn with pine-needles, through woods into which the golden sunshine fell only in streaks and blotches, she thus ludicrously attired.

But, on their way home, he halted on the wooden bridge that spanned the milky-green alpine river. Here, taking each glove in turn by one of the long, clownlike fingers, he drew it off, and rolling the two to a ball, dropped this in the swiftly flowing water. It bobbed about, twirled, was swept away.

"And that's that!"

For a moment he thought she was going to cry. Her lips pouched and trembled. But she said nothing; just hung her head and slid her naked hands back under her apron. After this, though, they were more carefully scrubbed; and gradually the ingrained black of the seams yielded, the nails grew less unsightly. And before she had finished, she could show quite a presentable little pair of paws.

This affair showed an artless desire to please, and he counted it to her credit. But it ended here, led nowhere: not an inch further did he get because of it. She seemed to sit entrenched behind a wall of her own making. A wall of mute resistance; an entrenchment of sulks and sullens. But her very dumbness spoke for her, and to him what it said was: you dragged me here against my will; I didn't want to come, I didn't want you. I'll give what I am bound to give, but no more; the rest is my own. And this, when all he really wanted of her *was* this intangible, incorporeal remainder! For the bodily intimacy they were forced into left him cold; sensually she meant as little to him as he to her. His mind hankered after just what she would not give; and day by day he grew more incensed at the persistence with which she withheld herself.

None of the little endearments of ordinary lovers — overflow of the closer bond — passed between them. He was never driven to smooth her hair, or to lay his arm about her and cup the place where arm and shoulder met, or to stoop and put his lips to her neck. Now, indeed, in his exasperation, he had to master a crazy inclination to hurt her. And, taking her by the chin, to jerk her stubborn face up to his, he would pinch her flesh between thumb and finger till she turned red with pain.

So it went on till that day when he first saw her cry. When he first made her cry.

In actual count of time they had been together but a week: but, as they walked that morning through the dewy freshness of the forest, he stalking ahead, she a couple of paces behind, he felt as if, for the better part of his life, he had gone with this mute shadow at his heels. There were men who complained of women's eternal clacking: God! give him rather one who talked from dawn to eve. And when they had reached their goal, and sat at a wooden table before a mountain inn, alone but for the hens scratching round their feet, and for a gaunt cat which, perched on a neighbouring table, watched them with unwinking green eyes — here he came to a swift decision. He would bring things to a head here and now, force her out into the open, compel her to speak — oh! to-day he felt ripe for a scene ... was regularly in the mood.

Leaning over the table, he snatched at rather than took her hand, gripping it till the ring on his little finger cut into her palm.

"Look here, my girl! — enough is enough. I'll stand no more. I'm done, finished, played out. Now you shall say — you *shall* say! ... what's wrong with you. Or else we part."

That got her. Wincing, she shot him one of her most furtive

glances, and tried to stammer out: "But nothing!" Her dry lips refusing, she feebly shook her head.

At this renewed prevarication, his last shred of patience fell away. Careless of the woman of the inn, who was advancing with a load of plates, he brought his fist down in a blow that made the table dance and the woman retreat, sent the hens scuttling, the cat flying. Then, with his eyes aflame, his head alternately thrown back or menacingly forward, his loose black hair tossing, the fingers of his free hand making spearlike motions, he gave his rage and indignation vent, pouring out all he had fumed over in silence, and so working himself up that he did not even spare her a recital of her physical shortcomings: her hands, her walk, her voice, her manner of speaking, everything about her that had jarred on his nerves: by this means setting free not only his present tangled emotions, but also the accumulated fire and passion which, given a creative work, would have found their outlet in that work: as well as the shame and misery his prolonged unproductiveness had caused him, him orphaned of the art that was his salvation. When, for sheer shortage of breath, he came to a stop, he was white and trembling. But relieved as of a load — relieved beyond the telling. — And she? The blood that had driven up over neck, cheeks, forehead, slowly ebbed again, leaving her, too, paler than before. There she sat, and, under the lash of his tongue, turned her head helplessly from side to side, like a tortured animal seeking refuge. But she could not escape: her hand was held in a vice. There was nothing left for her to do but weep, and weep she did; he had never seen such tears. They rolled out from under her lids like large round glass beads, slid one after the other down her cheeks and chin, losing shape as they fell, and dripping unheeded into her lap. It was a very child's way of weeping; she made no attempt to hide them, or to wipe them away. But when the sobs came, and twisted up her face, she let her head droop, lower and lower, till it ended by lying on the hand that held hers. And then both their hands were wet.

His anger had puffed out like a candle-flame. And to feel these tears on his hand did the rest. Lifting his other hand he put in on her hair, so that for a moment her head was shut between them.

But in her, too, her tears set something free. He felt her lips move, and bending, caught the words: "Oh, I've been so ... so afraid."

181

IV

AND summer passed. With this woman of flesh and blood in his arms, all thought of the phantom woman had faded from his mind.

So it was with a shock of something more than surprise, on unfolding his newspaper one morning, that he saw before him, black on white, the name he would once have given all he had to see. Now, his first impulse was mentally to jump away from it. With a quick glance at his companion, he turned over and crumpled up the sheet. But as soon as she had left the room he went back to it, and smoothed it outl What if his eyes had played him false? But there it stood: an announcement that the singer, Bianca Josefa del Sanseverina, would perform at a certain cafe, in the city of M., on such and such an evening.

He threw the paper from him and laughed. He could afford to laugh. What did she matter to him now?

But, matter or not, the mere sight or sound of the name had set something stirring in him again. And, that night, he lay and went back on all that had happened to him since the day when he hurled his manuscript into a drawer and turned the key on it; went back on his wild-goose chase and its fantastic issue; and, over this, the image of the unknown woman came oddly to life again. He began to wonder what his sensations would be, if, at long last, he found himself face to face with her. Did the mysterious hold she had had over him still persist? Curious? ... yes, curious he was — perhaps even more than curious. And admitting this brought on a fit of restlessness, in which he tumbled and tossed. Before him, on the whitewashed wall, the tiny, flower-encumbered window printed a silver square. Beyond the window, a black ridge of mountain cut across the sky. Not a sound broke the stillness. Or only that of his watch which, hanging above his head, had suddenly begun a frenzied ticking. He could close his eyes to the moonshine, to the mountains, but the noise of this ticking he could not shut out. And, as he lay and listened, it seemed to grow in strength, until it filled the room. He sat up in bed. To become aware that every nerve in his body was beating in unison with it, and that it had turned to a kind of menace, and what it said was: Time flies, time flies, time flies! He snatched it from its hook and buried it under the mattress, but this did not help, it had left its echo in the air; time was still in flight ... while he lay supine, inert. And now he knew that he would go — would have to go. Once more this stranger, this interloper, had thrust herself destructively in upon his life. — The old fury blazed up in him. He lay and cursed her.

To the girl beside him he said: "A day ... at most a couple of days, sweetheart!"

This for his own comfort as much as hers. For she did not murmur, or try to dissuade him, or even put a question about the business that was calling him away: a sweet reasonableness that made her doubly dear to him.

At the very last moment, he was within an ace of jumping from the train and letting his dreams go hang. Left standing alone on the gravelled platform, she looked so childish and forlorn that his heart misgave him. True, she smiled, showing all her dimples, but with lips pressed tight one on the other, to hide their trembling; while her fingers rolled and twisted without pause at a corner of the big black apron. But again something stronger than himself prevailed. All he did was to lean from the window, and wave to her, and swing his hat, till a turn in the line hid her from sight.

Arrived in M. he traced his way with ease, and that evening found him sitting among a cluster of portly burghers and their wives, who supped at tables set in front of a small stage. On this, when he entered, a sinister-looking individual in evening clothes and an opera-hat was cracking a riding-whip, to the strokes of which and his shouts of command, a madonna-faced woman, sheathed in black to her chin, to her finger-tips, her toes, with nothing of her visible but a lasciviously white face under an enormous black hat, capered like a horse. The performance earned scant applause. Then came the turn of the singer. Or should have come. But an interminable wait followed, in which raised voices could be heard behind the scenes. The audience grew restive. Whereupon the tawdry curtains rattled apart, and on to the stage walked ... a woman ... *the* woman, his woman! — oh! one look, one only, and it was as if, in a titanic burst of laughter, a merciless, sardonic laughter, a giant bubble exploded and collapsed. For this ... *this*! ... he had torn up his life by the roots, dragged himself over half Europe. His eyes sought the ground.

At odds with custom, however, the voice had not suffered the irreparable damage of the flesh. And over his lowered head it trilled its way, serene and pure, through some half-dozen ditties, each with a sting in its tail.

His first impulse had been to fly, to put distance between himself and the catastrophe this apparition was to him. But he was far from the entrance, and the right moment had passed. He remained sitting. And, the turn at an end, he abruptly rose and pushed his way through the papered door that gave behind the scenes.

Here the dispute had broken out afresh. Between the singer and the man of the whip. Money, it seemed, was owing her; and money she would and must have. But while she continued to vociferate, snatching breaths with the skill of the practised singer, she was also coolly taking in and appraising the young man who stood fixing her; and more than one meaning glance was sped at him from under her heavily blued and bistred lids. Still without ceasing in her flow, she edged near enough to him to press his arm, touch his foot with hers. Almost before he knew where he was, he found himself engaged to take her out to supper.

She was *hungry*. Under the glaring lights of a gilt and plush restaurant, he sat and watched her jaws go, in a kind of *perpetuum mobile* of mastication, of talk. Never had he seen such an eater, heard a like volubility. Whether her mouth was empty or full, she carried on at the top of her voice, chewing the while with many a juicy smack and suck, and much running of her tongue round her teeth. Moments came, when every eye was upon her.

But she had, it seemed, her own ideas of honesty. One of those who tried to diddle you, get something out of you for nothing, she was not ... not she! — if she said this once, she said it a dozen times; on her tongue it became a kind of theme with variations. And, her appetite finally glutted, he had no choice but to follow her to the mean little *hotel garni* where she lodged, and, at her heels, climb a bare stone stair to a room on the second floor, in the lock of which she fitted a key.

She switched the lights on, and he looked past a grimy portiere into a dingy, disorderly bedroom.

Holding back the curtain with one hand, with the other she signed to him to enter.

"Here you are! This is the way."

Not till the second morning after, did he succeed in making his escape.

Early though the hour was, a crowd of Saturday holiday-makers, armed with sticks, ropes and knapsacks, was hastening to catch the first train to the mountains. He mingled with them; pushed and shoved his way; joined in the rude scramble for a seat.

But no sooner was the train in motion than he wandered restlessly into the corridor, and planted himself at the window to watch the country fly by. Free ... free! And now for — But no! ... not again, not as long as he lived, would that name cross his lips. It was fouled for him for ever ... by arts indescribable. Salli — little Salli! In fancy he held her to him, felt her small head sleek to his chin, the skin of her neck blossom-soft and cool. Oh! once with Salli again, and all would be well.

But would it? Was that true? Would her presence pacify him? Free he might be, calm he certainly was not: deep down in him, a strange excitement was brewing. An unnatural excitement, that had nothing to do with Salli, or the joys of meeting. It recalled the throbbing unrest which the tick of his watch had set a-going in him, that moonlight night in the mountains. But was even more violent. He eyed himself in dismay. His heart hammered, his fingers trembled with suspense. He was like a man who stood waiting, with every nerve on end, for a bomb that is timed to fall. What on earth was happening to him?

With limbs as jerky as if hung on wires, he went back to the carriage, and turned to rid himself of his hat by tossing it on to the rack.

And then he knew.

He was still on his feet, still steadying himself by the rail, when the miracle happened. Quite suddenly, it was as if walls dropped away — from his brain, his sight, the carriage itself — walls that had shut him in, blocking and hindering. Now, with one accord they fell, but as noiselessly as soft curtains. For an instant their collapse seemed to leave him alone in space, without a hold, and feeling strangely shrunken. In the next it was he who filled space, swelled by a power that ran through him and overflowed him, magnificently spreading until it embraced all living things. Then he knew. The gift of creation was his again, he was one again with his daemon, his genius; with that mystic force which alone justified his existence. Humbly, like one accepting alms, he yielded to its oncoming; yet with a silent shout of exultation: received it into himself — as the prone, entranced body, lying deep in sleep, receives back the night-wanderer that is its spirit.

With a kind of groan he sank to his seat, and hid his face in his hands For, in this moment, in this lightning-flash of perception, he had seen his way: the link, the key was his, for lack of which his work had shattered: the handful of notes, the combination of tones, needed to start the chain of ideas that should carry him rapturously to the end. His now — all his! But he reached for neither pencil nor paper; before now he had known the prosaic act of transcription break the flow. He just sat with tight-closed eyes, and lived through, to its last intricate windings, the revelation that had been made him; with such intensity that each note might have been written in fire, each phrase burnt with a hot iron on his brain. Sat, and let himself sink into the state nearest bliss vouchsafed to mortal on this side of the great divide; a bliss that shares the quivers of a sheerly physical pleasure, yet is past expression subtle and pure: when the creative artist, freed from the trammels of time, lives through aeons in a few seconds of man's measuring.

At the first stop he left the train, and, some hasty purchases made, fell to the drudgery that must follow even the most inspired flights. The day passed; in a gloomy hotel-bedroom it was noon, it was afternoon, then dusk, before he finally lifted his head: pale, spent, famished; but a king again in his own right.

His first move was to seek for a calendar. And, this found, he began hastily to reckon and dovetail dates. Yes! it was still possible. With luck — oh, God give it! — he might yet be in time. Luck, and a toil beggaring description, was he to have his manuscript ready to lay in Maestro Ricchi's hands on the appointed day.

There was not a moment to lose. First to get food; then for the night train to the north.

But something troubled him; there was something at the back of his brain that he could not get at. He put a hand to his forehead. Then ... why, of course, blamed fool that he was! ... Salli.

Without a moment's hesitation he drew a sheet of paper to him and wrote:

My own love, my little Salli!
All day you will have waited for me and hoped for my coming — you are perhaps still waiting, still hoping — and

I ... I shall not come. Not any more, little love — or not for a very long time. And so I say to you, do not wait. Go back to your old life, and take it up where you laid it down for my sake. But don't forget me, child, or the many happy hours we have spent together. From my heart I thank you for them — though I am forced to act in what must seem an ungrateful way. I shall not forget. I shall treasure the memory of all you gave me ... like a lovely flower that time cannot fade. Who knows! Till then, farewell, my little love. I thank you again and again.

Your

Jerome.

But later in the evening, when he had eaten and drunk, and food and wine were insinuating their warmth through his veins, he tore this letter to small pieces. Salli! ... little Salli. A longing for her that was sharp as pain was upon him: to see her, to hold her to him again, seemed the acme of his desire. He was still so young; he stretched out his arm, the better to feel the youth and strength of it; and he loved her, loved her. In thought he lived through their meeting: the snatched hands, stammered words, the rush of body to body, the sinking to sleep, work-worn and passion-spent, on her breast. If he broke with her now, he would never see her but as in his last glimpse of her — a picture to haunt him all his days.

When his whole heart cried out for her.

And yet ... To go back now, let this unique chance slip his grasp, might — *would* mean hazarding his whole future as an artist. And that he would never forgive himself. Not in this way was happiness to be bought. When passion flagged ... as passion did — must flag ...

Feverishly he sought an alternative. What if he took her with him? ... wrote and bade her follow him? But even as the thought came to him he swept it aside. Absorbed in his work he needed no one, could tolerate nobody beside him ... let alone a woman: he the "Saint Jerome" of his friends' gibes! To be perpetually aware of a presence, no matter how mute, how humble, would hang him with chains. Nor was it he alone who came in question. What of her, who had so far known him only in a summer mood of idleness, of relaxation, when he became cold, preoccupied, a victim of the fierce nervous irritability to which creative work condemned him?

And then ... his friends ... the clique his life was spent

amongst. What, take her, his little love, back among this ribald, scoffing crew? — this artist-pack that respected no one and nothing outside the products of their own genius? She would get scant mercy at their hands. For it was not even as if ... The plain truth being, love had stolen a kind of march on him, dimming his vision, making him in the end fond even to her unlovelinesses. But *they* would judge her as inhumanly as he himself had once done; each of her defects serve as the butt for a coarse witticism, an obscene joke: he could imagine them, from Arped down, cynically winking and chuckling. At the thought, such a wave of protective tenderness ran through him, in this moment he so truly loved her, that doubts and hesitations were swept away. Rather than expose her to so bitter an obloquy, he would never see her again.

The rest was easy.

He wrote no second letter; better, since the break was inevitable, that it be short and sharp. And having found a telegraph-office, he pulled a form to him, and wrote the few words that were all that remained to be said.

Am not coming back. Return home.

This done, he flung out and strode through deserted streets, where a gusty wind buffeted him at every corner, and the branches of half-bare trees thrashed despairingly. Afterwards, in waiting for the train, which was late, he paced a station open at both ends to the dark, and cheerless as the night itself: a place of murky shadows, and hollow, clanking sounds; of tears, partings, irremediable regrets.

The thunder of the express, cries of porters, opening of doors roused him; hoisting himself up, he picked his steps among disgruntled sleepers. And soon, with more banging and shouting, the train slid into motion, and began to bore its way through the night, shrilled round on the high plains by the whistle of the wind. In the corner of a shaded carriage, Mocs sat and listened to the grotesque distortions ground out by the wheels, now of this theme, now of that. And oftenest what he heard was one of a tossing sea, sailed by a ship carrying lover back to lover. In its broken rhythm, its restless upward surge, his own unrest, his growing exaltation found vent: he, with his face set once more for what, to him, had never ceased to be the one Reality ... all else but a ghostly surrogate.

MARY CHRISTINA

MARY CHRISTINA was going to die. — For sixty years, come March, she had been an inhabitant of the earth, and had suffered her full share of life's vicissitudes: she had passed from girl to woman, had loved and been loved, had borne children and tended children, had watched young faces lose their youth, and harden, and grow unbeautiful; she had cared for graves; had resigned herself, in the course of years, to the creeping on of age: she had wept, and laughed, and been indifferent, mostly indifferent, as is man's way; but now she was going to cease to be, and nothing would please her, or sadden her, or leave her merely cold, again.

She knew what was coming, before anyone else; for she had had a presentiment; so, at least, she called it, one grey November afternoon, when, with icy hands outspread, she crouched low over a fire from which she could derive no heat.

That day, while a sharp wind was causing the last, tattered leaves to whirl madly on their stalks, Mary Christina had journeyed to a distant quarter of the town. Her business done, she entered a crowded conveyance. As she sat and let her eyes range over the row of faces opposite her, faces worn with toil, and reddened with exposure to the wind, she said to herself: "My God, how ugly people are!" But, in the same breath, a small, inner voice rebuked her: "Be thankful to be among them, Mary Christina! What if you were never out of doors again?" To which, elliptically, she made answer: "Better now than in spring, when things are freshening up."

Mary Christina was going to die.

That night, the hour being come, she took off for the last time the wrappings in which the world had known her, and, with as little covering as she would ever again need, lay down between the sheets that witness the incoming and the outgoing of mortals.

But the lying down and folding of the hands is not enough; it is no such easy matter as that to die. The way out of life is as darkly mysterious as the way in.

Thus, after having ever been one of those stoics who look upon illness as a moral failing, to which it is dishonourable to yeild; after having borne her casual ailments as mutely as a suffering animal, Mary Christina now began to fling about on her bed, in such a manner that every one within call was needed to restrain her; and to utter shrill, shameless cries, which echoed through the house. Beads of moisture rolled from her forehead and made round spots on the sheets, or splashed the hands of those who held her.

A stranger, summoned in haste, sat beside her bed. Before him, a scrupulous, womanly reserve dropped like a rent veil.

The well-known faces of her children — children now in the eyes of Mary Christina alone — hung over her. Hand after hand sought hers, sweat-bedewed; and from the lips of the youngest broke man's most human cry: "Oh, Mother . . . Mother!"

But though these, of all living creatures, had been in Mary Christina's thoughs ever since they had come into the world; though she had watched, night for night, till she knew their eyes closed in sleep, harassed by the fears that only a mother knows; though up to the last, her love had thrown out a thousand arms, to safeguard them on their divers ways, she was now as indifferent to them as to the several strangers who moved round her bed. And the withdrawal of her warm affection seemed, to those who had been used to shelter beneath it, like the first significant victory gained by death over life.

For Mary Christina, the centre of existence had shifted: henceforth, her desire was only to herself. First came the idolatrous attention demanded by her body — this strong, personable body, still ablaze with energy, and resolutely desirous of living. It was made the object of a religious care; untiring were the endeavours to ward off the inevitable. The minutest variations in the heat of the blood, in the pulsations of the heart, were verified and controlled. Hitherto, she had lived unconscious of her vital functions; now she, too, shared the palpitating interest in their course. For all these things, now of a morbid importance, were possible disarmers of the great enemy, of the griping, gutting pain, to repel which was her chief concern. This came at intervals. It began somewhere in the distance, far away, drew rapidly nearer, darkening the bed with the shadow of its wings; it hovered over her, circling like a vulture, she lying defenceless and terrified; then, with one swoop, it descended and settled on her, plunging beak and claws into the shuddering flesh. She looked at those about her with wild eyes, dumbly imploring them, praying to them, as to gods, to shield her from it; but they did nothing. It tore at her, sick and faint with anguish; the muscles of her body twisted into knots; she heard her own shrieks rend the air.

For longer than eight long days she fought this fight, returning time and again to the encounter, in which, each single time, she left more of her strength. Gradually, however, the force of her struggles declined, and the hope that had sustained her, the hope of once coming off conqueror, died out. She still swallowed, with avidity, the bitter draughts that were held to her lips; she submitted, gladly, to the importunate services of the nurse, which broke in, by night and by day, on her hard-won rest; she still gave desperate battle, when the agony sucked at her; but it became a mere blind instinct to live, without faith in the issue. — And the watchers round the bed began to avoid her eyes, in which, at moments, the death-secret was legible.

For eight days and over, she disputed each inch of ground, and those whose lot it was to stand and look on, felt the limits of human endurance strain to breaking-point. Then, however, a change was visible. The pain still wrung her, in savage bouts; but Mary Christina did not answer to it, as at first: her nerves were losing their fine power, both to feel, and to interpret the feeling. She ceased to resist so ardently, let the anguish engirdle her, do its worst. Now that her nerves were drowsier, too, she was able, the moment she ceased to suffer, to sink into repose; a tranquil, twilight state, on the borderland between sleeping and waking; and the experiences of a lifetime had numbered no goodlier pleasure than this: the wishless well-being that follows on a vanishing pain.

Her dark hair, fine as silk, was gathered loosely round her head; iced cloths were strapped to her brow; her large, worn hands lay folded on the sheet. The watchers stifled their own flickering hopes, and gave up asking her how she did; for she could hardly bring herself to return a pressure of the hand: all else was immaterial to her, so long as the agony was kept at bay, and she not roused from her present sweet reprieve. They moved on tip-toe, fearful of disturbing her; for they believed she slept. But she was not asleep — as one saw, who bent more nearly over her: the dark pupils were fixed, beneath the half-fallen lids, like the unclosed eyes of one already dead.

In these benign moments, when her torture slackened, Mary Christina lay and let pictures pass before her — pictures, fragments, flashes — of the life which, until now, had been hers; and, compared with this intensely personal past, which had its rise in mistiest morning memories, even her children seemed unfamiliar to her — the chance associates of an hour.

Fifty years ago! ... The walls of the room expanded, then fell in, like the sides of a card house. It was a wide and sunny square; before an old-fashioned house with a shiny brass knocker, under a pale-blue English sky heaped with bulbous masses of cloud, a group of children that played. One had hair of a light, flaxen colour, which flapped to her waistline, floated behind her as she ran. She was the wildest and merriest of all; she threw the ball highest; she caught it most surely as it came to earth again. In a spirit of wantonness, elated by her own skill, she threw it so high and so far that it did not return: it had gone over the wall of a neighbouring garden. They were not allowed to enter this garden; the ball, her ball, of which she had been so proud, was lost for ever, and through her own folly. She sat down on the steps, and wept bitterly. Her play-fellows, unable to comfort her, stole away ...

Years had passed. Overhead, a lowering grey sky; which was yet no greyer than the flat stretch of earth beneath. Snow was in waiting, but, so far, only a few detached flakes had fluttered down. On a hard-frozen pond, people were skating; a young girl stood at the edge, and followed their bird-like dartings and skimmings. She wore a scarlet hood on her head. Seen against the prevailing dullness, this hood burnt like a flame. Two young men passed, swinging their skates; one turned to look at her, and she caught an admiring word. He had bright, merry eyes. She reddened; then, obeying an impulse, took to her heels and ran, never pausing till she had crossed the home threshold. Too big for such frolics, they rebuked her; but she only smiled at them in return, not grasping what they said. Her thoughts were singing: life seemed suddenly to mean undreamed-of wonders — the unravelling of a magic coil ...

And again the years moved forward. It was summer now. The sun went down, huge, flamboyant, in a violet-steaked sky. At the bottom of a tangled old garden, in a thicket of raspberry-bushes, she stood with heaving breast, striving to repress tears of shame and disappointment. Throughout the afternoon, he had seemed to avoid her, had kept at the side of her friend. Now, she made as if she were gathering fruit; but the basket on her arm was empty: she stared unseeingly at the streaky red and gold of the western sky. While she stood thus, a world of bitterness in her young heart, a hand was laid on hers, and a kind voice said: Mary Christina ... I missed you ... I came to look for you ... The little fancy basket dropped from her nerveless fingers, dropped among the bushes, and there it was left, to lie and rot. How foolish of her it had been to forget that basket! It was made of green straw; had a pretty twisted handle. Why had she never gone back to look for it? — what had blotted it from her mind? Did it still lie, where it had fallen — a shapeless, sodden mass? Or had strange hands recovered it? ... Who lived now in the home of her girlhood? Did other young lips meet beneath the flames of the evening sky? ... other feet tread the familiar paths, whence hers had for ever passed?

The sick woman stirred uneasily, and moved her head. It was deep night; the house was still, the room sunk in shadow. The darkness oppressed her; she tried to look about her, and moaned. At the sound, a soft-footed Sister of Mercy rose from out a patch of gloom, and bent over her, presenting a cup to her dry lips: as she drank, Mary Christina's fixed and feverish eyes met the stiff white linen of wimple and bands. The draught soothed her; at once her lids half-closed again; and the watcher shrank back into the corner from which she had sprung.

Before she had reached it and sat down again to her beads, Mary Christina seemed to hold a living child in her arms, gathered two tiny feet into the cup-shaped hollow of her hand. A fire burnt in the grate; wine-red curtains were drawn against a night of lashing rain. Out on the highways, and in the storm-swept fields, these icy rain-stripes spelled a shuddering desolation; within, in the safe, warm room, husband and wife knelt to examine each soft line and curve of the miracle that was theirs. — Surely there was no better joy than this joy . . . See! — how his hand grasps mine! He listens . . . he smiles. Never was such a child born before!

Another turn of the wheel, and the babe was cold to the touch: she stood pressing a little dress to her face, and eating her heart out in vain regret. How she had struggled, and rebelled! She had then believed that no after-grief could equal this grief for the little dead child (so long since become one with the earth it lay in); for this faint life-spark, of which all but herself speedily forgot the existence. It had not been so; many a greater grief had overtaken her: with the passing of the years, it sometimes seemed as though sorrow's bowed and grey-veiled form would never again quit her side. She had learned that it is easier to see a child die, unspoiled, than to watch it change, grow hard, betray its soul; had even come to rely on death, as on the fundamental stay of life — the bed-rock, beneath loose and shifting sands.

But after this last precise vision of the waxen babe that awaited her in the land of shadows, the memories came crowding thick and fast: she could not follow each singly to an end. The later years, too, had been so like, one to another; and they had flashed past with a dizzy quickness: one day she had been thirty, and it seemed only on the morrow that she was sixty — an old woman stretched out to face death. With the far-reaching sight granted to dying eyes, she lay and looked back at the confused pattern of her life, as at some richly-worked arras, and surveyed it; but without emotion. Now, the many happenings that composed it struck no answering chord in her; and it passed belief to think that she had once been stirred to the depths of her soul by them. In this hour of profounder knowledge, she saw that they had only been dreams and shadows — delusive images that had tricked her brain. Nothing of them had persisted; nothing been real or lasting: her hand had caught the frayed edge of no perdurable garment. The wonders had been a chimera; the evils, too. And their hold upon her had been a imaginary one: her inmost self, the vitalest part of her, had remained unmoved by them, and unharmed. She had not striven in mortal combat; for there had never been a combat to engage in. That was still another illusion — perhaps the greatest of all. Life, tapped at its core, stripped of its rainbow gauds, meant — she knew it now — a standing dumbly by, to let these dream-things pass. Now that she was done with it, with life and living, and could view it as a whole, she saw that this was what it came to: one was never really of it; it only seemed so, at the moment. One's soul held aloof, shy, proud, chill, while past it bore an unsubstantial pageant of varying places, and their accompanying ghosts. Sometimes, these shapes held out their arms to us; sometimes, we stretched yearning hands to them. For a brief suspense, there appeared to be an entanglement; then, one or other yielded, and the procession went on as before. Love had no more reality, no more enduring-power, than the lover's arms; the dream-child we reared, changed and passed; joy passed and pain, and the windy excitements of the day. — And memory, turning on the steps of death's threshold, for a last backward look at the sun-tipped mirage, could impossibly distinguish one transient image from another. Now, they all seemed alike; they *were* alike: there had been no real difference between them. Joy and grief, love and hate, rapture and despair, were, in very truth, one and the same — the thin, blue spire of smoke, that ascended from a phantasmal fire.

And having achieved this ultimate wisdom, the dying woman was lapped by a great peace: not again would she choose to be of life. Now, she asked for rest — only rest. Not immortality: no fresh existence, to be endured and fought out in some new shadowland, among unquiet spirits; but deep, deep rest, with the heavy brown earth flattened down above her, and every wish stilled at last. Without substance, without meaning, it had all been an idle beating of the air; but it was over now; and she thanked God that it was so. Never again, the laceration of a sunset, the agony of a fading autumn day. Only sleep; the sleep of nothingness: an eternal forgetting ...

She lay and let death's torpor steal over her, dimly noting its progress. But towards evening, when the cold blue eastern shadows fell, she made the instinctive effort of the dying: sought to flee the unfleeable, while there was yet time.

"I will get up and go away ... far away."

She was raised in her bed and propped by loving arms; then laid down again; for she was unable to support the weight of her own body: her head, all a-tremble, sank from side to side, like a top-heavy flower on its stalk. — And the sensation of sinking, of being sucked under by a current she could not stem, began anew. It was as if she were caught and swept round in a whirlpool: for a time she would ride high, on the same level; then came the dizzy, downward drop, and she was by so much nearer to the black, serpent-like, central shaft, so much farther from the blue roof of the sky. Down ... down ... down! — a giddy whirl towards the horrors of the dark; and so it would go on, in ever-contracting circles, till the awful moment when she whirled no more, and when the churning waters met, with a crash of thunder, above her head.

Then, the vertigo ceased, and a merciful weakness came to her aid. Her thoughts, drawing to an inseparable tangle, escaped her, and were reabsorbed in the Supreme Thought, from which they had primarily come forth. Though her eyes remained open, doctor and nurse no longer hushed their voices when they spoke of her: for them, she was already numbered among those mute or inarticulate things, which, because they cannot make protest, are held insensible to hurt and affront.

Life ebbed lingeringly, unwillingly. A muddly pallor overspread her face; her breath came snortingly; the pinched nose strained upwards. But the heart beat on, throbbing through the dead body till long after midnight.

Then this, too, ceased.

The weeping watchers retired, with the sense of relief in their breasts that accompanies death accomplished; and the withdrawal of their lamentations left a great vacancy in the room. The black-robed woman who remained, raked out the embers of the fire, and pushed back the chairs from the bed. On the eyes of the thing that had been Mary Christina, she laid two squares of damped muslin; and, as she did so, she made fervid intercession with the other Mary — the Gracious Namesake of this poor soul that had gone unblessed into the darkness. The coverings decently stretched and folded, she turned out the gas, and set a night-light in a glass of water. — It threw living shadows on the wall.